WHERE NO ONE WILL SEE

Felicia Watson

DX VAROS PUBLISHING

Published by:
D. X. Varos, Ltd
7665 E. Eastman Ave. #B101
Denver, CO 80231

Book cover design and layout by DX Varos Publishing
Featuring artwork from:
SelfPubBookCovers.com/billwyc

ISBN: 978-1-955065-78-8 (paperback)
ISBN: 978-1-955065-79-5 (ebook)

This novel is dedicated to Ed for being my sounding board, my beta reader, my cheerleader, and my biggest fan.

Enormous gratitude is also due to Dorrie for her invaluable insights and to Dave for his unwavering support.

And lastly, in memory of Rocco, who will never be forgotten.

CHAPTER 1

The Past, Present and Future

"Family faces are magic mirrors. Looking at people who belong to us, we see the past, present and future."—Gail Lumet Buckley

Lucia Scafetti was not a good person. At least, she'd long suspected that might be true. In the red glow of the darkroom safelight, she developed the latest series of photos she'd taken of a stranger's illicit bedroom activities, feeling a little more doubt slip away. Once the images emerged, Lucia cocked her head in contemplation, imbued with an odd mixture of satisfaction and disgust. "Yikes. Mr. Shapiro, you are so busted." Shaking her head, she hung the eight-by-ten photos up to dry in the spacious darkroom belonging to the Community College of Philadelphia.

By noon, Lucia was heading home to West Philadelphia. She hesitated at the entrance to the

Broad-Street subway. Considering that the summer of '95 was setting records for both heat and humidity, it would be cooler to take public transit all the way. On the other hand, if she walked the few blocks to the Market-Frankford Line, she'd pass right by Marco's Pizzeria where she could grab a couple of slices for lunch. Marco's was neither a particularly clean nor congenial place but two slices of plain pizza could be had for a buck. Her stomach growled, protesting that the only sustenance it had known that day was a large coffee and a small soft pretzel. Lucia considered that complaint as the deciding vote—she'd make the walk to Marco's.

Upon entering the pizzeria, she saw that the counterman was Andre Bradley, a fellow student and sometimes dinner companion at the community college. Bradley, handsome, courtly, and good-natured, was like Lucia, in his late twenties, older than the average CCP student so they'd gravitated towards each other in their "Introduction to the Internet" class. Lucia had initially hoped his interest in her was more than friendly but she'd quickly discovered that his taste in women ran to the petite and dainty side. At six-feet, and a muscular 200 pounds, neither descriptor had been applied to Lucia since long before puberty, making this a familiar disappointment which she accepted gracefully.

Andre greeted her with both a smile and advice to wait for the fresh pie he had coming out of the oven shortly. After she agreed that fresh pizza was well worth the slight delay, Andre asked, "Where are you coming from, CCP?"

"Yeah, I was using the darkroom." Lucia held up a manilla envelope full of her morning's work.

"How is it Banco still lets you use the darkroom when you finished with her class years ago?"

"Because I asked her." Andre tilted his head, obviously waiting for the whole story so Lucia admitted, "I asked...and I also gave her a sob story." Laughing, she added, "Sob stories being the most important weapon in a private investigator's arsenal."

"Not your Glock?"

"Nope." To her everlasting regret, Lucia had once told him that she occasionally carried a Glock-22 on dangerous outings and Andre had since considered it to be the most interesting thing about her. "Being a PI in real life is nothing like those TV shows."

Andre's retort was preempted by two men entering the restaurant. Lucia automatically stepped aside to let them place their order. The older, shorter man informed Andre that they were there to pick up a takeout order of twelve hoagies for a nearby construction site.

"It better be ready—and right," barked the younger one, sporting an impressive mullet and an obvious chip on his shoulder. "Or I'll come back here and take back your tip and something outta your hide to boot." Ignoring the belligerence, Andre cheerfully informed them it was in the back, ready to go and he had checked it thoroughly. When he went to get it, the mouthy man lounged against the counter, made a casually racist remark about Andre to his companion and then eyed Lucia. "Wowee. You're a big gal, ain't you, honey?"

Lucia heard observations like that more frequently than she heard hello. She usually shrugged them aside but this guy had gotten on her shit-list in record time. "What is it you bring to the world besides ignorance, an ugly haircut, and your fascinating grasp of the obvious?"

He straightened up and glared at Lucia. "What's a' madder? You a lezzie?"

"If you think every woman who's not attracted to you is gay, you must run into a lot of lesbians."

"What the fuck does that mean?" His friend warned him to let it go but mullet-guy persisted. "Bet I know why you don't like men. Bet you used to be one, huh?"

"Wrong." She smiled coolly down at him from her slight height advantage. "I'm no more a man than you are."

"Here's your order!" They all turned to find Andre holding out two large paper bags by the twine handles.

The loudmouth, who appeared to still be searching desperately for a crushing comeback, made no response while the older man took the bags and headed towards the door, saying, "Come on, Mitch. The guys are waiting."

Shaking off his stupor, Mitch nodded. "Yeah, let's get the hell outta here." He headed for the exit with his friend, pausing long enough to look back and snarl, "That bitch ain't worth it."

"You say 'bitch' like it's a bad thing," Lucia called after them.

While Andre bagged up her pizza he said, "I guess those guys are lucky you *don't* carry your gun everywhere."

"I don't need a gun to handle losers like that. I never did."

"Yeah," he chuckled. "I guess you've always had your last name for that."

Somewhat irked by that quip, Lucia still mustered up a forced laugh. After all, Andre was just repeating the kind of joke she often told on herself to put new people at ease. She couldn't blame him for buying her act—could she?

Thirty-minutes later, Lucia paused at the entrance to the Overbrook Commons Office building, distracted by the sight of a shiny new plaque, advertising the services of Siskin and Narváez, Attorneys. She smiled broadly, having already targeted her new neighbors as potential clients. She was working diligently to move her business away from mainly spying on cheating husbands and had already signed on as the house PI for one small law firm. Making it two could really boost her profile in the legal community.

Buoyed by the thought, she dashed through the front doors, and ran down the steps at the left of the lobby to her own office in the basement. That wing of the basement housed only the office of Fidelia Investigations and the long-deserted Goldstein's Tailoring & Dressmaking Shop. As soon as she slotted her key in the door, a chorus of barks announced the presence of her dachshund, Rocco. Seeing his silhouette appearing over and over at the frosted glass window in the door she yelled, "Stop jumping, it's bad for your back."

He obeyed that order as well as he did all others—which is to say, not at all and she was nearly knocked down by the force of a thirty-pound bullet of muscle and fur. "Okay, okay, I know, your lunch is late." She surveyed the office carefully. Other than a few strands of black fur on the leather couch positioned to the right of the door, there was no evidence of dachshund wrong-doing. "But you get a walk first, since, thank God, you didn't already take care of business."

Upon returning from their walk, she retrieved the bag of dog food from the lowest drawer in the huge, battered filing cabinet, and noticed the light blinking on her answering machine. Her hope that it might be a client was dashed when Lucia leaned towards the desk and saw that though there was but one message, a good third of the cassette tape had been used up.

After feeding Rocco, she pressed the button to listen to the message, saying, "Whata' ya' want, Ma?"

"Lucia, it's your mother."

"Duh."

"I'm coming into town tonight. My flight don't get in 'til after ten—"

While throwing on a blazer and preparing a Fidelia brochure to take up to the new tenants, Lucia carried on a one-sided "conversation" with the answering machine. "Thanks for all the notice."

"...so don't bother meeting me; I'll take a cab. I don't want you driving that damn Chevelle on the Schuylkill that time a' night." There was a slight pause and Lucia braced for the inevitable addition. "If Baccaro'd been a decent sort, he'd've left you a safer car...but if he'd been a decent man, he'd've married you."

"At least he didn't kill people for a living."

"I'll be staying at Patsy's 'cause God knows I can't stay with my daughter. Patsy says you should come have breakfast with us tomorrow. Be there 'bout nine—"

"Sounds great."

"...and the whole family is having Sunday dinner at Carmela's."

"Oh, shit."

"She's making homemades and gravy. Wear a dress—"

"All right."

"...as long as you shave your legs—"

"Geez, that was one time!"

"And it wouldn't kill you to put on some nylons."

"Yes, it would, it's July. And they're called pantyhose."

"I don't know about bringing that dog of yours to dinner. Zia Carmela don't like him."

"The feeling is more than mutual; I'll leave him here."

"See you tomorrow, honey. I love you."

"I love you, too, crazy lady."

Enrique Narváez was crouched down at his floor-to-ceiling bookcase, shelving books in his new office. Well, it was new to him anyway. The fresh coat of paint did little to hide the wear and tear and the olive-colored carpet looked to be a relic from World War II. He heard a voice call out, "Knock, knock, anyone home?"

Assuming it was their first potential client, he dusted himself off and ran a comb through his thick brown hair. By the time he made it out to their tiny common area, his best friend and partner, Max Siskin, was already in conversation with an Amazonian woman as tall as Max. She had a mass of dark curly hair and her jeans were topped by what looked to be a custom blazer, based on the way it fitted her impressive shoulders. She stuck out a hand in greeting. "Mr. Narváez? I'm Lucia Scafetti."

Max said, "Lucia is our downstairs neighbor. She's here to welcome us to the building and offer her services."

"Nice to meet you, Lucia. You can call me Hank." As they shook hands, Lucia explained that her accountant, Julianna Channing, had told her they'd be moving in and she'd been looking forward to meeting them. Hank smelled a sales pitch and decided to cut to the chase. "What services are you offering?"

In lieu of an explanation, Max silently handed him a marketing brochure for Fidelia Investigations. Hank immediately shook his head. "Oh, we're just starting out. We can't afford to hire a PI."

"Yes, your partner said that but if you'll have a look at the data on the inside cover, I think you'll see that you can't afford *not* to hire a PI." More to humor her than anything else, Hank flipped open the brochure, to find several graphs showing how many billable hours lawyers "wasted" on investigative activities. "Notice the introductory package available to lawyers just starting out, like yourselves. For a low yearly retainer of—"

"Miss Scafetti—"

"Lucia, please."

"Lucia, we haven't even booked our first client. Maybe we'll consider hiring a PI later. If so, you'll be at the top of our list." He went to hand the brochure back to her but she waved him off, saying they should hang on to it.

Max took it back, perusing the material more thoroughly. "This is really nice." Addressing Hank, Max declared, "We should get something like this to hand out to potential clients." He then asked Lucia, "Who did this for you? Are they reasonable?"

"Very." Flashing a proud smile, Lucia explained, "I did it. As the final project for my marketing course. Got a B-plus."

Surprised that the brochure in question was amateur work, Hank asked, "You're a student? At Penn?" It was a natural assumption, his alma mater being in the neighborhood.

"I'm sort of a student, but at CCP. I got my Associates Degree in Business a few years ago and now I'm taking some computer courses."

"Do PIs use computers these days?" Hank pointed at the shiny black Dell sitting on the desk in the common area. "Max swore we needed one for our office but we're still debating exactly what we'll use it for—besides e-mail."

Lucia glanced at the computer. "Maybe some PIs use them but I'm just trying to figure out what a web page is and whether or not I need one to promote Fidelia."

"When you figure that out—can you let us know?" Max murmured, chiefly occupied with reading the back cover of the brochure. His head jerked up and he looked at Lucia. "Wait, you've been in business for nearly twenty years?" His voice dripping with skepticism, he protested, "Come on. Did you start as a PI in kindergarten?"

With a wry chuckle Lucia admitted, "No, not 'til high school." She pointed to a small picture at the bottom right of the brochure. "Former FBI agent Robert Baccaro started Fidelia in 1977."

Max squinted at the image. "Good looking guy. Where is he now?"

"He died nine years ago, that's when I took over."

"You've been doing this that long?" Hank scrutinized the young woman who appeared to be about his age. "You really were in high school?"

"Yeah, I started in my last semester." After the men simultaneously insisted on clarification, Lucia explained that one night she'd been playing pool with Baccaro and had him thirty-seven dollars in the hole. "Instead of paying me, he offered me a job doing legwork for Fidelia. I took it."

"Your family was okay with that?" Max asked. "My choices were law school, medical school, or being disowned."

"They were okay with what I told them...." A mischievous smile lighting her olive complexion, she continued, "Which is that I was working at Fidelia as a secretary."

Hank shook his head in mock disapproval. "When did they learn the real story?"

"Any day now," Lucia laughed. When Max wanted to know if she was serious, she explained, "They kind of figured it out when I started carrying a gun."

Since she'd mentioned one of Hank's favorite pastimes, he deliberately circled the conversation back to her mention of pool. "It sounds like you were a pretty good pool player in high school." With a grin he amended, "Or your boss was pretty bad. Do you still play?"

"Careful, she not only plays—she's a shark." They all looked up to find that Juli Channing had entered the room.

"Juli!" Lucia crowed. "As their accountant, please explain to these gentlemen—"

"Sorry, girl. I just helped them find some cheap office space here in Overbrook. I'm not their accountant." Hank mumbled that they'd hire her as soon as they had enough money coming in—*any* money coming in. In the meantime, Juli was explaining to Lucia, "They're friends of Dan,"

11

referring to her husband, City Councilman Daniel Bennett.

In response to Lucia asking how they knew Dan, Hank was dismayed to hear Max fire up one of his favorite speeches—lauding Hank for volunteering his legal services for Bennet's Fair Housing Initiative, which had inspired Max to join, too. He cringed as Max went on about Hank's passion for justice, ending with the information that they'd opened their office in West Philadelphia to better serve a community often denied any semblance of justice.

"Step down from the soapbox, Max. Let's get back to something interesting—like our neighbor here and her reportedly awesome pool game." Hands on hips, he looked up at Lucia. "I can't resist the challenge of a worthy opponent. How about a game? You ever play at Otto's Tavern on Delancey?"

To his surprise, Lucia said she hadn't, but accepted their invitation for a few rounds of pool after work that night. Juli agreed to join them, declaring that with her kids away at camp and Dan working late, their offer sounded much better than sitting home alone.

Lucia spent the rest of the afternoon delivering the bad news to three women that, yes, their husbands were cheating on them. Years as a PI had made her both wary and wise, so she prudently collected her final fee before handing over the photos. In the early days, she'd suffered mightily from a "Kill-the-

Messenger" customer mentality and now tried to exit the scene before her clients opened those manilla envelopes. Business concluded for the day, her thoughts turned to the prospect of a pleasant evening, starting with a leisurely walk with Rocco.

An afternoon rain shower had cooled the city enough that Rocco seemed to actually be enjoying their walk. His long luxurious fur was the reason he loathed the heat and his coat glinted like ebony in the early evening sun, swaying to the rhythm of his lively steps. Lucia's mood matched Rocco's and she was whistling in happy anticipation of the night ahead. A couple of games of pool was always a welcome diversion and she was toying with the idea of trying to persuade the guys to sign her on as their PI in name only. Even if no money changed hands and the job was strictly ceremonial, she could add that achievement to her marketing materials. They rounded the corner onto Ludlow Street where the office was located and Rocco hiked his leg against a light pole to no effect. "That's just bravado, boy, you're on empty. Stop dawdling."

When they reached the stairs leading down to the basement, Lucia saw a man wearing a stiff gray suit waiting outside her office. A new client was her immediate hope and she whispered to Rocco, "Be cool, okay? I don't need you scaring him off." The dog, more fearful than aggressive, generally ignored new people as long as they left him alone but he occasionally took a puzzling and immediate dislike to an innocuous stranger.

She clattered down the steps, calling out, "Hello? Are you here for Fide—" The man turned to face her and the shock of recognition stole the rest of the sentence and nearly her breath away. She gripped the banister in an effort to remain upright, loathe to show any weakness. Finally, she recovered enough to close her mouth and croak out a puzzled, "Dad?" The answer he gave was drowned out by Rocco, barking furiously, and lunging at the man who was studying them dispassionately.

CHAPTER 2
The Wound Lasts

"Stab the body and it heals, but injure the heart and the wound lasts a lifetime."—Mineko Iwasaki

Lucia quickly realized that no explanation would be audible until she quieted the agitated dog. She unlocked the office and motioned for her father to follow her in. As usual, once Rocco was secured in his crate, he calmed down, satisfied with emitting the occasional low growl. She straightened up after locking the crate, faced Carlo Scafetti, and gathered her wits. Coolly perching on the edge of the desk, she looked up at the man who, as in her youth, towered over her. "What are you doing here?"

"That's all you got to say after all these years? How 'bout, 'It's good to see you, Dad'?" When she refused to respond, Carlo muttered, "I guess it's not good. I guess if you'd've wanted to see me, you wouldn't've stopped coming to visit after my mom died."

"You weren't due to be released until September," she insisted, as if stating that bald fact could somehow cause the apparition before her to vanish and give her back those weeks she'd been counting on to prepare for this event.

"The DA arranged for it. They call it a quiet release." With a casual shrug he admitted, "I got a lotta enemies."

"I'll bet." She smacked herself in the forehead. "Oh, this is why mom is coming into town. She's here for you."

"That's right—we're going away together. I gotta take care a'some business and then we're leaving right after Sunday dinner."

"What business—" she started to ask before saying, "You know what? I don't even wanta know." While recoiling at the thought that she'd never again see her mom without having to see her father, too, she reconsidered the implications of her mother's message. "Does the rest of the family know about you getting out?"

"Most'll find out on Sunday. Only a few—Zia Pina, Zio Vince, Patsy—already know." He crossed his arms and glared at her. "The few who visited me this decade."

"Sorry I didn't wanta keep visiting the man who turned my world upside down and marked me with his name." Carlo shook his head in disgust, angling his body away from her while her complaints gathered steam. "Growing up, I thought you were a *good man*—a baker who visited his mom every day and walked me to church every Sunday. The man who bought me the fancy dress for my First Holy Communion when Mom worried it cost too much and Grandma said it would look silly on a girl my size. Then I lost that man—in the worst possible way."

Turning back, he pleaded, "You didn't lose him. He's right here."

"No, he never existed. I never had that father. I had the man who murdered people for money."

"You always do this," Carlo growled. "You make it sound so bad...it wasn't like that."

"Yes, it was," she snapped. "I wish I was smart enough to make what you did sound worse than it was."

With a curled lip, Carlo shot back, "You think I don't know you got a notch on your own gun?" She glared while he explained, "Your mom told me all about that."

"I'll bet she did. I'll bet she told you it was in no way comparable to murdering eight people in cold blood!" Saying it out loud, opened the wound that never seemed to heal. "*Gesù, Giusep, Marie,* eight people."

"I wasn't killing no choir boys. Anyone I took care of...they had it coming."

"Well, now I know where mom learned that particular line of bullshit."

"How do you know she learned that from me? Maybe I learned if from her." With an insolent grin, he added, "I learned plenty from her."

17

"Okay, we're done here."

"No, we're not. Where's my stuff?" She stared at him, at a loss for words, until he clarified, "The trunk of stuff Grandma left for you to hold on to for me."

"Oh yeah. It's out in the hall bathroom."

"What!" Carlo bellowed. "You left my stuff out where anybody could've stolen it? What the hell's wrong with you?"

"In the first place," she stated through clenched teeth, "only I have a key to that bathroom, and in the second, who in the world is interested in stealing twenty-year-old suits?"

"It ain't just suits! Where's your grandma's things? The mink I bought her and—"

"It's all there. I just...checked on that mink last year."

They were both startled by a knock at the door. Juli called, "Lucia? You almost ready to go?"

Lucia dashed over to the door and cracked it open, trying to shield Carlo from Juli's line of sight. "Hi. Um, I'm with a client. You guys go on ahead and I'll meet you there."

"Okay." Juli didn't immediately leave, studying Lucia's face instead. "Is everything all right?"

"Yeah...everything's fine. I just gotta settle up with this guy and then I'll be on my way."

With that assurance she left, calling out, "Hurry or you're gonna miss the free wings. We'll warm up a table for you."

Lucia turned back to her father who immediately asked, "Who's the—"

"You better think very carefully about your word choice here."

"Or what?"

"Or maybe you don't get your stuff tonight."

He shrugged and snickered, "We *all* used that word on the inside, you know."

"You're not in Graterford, Dad. You're in my office, on my turf."

"Fine. Who's the colored lady?"

She winced at the term he had settled on but let it go, figuring he had chosen it purposely to irk her. "Juli is a good friend of mine. Now, let me get your trunk and you can be on your way. Wait here."

She dragged the heavy trunk out of the bathroom and into the office, finding that her father had made himself at home. He was sprawled on the couch, examining the ash tray and lighter she kept on the low coffee table for clients. "Since when do you smoke?"

"I actually smoked from ninth grade up until a few years ago. You might've missed some stuff—you know, being locked up for most of my life."

"Yep, we got a lot to catch up on." He stood up and grabbed the trunk from her. "It'll be great— won't it?"

"Yeah, it'll be a blast," she snarked, watching her father easily hoist up the heavy trunk, impressed in spite of herself. "See you for Sunday dinner. Try not to murder anyone between now and then."

Appearing not to hear that barb, he paused at the open door, looking back to ask, "You ain't coming to breakfast tomorrow?"

"What? Patsy's putting you both up?"

"Of course. Why not?"

She loved Pasquale but felt he was a sucker for the idea of *La Famiglia* and let them walk all over him. Lucia muttered, "He is such a—"

"Hey, you watch your mouth. My cousin's always been one who understood how the world works." Carlo shook his head and assumed a fatherly tone that stoked the fires of her annoyance. "Maybe someday you'll wise up and figure it out, too."

"I know how the world works. I've been making my way in it for a very long time."

"Uh-huh." He glanced around the office. "I can see how good you've been doing at that—living here like you do."

"Beats a prison cell all to hell, don't it?" She swept a hand around the space. "Not a toilet in sight."

"Grow the fuck up, Chichi."

She wanted to object to that hated nickname but refused to let him know he'd gotten to her as much as she'd apparently gotten to him. Instead, she pointed out into the hall. "I'm sure you have to be going."

"Yeah, that taxi's waited long enough." Carlo called out, "See you at breakfast, kid," as, to her immense relief, he left.

Clenching her teeth, Lucia ensured no tear escaped until after her father's footsteps faded away. She let Rocco out and hugged him tightly, sniffling into his fur while he valiantly tried to lick her face. She thanked him for that bit of mammalian comfort by giving him a little extra dinner, then grabbed her pool cue and headed off to Otto's, stopping briefly in the lobby bathroom to splash cold water on her still-flushed face.

Otto's was dim and smoke-filled so it took Lucia a minute to spot Juli waving her over to a pool table in the back of the bar. Gratefully accepting the plate of wings the group had saved for her, she ate while observing the game they were finishing up. Hank won handily and then volunteered to procure the next round.

"Sam Adams okay for everyone?" he asked.

"Works for me." Lucia wiped her hands clean, then took her cue out of the case and started fitting the pieces together.

"Oh, how fancy," Max cooed. He called over to Hank, "Get your game face on, Narváez. She's got her own cue."

A minute later, Hank set the beers down on a nearby table and stooped to examine the small plaque on Lucia's cue case. "No, she *won* her own cue." He read the inscription aloud. "WPBA, Delaware Valley Tournament, 1988, Fourth place." Straightening up, hand on hip, Hank stared at Juli. "You said she was good; you didn't say *she was a pro*." He turned to Max. "All bets are off—literally."

"As officers of the court, I'm sure you wouldn't engage in illegal gambling either way, right?" Lucia laughed. "And I'm not a pro. I tried—but that tourney convinced me to give it up." She pointed to the case. "A local event and I came in fourth. Didn't even finish in the money. Buying a cue would've cost me less than the entrance fee."

Max chugged some of his beer and cocked his head at Lucia. "So, what you're telling us is that we have nothing to worry about because you're only the fourth best woman pool player in the tri-state area?"

"That was seven years ago." She chalked her cue, then offered, "Are you looking for some weight? Let's play a game first and then, if need be, I can give you that."

"Some weight?" Hank asked.

"You know...a handicap. Like, are you looking for me to spot you some balls or do you wanta play wild eight or—"

"This is getting way too complicated for a friendly game of pool," Juli interjected. "The old lady is the worst player here. I'll team up with Lucia; that evens things out. Right?"

The guys agreed to that compromise, and soon Lucia was making shot after shot while regaling them with stories of her most amusing cases. "But then the hooker turned to the judge and said she didn't lie to me, she just didn't recognize my client's husband with his clothes on."

Max's laughter died abruptly when she finished the game by banking the eight-ball into the side pocket. "Were you being kind to us with those first few shots or lulling us into a false sense of security?"

"Just getting the feel of a new table," Lucia admitted. She looked at Hank and Max. "You've been playing here since law school?"

"Undergrad *and* law school," Max volunteered. "Otto's is *the* hangout spot for Penn students."

"Ah, that's why I've never been here before." Lucia racked up the balls for a second game, then told Juli she could break. "Us community college types hang out at Westy's on Callowhill. Never the twain shall meet."

"Do you live up near Spring Garden?" Hank asked.

Juli missed her shot and grinned, awaiting the answer. Ignoring her friend's obvious amusement, Lucia said, "No, I live here in West Philly." Juli raised her eyebrows, silently calling her out on that slight deception so Lucia added, "On Ludlow, between 48th and 49th Street."

There was no immediate response as the guys were consulting on Hank's opening move. Max pointed out his recommended shot, murmuring, "I didn't know there were apartments in our office building."

"There aren't," Lucia admitted with a shrug. "I made a deal with Belsky...the old man, not that creep son of his," she clarified. "He lets me live there full-time for a few bucks extra a month. When I took over Fidelia, I couldn't afford the office and an apartment. These days I could, but I'm saving for a house."

"Tell them why," Juli laughed.

Sighing, Lucia answered, "Because of Rocco. He wants to live in a house with a yard and a screened-in porch."

After making the shot Max had suggested, Hank bounced the butt of his cue on the ground, studying

23

the table. "Rocco is your boyfriend?" When she corrected him, he looked at Lucia, his head cocked, lips parted slightly. "Your dog told you he wants to live in a house?"

"In a way. I housesit for Juli whenever she's on vacation and Rocco loves it. So, I'm saving up to buy a twin there in Mount Airy."

"That must be one great dog," Max said, missing his shot and turning the play over to Lucia.

"Oh yeah, he's great at getting her in trouble." Lucia concentrated on sinking the eleven-ball, while Juli continued, "If he snaps at Belsky's son one more time, the old man might be forced to give you the heave-ho."

"Speaking as a lawyer," Max interjected, "a snappy dog can be a real liability."

"He's not a liability. Who wouldn't snap at Donny Belsky if they had the chance?" As Juli laughingly conceded her point, Lucia left off her defense so Juli could shoot in peace. When she finally missed, Lucia picked up the subject, saying, "Give him a break—Rocco likes *you*."

"Yeah, he's a love to me, but he *hates* everything else—people, other dogs, cats, squirrels, water, loud noises—"

"Aww, only 'cause he had a rough start in life." As the guys took their turns, Lucia described how Rocco had been bred as a show dog but was stolen from a puppy show at four-months-old. "His breeder hired me to find him. By the time I did, he'd developed some...issues. When he bit a show judge, the breeder offered him to me in lieu of paying her overdue bill."

Hank considered his options, then told Max he was going to try a safety to stave off a second defeat. After he completed the task, he laughed at Lucia. "You took a problem dog over cash?"

Her forehead crinkled in concentration, Lucia studied the table, responding absent-mindedly, "I had to, we bonded during his ordeal." She then bent to work, pulling off a semi-massé shot to seal the victory. "Some connections defy logic."

"This certainly sounds like one of them," Max answered with a chuckle. "Rack 'em up again, Scafetti. I finally got a handle on your weaknesses. Victory will be ours this time."

Whether it had been over-confidence or mere bluster, Max's game didn't live up to his boast. Watching Lucia sink the eight-ball for the third time, Hank said, "I'm out. I've had enough of the agony of defeat." He smiled at Max. "Thank God, we're law-abiding officers of the court so financial loss wasn't part of it."

They ceded the table to some waiting students and easily found seats at the deserted bar. Hank raised his nearly-empty bottle of beer in a salute to the victor. "I guess the PI business leaves a lot of time for playing pool?"

Lucia was digging through her pockets, collecting loose ones for her portion of the tab. "Actually, it's busing tables in a restaurant that leaves lots of time for playing pool on the ratty old table in the back room."

"You work in a restaurant, too?"

"I did, as soon as I was strong enough to handle a bus bin. Which for me, was age ten." Lucia explained that her great aunts and late grandmother owned a restaurant together and the whole family was expected to pitch in. "Most of the other girls graduated to waiting tables in their teens but I was never considered pretty, graceful, or deferential enough. All true, and fine by me."

Hank gallantly objected to her self-deprecation while Max inquired, "Deferential? What does that mean?"

"Le Sorelle is frequented by...a very special clientele—and Zia Carmela didn't trust me to be nice to them." She polished off her beer, muttering, "Can't fault her on her perceptivity."

"Le Sorelle on south tenth?" Max asked. "No offense, but I always heard that was a mob hang-out."

Lucia raised her eyebrows at Max, while Juli leaned forward, explaining in an undertone, "That would be the special clientele she was talking about."

Her voice raspy with emotion, Lucia said, "Yep. My family associates with criminals, murderers, and thugs. Even worse—a lot of them *are* criminals, murderers, and thugs."

Hank had been staring at her throughout the last few conversational exchanges. He swallowed visibly. "Scafetti. Are you related to Carlo Sca—"

"He's my father." Rather than admitting that the man in question had visited her a few short hours ago, she slapped her money on the scarred wooden bar top. "I come from a long line of terrible people, but he's the worst." Grabbing a paper napkin, Lucia swiped it across her damp brow. "When I found out who he was...what he was, I thought that was as bad as it could get. But then came a lifetime of people treating me...." She tossed her head, running out of steam and figuring they could fill in the blanks.

"Like you were one of them," Max said. "Presumption of guilt."

"Exactly." She shrugged her shoulders and rolled her head, admitting, "I've even thought about trying to escape it by using my mom's maiden name: Luna. Lucia Luna." She looked up with a faint smile. "Has a certain 'movie-star' ring to it, doesn't it? But my family would disown me for sure if I tried that. Even my mom."

Not looking up from the label he was peeling from his beer bottle, Hank asked, "Are you sure you care?"

"No. I'm not sure. Except for my mom and one of my cousins, I mean. But...like it or not, they're the only family I've got." She clapped her hands on her thighs, and briskly announced, "Well, I had a great time but I'm ready to call it a night, guys." She turned toward Juli. "I'll walk you to your car, if you're ready."

Everyone agreed it was time to go. Hank and Max headed for the El stop at 40th and Market, while Juli and Lucia went in the opposite direction.

On the way back to her car, Juli Channing shot down Lucia's idea of trying to sign Siskin and Narváez as faux-clients. "It borders on fraud and I'm sure those two aren't down with that." Her young friend quickly saw reason but was obviously disappointed. "You've come a long way since the days you were putting up flyers in hair salons and laundromats to scrounge up business. Fidelia's headed in the right direction— you'll get there."

"I hope so." Lucia was silent for a time before venturing, "Since you know the guys so well...."

"It's Dan that really knows them but ask away."

"Is Max single?"

"Ah, I see. The good news is your taste is improving—the bad news is your luck isn't."

"Aww, I knew it—he's taken."

"Not at the moment, but he is gay." When Lucia started lamenting that all the good men were one or the other, Juli asked, "What about Hank? No interest there?"

"Yeah, right. The guy who looks like he's the result of someone asking a Disney illustrator to design a Hispanic lawyer, is gonna go for me."

"How can you be such a good PI and miss such obvious clues? Didn't you see how he reacted when he thought Rocco was your boyfriend? And how he objected when you said you weren't pretty?"

"He was just being nice."

"No, he wasn't. You're a very striking young woman. Stop selling yourself short. *That* is how you end up in...unhealthy situations."

"Why don't you just come right out and say it? 'I never approved of your relationship with Robert Baccaro.'" Juli threw her hands wide open, acknowledging the obvious, and Lucia continued, "You know, those first few years, I thought you didn't like me, I didn't realize it was actually Bac you didn't like."

"I liked him well enough. What I didn't like was how he thought he could get whatever he wanted from a woman by just flashing those baby blues at her."

"His eyes weren't baby blue, they were turquoise...." In a dreamy voice she finished, "...like no other eyes I'd ever seen."

"That's what I'm talking about. They sure worked on you." Lucia had no response other than a sheepish shrug. Juli prodded, "Maybe, give some deep brown eyes a chance for a change."

"You think I should ask Hank out?"

As much as Juli admired Lucia's headfirst nature, she thought Narváez just might be a slightly old-fashioned guy in matters of romance. "*Or*—you could flirt a little and wait for him to do the asking."

"Waiting is not my style."

"The meek will inherit the earth, hun."

"Maybe—but they sure don't get anything right now."

A few minutes after seven the next morning Lucia breezed into the lobby, feeling invigorated by her morning swim at the YMCA. She ran a hand through her hair to check how much it had dried on the walk. With July humidity blanketing the city, the answer was not much. When she was younger, she often attempted to blow-dry the unruly mass into a smoother style. Age brought wisdom and she now accepted that beachy waves were not part of her genetic legacy, and so let her curls run wild—and that they did.

"Good morning!" Lucia turned to see Hank Narváez, dressed in spandex shorts, walking his bicycle into the lobby. She returned the cheery greeting, also taking a moment to discreetly admire his strong, shapely legs, before commenting on his chosen form of transportation. He explained, "I live in Powelton Village, so biking here makes the most sense."

"I can see that. Except it might not make as much sense on a day like today. Especially on your way home—in the scorching sun." While Hank avowed a life-long indifference to heat and humidity, Lucia was scrambling for a segue into more personal matters. "I had a really good time last night." If she could have smacked herself for the lameness of that comment without him noticing, she definitely would have done just that.

"Me, too." With a merry laugh he added, "Probably not as good as you, though."

"Oh, well, I'm used to that. Winning at pool, I mean." Frantically trying to erase the casual boast she'd just inadvertently made, Lucia blurted, "But you gave me a good game."

"No, I didn't. That's why I was thinking of us maybe trying something that didn't involve you and your pool cue." She stared at him, afraid to assume he'd just asked her out until he added, "You know...like dinner? Say, this Saturday?"

"Dinner! Yes, I love dinner. I was actually gonna—" She took a breath, gathering her scattered wits. "I mean, I'd love to have dinner with you."

"Great. How about Striped Bass? Do you like fish?"

"Oh my God, Striped Bass—that would be awesome. I've been dying to try that place, but from what I've heard, it takes at least a month to get reservations for a weeknight let alone a Saturday."

"True, but it just so happens that I already have a reservation—for this Saturday at seven-thirty."

"For two?"

"Yes, I was going with a friend...but...he canceled on me."

Grinning widely, she said, "I see. Well, since you got the reservation, seems like I should pick up the check." After he loudly objected, they went back and forth for a while, finally agreeing to split the tab. She waved good-bye as Hank walked his bike into the elevator, calling after him, "Tell Max I said thanks and I will definitely make it up to him!"

CHAPTER 3
Rumors of Death

"We wake, if we ever wake at all, to mystery, rumors of death, beauty, violence...."—Annie Dillard, *Pilgrim at Tinker Creek*

In the glare of the Friday morning sun that was already feeling a touch oppressive, Patsy ushered Lucia and Rocco into his immaculate rowhouse. His greeting included a smile and the news that he'd procured some imported mortadella for breakfast. Knowing he'd done that explicitly for her sake, she thanked him lavishly; that particular cold-cut was expensive and she rarely got to enjoy it.

Her Great-Aunt Giuseppina's youngest child and only son, Pasquale Rinaldi was strong and handsome, if slightly squat of build. A faithful Catholic, he refused to even date though his wife had left him almost ten years earlier for another man. He devoted himself to the son he saw every other weekend, his father's butcher shop where he was the most skilled butcher on the premises, and his extended family. He loved them all, though, like Lucia, he stayed firmly out of the more questionable aspects of the family businesses. Unlike her, he did not condemn those who chose otherwise. His tender heart was the main reason he was, other than her mom, Lucia's only ally in the family.

"Your parents are upstairs," he explained as they walked to the back of the house and into the kitchen. "There's been some...commotion going on since last night."

With a wince, she said, "If that's a euphemism of some sort I will have to kill you and then myself."

He handed her a mug of coffee, with a puzzled look on his face. "A eupha...no! There's some money or...I don't know...something missing from your grandmother's trunk."

"Money? There was no money in there."

"You went through it?"

"No, Patsy, I stored the belongings of a convicted felon for almost seven years without knowing what was in there. Of course, I searched it!"

Her father burst into the room, followed closely by her mother. A tiny woman, Angelina Scafetti was dwarfed by her hulking husband, who was unshaven and carelessly attired in a yellowed t-shirt and creased trousers. In contrast, Angie, still a beauty at fifty-five, was carefully coiffed and dressed.

Breathing heavily, Carlo charged over towards Lucia, causing Rocco to dash under the kitchen table, making his presence known through his nonstop growling. While Lucia hugged her mother, accepting her warm greeting, Carlo demanded, "Where is Lidia's scapular?"

"What?" She was completely thrown by the question though she knew about her grandmother's extensive collection of scapulars, a Catholic devotional item featuring various saints. Most of them consisted of two small cloth squares joined by shoulder tapes, meant to be worn under clothing, one square front and one square back. And they were the last thing she'd expected her father to be looking for.

"The Green Scapular," he insisted. "The one Grandma gave Lidia when she first got sick."

Patsy walked over to him, murmuring, "Carlo, Lucia was still a baby when your sister died. She's probably got no idea what you're talking about."

"It was in that trunk. My mother kept it there, always! Last she told me, it was in her mink. I even tore the lining outta that coat, it ain't there!" He turned back to Lucia. "Did you take it?"

"No! All of Grandma's scapulars are in her pocketbook that was in the trunk. Did you look there?"

Angie entered the fray, saying, "Those are the ordinary brown ones. Your father needs that special green one."

Looking up at Carlo, Lucia asked, "What for?"

"None a' your fucking business. You told me you checked the mink last year. Was it in the pockets?"

"No," she answered automatically, though she was frantically casting her mind back to when she wore the mink to the wedding she'd attended with Davis Rockingham. Surely, she would have remembered finding a scapular in the pocket. She stared up at her father, declaring, "There was nothing in that coat."

"What were you checking it for?"

"To see if the moths had gotten to it." Which was the truth, though only part of it. "You're not supposed to store furs like that."

Carlo slammed his fist on the counter, causing Patsy to jump and Angie to rush over and rub his arm in a soothing gesture. In a low voice she asked, "You sure she said it was in the mink? It's been a long time."

"I think so—she kept moving it, goddamn it. Every time I talked to her it was in a different place."

"Let's go up and check the trunk agai—"

"Forget it, we've wasted enough time. I don't need the fucking key. There's other ways to get at it."

Angie asked what he meant while at the same time Patsy suggested, "Maybe your dad knows—"

By then Carlo was halfway out the back door that opened onto a narrow alley. He called back, "I'm taking your car, Pats."

When the dishes on the table had stopped rattling from the force of Carlo's departure, Lucia turned to her mother. "Ma, what in the hell is going on? Why's he screaming about a scapular?"

"Your grandma was keeping some...money for your dad. He needs a key to get at it—and the key was with that scapular."

"What kind of key is it? What does it open?"

Still staring at the kitchen door, her mother answered in a distant voice, "He wouldn't say."

"Was it for Grandma's safety deposit box?"

Eagerly, Angie spun around to face Lucia. "That must be it! Where is that key?"

"I don't know," Lucia answered as she gulped some coffee. "I only saw it one time when I went to the bank with her." She rolled her eyes. "She kept all her canceled checks there though I told her she didn't have to hang on to them forever. Patsy's right, maybe Nonno knows where that key is."

"I'll go see Zio Tony today," Patsy volunteered. "Ask him about it."

"Save your breath." Waving a hand at Patsy, Angie scoffed, "Tony don't even know his own name these days, I hear."

"Ma!" Lucia admonished. "That ain't nice."

"Yeah? When was he ever nice to me?"

Lucia had no rebuttal since it was true, her grandfather had never bothered to hide his animosity towards his daughter-in-law. Dropping the matter, she offered, "I have nothing much on the schedule this morning, so I'll go with you to the nursing home, Patsy. It's worth a try." She looked towards the door her father had exited so hastily. "If Dad goes roaring into a bank trying to get into that safety deposit box with no key, he's gonna be back in the slammer before dark."

"Let's eat first," Patsy answered. "Come on, Angie, you, too. We'll all feel better if we have something to eat."

"The Italian-American motto," Lucia muttered, taking her place at the kitchen table, after calling Rocco out from under it.

Lucia and Patsy walked back from St. Agatha's Rehabilitation and Nursing Center in a subdued mood, having received the news that Antonio Scafetti was not expected to live much longer. Lucia's grandfather had suffered his first stroke when she was a teenager and was eventually incapacitated by a massive one a few years later. Still, hearing that he'd been put in hospice was something of a shock.

Waiting to cross at a red light, she studied Patsy, trying to decide whether she should give voice to her principal thought. She was aching to complain that her father should have gone to see his dad immediately, rather than worrying about that stupid money. In the end, she held her tongue. Patsy would just defend Carlo, as he would the devil himself if they were related, and Lucia was in no mood for an argument with her favorite cousin.

Angie and Rocco met them at the door. "Well?" Angie demanded loudly, struggling to be heard over Rocco's joyous barks. "Did the old man have anything to say? Anything you could make out clear?"

"He couldn't talk much," Lucia answered, while attempting to keep Rocco from jumping into her arms. "But he did have this." She held up a white and green scapular, consisting of one piece of plastic-covered rectangular cloth, hanging from a green cord. "No key with it though."

"Well, that's just great," Angie groused.

Patsy put a consoling hand on her shoulder. "We don't know that's the same scapular Lidia had. Zia Sofie used to give those green ones out to everyone who was...you know, dying."

With a snort of bitter amusement, Angie declared, "Yeah, all those years Sofie took care a' Tony, did everything for him, worried about him dying—and then she went first."

Throughout her childhood, the undercurrent of hostility between Tony and Angie had puzzled Lucia. As an adult, she'd finally deduced that her old-world grandfather had probably opposed his son's marriage to a Las Vegas cocktail waitress who was not only a stranger to the family but two years older than Carlo. "Well, now he really is dying, Ma, so maybe you can let the feud go? They said he won't last the month."

"Oh, honey. I'm sorry to hear that, I really am," she said, embracing her daughter. "I know you love him and he sure loves you."

Lucia nodded sadly, remembering how her grandfather would let her help out at his newsstand. Her help consisted mainly of reading comic books and eating candy, with the occasional duty of delivering small brown bags to a bar down the street. It was a sorry day when she realized the stand's popularity was not due to the great magazine selection but because Tony was booking bets and running numbers for the neighborhood. "Dad better go see him as soon as he gets back." No longer able to hold in her anger, she added, "In fact, he should've done that before he went after that damn money."

"Can you just once cut your father some slack? He's been waiting for that money all these years."

"What money is it?" Angie just shook her head, so Lucia repeated, "Ma, what money?"

Angie sighed, "Money...from your father's business."

As Lucia was staring at her mom, trying to parse that evasion, Patsy announced he had to get to the butcher shop for his afternoon shift. Lucia suspected he mainly wanted to escape the tense atmosphere that had suddenly developed in his kitchen. Not able to blame him, she bid him an affectionate farewell.

As soon as he was gone, Lucia returned to the subject. "The money couldn't be from the last job Dad pulled because that was a bust." Slowly putting the pieces together, Lucia stared at Angie. "Oh my god, Dad didn't get the goods off of Guenther because he'd already fenced them. So, he took money off of the body, instead. Is that it?"

"Don't ask me for the details, you know your father never talked about his work. It's money and it's related to the Guenther job. That's already more than he'd want anyone to know. Especially you."

"Ain't that the truth," Lucia whispered. Out loud, she started, "Are you sure this is...." She walked over and put an arm around her mother's shoulder. "Mama, are you sure you want back into this life with him?"

"Lucia, don't be silly. Your father ain't picking up the trade again. That's what the money is for—it's enough to give us a start on a new life together."

"A new life," Lucia repeated softly. "Are we talking like...hundreds of thousands?"

Angie laughed. "Oh yeah, I waited tables at Le Sorelle all them years 'cause we was sitting on a fortune in cash. No, nowhere near that much." She slipped out from under Lucia's arm. "Now, sit down. I'll fix you a hot lunch for a change an' you can fill me in on what you've been doing."

Sighing heavily, Lucia contemplated trying to puncture her mother's naiveté, but abandoned the notion immediately. If her was willfully blind to the fact that no amount of money was going to suddenly propel Carlo Scafetti into an honest life, then Lucia telling her so wasn't going to open her eyes.

Since her father did not reappear, Lucia enjoyed the time she spent with her mother despite the list of directives she received during lunch. Angie walked Lucia and Rocco to the front door. "What we talked about," she said, "are you gonna get any of that done today? Do you want me to call Donna for you? She might be able to fit you in this afternoon."

"Ma, I am not getting my hair done at Donna's salon; everyone comes outta there looking like it's 1965. As for the rest of it, I like wearing Lidia's cast-offs, it's called vintage, and I can hardly lose ten pounds today." Without waiting for her mother's reaction, she headed out the door.

"I didn't say *that*! I just asked if you were living on junk, which how could you not be with no kitchen and no way to cook?"

Halfway down the marble steps to the sidewalk, Lucia turned and smiled up at her mother. "Okay, so I don't need to lose any weight?"

Angie hesitated, rocking her head back and forth. "If I'm being honest, honey, a few pounds wouldn't hurt."

"See you Sunday, Ma."

After leaving her mother, Lucia spent the rest of Friday wrapping up two missing persons cases. The first was good news—Lucia had located the client's dead-beat ex-husband and she could start the process of getting her back child support. The second case had no such happy ending. There was a positive ID on the clients' daughter, Billie Hansell, as a girl who had died weeks earlier in a crack house in Camden. Lucia had become painfully familiar with delivering that sort of news and handled it well. Still, it never got easy, but she thought maybe that's how it should be.

With those cases done, she devoted Saturday morning to an insurance fraud job: a slip-and-fall where the list of injuries was suspiciously long. Nothing fancy or dangerous required, just old-fashioned surveillance of the suspect's home. She also discretely canvassed the woman's neighborhood looking for that jackpot of a busybody with a lot of time and a loose tongue. However, the suspect didn't make an appearance and she had surprisingly incurious neighbors, so Lucia came up empty. She'd try again later.

That wrapped up all planned work for the weekend, and she walked Rocco while mentally cataloguing her wardrobe choices for that night's dinner with Hank Narváez. It seemed like the occasion called for a knock-out dress but was that trying too hard on a first date? Perhaps a dressy skirt and simple top would be a better choice? By the time she and Rocco returned to the office, Lucia had settled on her bottle-green brocade cocktail dress— she always said, 'Go big or go home,' and saw no reason to change that attitude now.

Her phone rang and Lucia's first thought was that it might be Hank canceling. She answered while praying that wasn't the case and was relieved to hear Patsy's voice. "Miss me already? Or did my mom forget to mention that I need a manicure?"

"No, it's nothing like that. It's...I need you to come over to my parent's house, right now."

"Is something wrong?"

"Yes, but I'd...we'd rather tell you in person."

"Is it *Nonno*?" When Patsy didn't respond, she said, "Oh my God, it's not my mom, is it?"

"It's neither of them, please just come over as soon as you can."

"On my way."

Lucia was greeted at the door of the senior Rinaldi house by Patsy's sister, Donna, who had moved back in with her parents after her husband died of most unnatural causes. She and Angie had

43

always been friendly and Lucia wasn't surprised to see her mom sitting on the couch between Zia Pina and her husband, Vince Rinaldi. What did give her pause was the shellshocked look on her mom's face and the large crowd in attendance.

Quickly scanning the room, she noted in addition to the Rinaldi clan, her Great-Aunt Carmela, Carmela's dour son, Dominic "Micky" Vetere, his daughter Gabby, and son-in-law, Frankie Tumino. Lucia had mixed feelings about Gabby. On one hand, she was a back-stabbing little gossip, on the other, her father made Lucia's own look like Mr. Rogers. Moreover, she was, at twenty-one, already married to one of the densest, meanest thugs in South Philly. Reflexively, Lucia checked to see if Micky and Frankie were carrying and upon spotting the telltale bulges under their shirts, got the usual answer.

Patsy stood up from his chair and gestured that Lucia should take his place. She shook her head. "I'd rather stand. What's this about?"

"Your father never came home last night and they found my car abandoned on Oregon Avenue. Now, there is word...we have reason to believe he won't be coming home. Ever."

"Are you saying...he's dead? My father is dead?" She looked over at her mom who just stared back at Lucia, her face painted with an inarticulate grief.

"Yes," Patsy answered very deliberately. "We think so."

"Wait—you think he's dead, or you know he's dead?"

Patsy kept looking at Frankie, who finally spoke. "Signs point that way. I can't say no more."

A variety of emotions surged through Lucia, so numerous and tangled were they that she couldn't immediately identify her reaction. She pulled at the dominant thread and found anger. The emotion Bac always warned against, the one that got people killed. With effort she shoved it back into the snarl. "What signs? Why would anyone want to kill him? He literally just got out."

"You know better than to ask those questions," Micky retorted. He went over to Angie, imperiously offered his condolences, and left. With Micky gone, everyone but Carmela and Gabby looked more relaxed, Frankie most of all.

Zia Pina stared at the door where the white lace curtains still swayed from Micky's exit. "D'Amico didn't waste any time." She sighed mournfully. "He never forgets or forgives disrespect. Carlo should not've struck out on his own. Salvatore has a long memory...and is a most patient man."

"It wasn't about respect," Angie answered woodenly, finally finding her voice. "They were after the Kimberley Star and those coins—"

Rubbing her forehead to ward off a looming headache, Lucia turned to her mother. "Why would they do that? *Everyone* should know that Dad never got them. Otherwise, he would've traded them for a better deal back then. He wouldn't've sat in prison for nearly twenty-years."

"You could both be right," Vince said. "Carlo would'nt've sat on them all this time—but it was enough if D'Amico thought he did."

Frankie scoffed, "Like always, none of yous know nothing about how things work. Why wouldn't he do just that?" With a shrug he added, "I woulda. Just do your time and then live large for the rest of your life. No wonder Carlo wasn't gonna let D'Amico take 'em away. He forgot—D'Amico takes what he wants."

Lucia spun around to face Frankie. "You seem to know an awful lot about it for a...." She paused and her tone curdled as she finished, "...messenger boy. If I find out you had anything to do with this, you *strunz*, you'll be the sorriest man in Philadelphia."

"You sure like to talk tough don't you, Chichi? Well, girlie, just in case you ain't all talk, remember this...." He puffed out his chest, gloating, "You come for the king, you better not miss."

"Here's two pieces of news everyone else in this room already knows." She strolled over until they were nearly toe-to toe. She stared him down, eyes narrowed. "In the first place—you're no king. And in the second...." Her voice dropped to a menacing hiss. "I never miss."

"Lucia, *che fai*?" Zia Carmela exclaimed. "Show some respect for once in your life! Especially in front of your mother. She's a widow now."

"Is she?" Lucia threw up her hands in disgust. "Why are you all so sure my dad is dead?" She jerked her thumb in Frankie's direction, asking, "Because he thinks so? If that one told me the sun was rising in the east, I'd still check for myself. He's the mushroom boy of the mob. They feed him bullshit and keep him in the dark."

"Like anyone cares what you think," Frankie sneered.

Her mouth twisted in a grimace, Lucia eyed him silently for a moment, her mind racing. "You still carrying water for Paulie Lugano?"

"What?" His demeanor shifted suddenly from feigned indifference to barely controlled fury. "I don't carry water for no one! If anyt'ing Paulie is my stooge!"

She nodded, smiling to herself at Frankie's gullibility. She made no reply to Frankie, and walked over to her mother, still sitting on the couch in stony silence. Vince stood up and Lucia took his place. "What do you want me to do, Mama? What can I do for you?"

Angie hugged her tightly. "Nothing. And I mean that, Lucia Marie. You are not to go digging into this. We wait. If your father's dead...." her voice cracked. "You can't fix that. An' if you're right that he's alive then...then he don't need you getting in his way." Angie took Lucia's face between her hands and stared into her eyes. "Stay out of this. Promise me! Swear it."

"I promise. I swear on Grandma's grave I won't do anything."

Angie appeared satisfied and allowed Lucia to get her a glass of Zio Vince's homemade wine from the kitchen. After she drank it, Lucia asked if she needed help getting back to Patsy's house. Angie waved her off, saying she could walk six goddamned blocks and Patsy would be with her anyway. Lucia stood up and bent down to kiss her mom on the cheek. "I'll see you early tomorrow morning, Mama."

Eyes narrowed in suspicion, Angie asked, "Where are you going?"

"Don't worry, I'm not investigating anything—I have a date." Lucia ignored the murmurs of shock from her great-aunts at the callous indifference she was displaying to her father's supposed death.

As usual in family gatherings, Angie came to her defense. "Let her go," she snapped. "Can't you see she ain't accepted this? Let her put the pain off a little while. I wish I could." Lucia kissed her mom again, quietly voicing her gratitude. Angie said, "You really wanta thank me? Tell me about—"

To belay her mother's third degree, Lucia chanted, "I didn't mention him to you because we just met, he's a lawyer, not Italian, but yes, Catholic. I think. Yeah, I'm pretty sure he is." Lucia headed for the door, tossing back, "And no, you can't meet him. Yet."

"*Che disgrazia!*" Zia Carmela thundered. "This is how you speak to your grieving mother?" Lucia exchanged a few quiet words with Patsy as her great-aunt started in on Angie. "This is what you get for spoiling her. You and Carlo both spoiled that girl rotten, with Tony helping out. Only Sofie ever tried to curb her. Now you see what that got you, she's got no respect for anyone or anything."

Lucia was tempted to turn around and point out how much Carmela's own widow-comforting skills sucked, but wisely, she tucked that incendiary device away and wordlessly left the house.

CHAPTER 4

In Every Scar

"I realized that there is a lesson, which was, in every scar there is a story."—Emily Bernard, *Black Is the Body: Stories from My Grandmother's Time, My Mother's Time, and Mine*

In the crowded bar of *Striped Bass*, Hank wended his way back to their small table where Lucia stood, looking around, admiring the décor. It was impressive: marble columns, thirty-foot-high ceilings, and dozens of mullioned windows. He'd gone to see if their table, now thirty-minutes overdue, was ready yet. She smiled at his approach, saying, "And the word is...?"

"The word is that they've run into some unspecified issues and it will be, quote—unquote, 'a little while longer'."

"I'd be annoyed if it didn't just mean more time with you." Hank was about to ask if she wanted another glass of wine when she muttered, "Oh, shit."

"What? Did you just see the price card?"

"Worse—I just saw my asshole ex."

"Where?"

Lucia inclined her head towards the entrance where a group of dark-suited men were in conversation with the maître d'. "The incredible hulk over there—with the high forehead." She added with an unkind snicker, "That keeps getting higher."

Hank studied the man, assuming she meant the one towering over his companions. "Why does he look so familiar?"

"Maybe because he is the most prominent assistant district attorney in Philadelphia?"

"Davis Rockingham." Turning his head back towards Lucia in surprise, Hank exclaimed, "You dated him?"

"Don't hold it against me—we all make mistakes."

Before Hank could formulate a response, the tall broad form of Rockingham was casting a significant shadow over their tiny table. "Lucia? I thought that was you! How are you?" Lucia performed a short, perfunctory introduction. After a handshake that Hank felt was unnecessarily forceful, Rockingham asked, "Are you waiting for a table? Need any help getting seated?" He pointed back towards the group he'd entered with. "My Kappa Sig brother, Pierce Riddle, is a friend of Alison Barshak. She's the chef-owner—"

"Yes, we know who she is," Hank said. "Thanks for the offer but we have a reservation. I'm sure we'll be seated soon."

"In a place like this, reservations have been known to get lost." Rockingham smirked. "I assume that's how we got a table on such short notice. But—suit yourself." He sauntered off.

As soon as he was out of earshot, Hank rolled his eyes at Lucia. "Wow. You weren't kidding when you said he was an asshole. Is he always like that?"

"Yeah, pretty much. Thing is, I'm sure he thought he was being gracious."

"I can definitely see why you made him your ex."

"Oh, it wasn't that."

"What was it, then?"

"Probably the fact that he dumped me."

"Oh. Sorry."

"Nah, it all worked out for the best." She smiled warmly at him. "Rockingham went back to dating Muffy von Trust-Fund while I get to date handsome, highly-principled young lawyers."

"What? You got another guy coming tonight?"

"We can throw modest into that mix," she answered with a light laugh. "No, no one else is coming—and it looks like that includes our waiter." After another twenty minutes, having been once again told that their table wasn't quite ready, Lucia drawled, "You know what? I'm not in the mood for fish anymore. How do you feel about pizza?"

"I love it."

Twenty-minutes later they were seated at a table in Pietros Coal-Fired Pizzeria, a mere four blocks down Walnut Street, but a world away from Striped Bass. Hank studied the warm walnut woodwork and the friendly bar. "This place is great. I haven't had pizza from a coal oven since I left New York."

"I knew you'd love it. Everybody does, even—" Lucia stopped short, amending her statement abruptly, "Just...everybody loves it."

Hank chuckled to let her know he'd caught her slip and it was okay. "You brought Rockingham here?" When she nodded, he asked, "How did you and the Main Line Meathead ever even cross paths?"

"I was a star witness in a case he was prosecuting. This sleazeball car dealer killed his wife so he could marry his stripper-mistress without paying out a dime. Little did he know his wife was wise to him and had already hired me to get the evidence."

"Oh, the Bandey case. You were the PI on that?"

"I was." She acknowledged the achievement with an exaggerated nod of her head. "Not surprising considering almost seventy-five-percent of my business is from wives who think their husbands are cheating on them."

"Hmmm," he drawled mischievously. "I don't remember *that* statistic in your brochure...."

With a laugh she admitted, "That brochure exists because I'm looking to branch out. But I'm not there yet, so yeah, I had photos of Bandey with Candy and that was it. Murder in the first."

"Nice. Rockingham got his man—and his woman."

"Until his mother put a stop to it. The woman, not the conviction."

"His mom? You're kidding, right?"

"Circumstantial evidence points that way." He looked at her, eyebrows raised. "He broke up with me two days after I went with him to a family wedding. Grand Dame Rockingham had cornered me in the ladies' room and tore into me. Said I might think I was hiding my...." Lucia made finger quotes as she continued, "...noxious nature and despicable background, but a discerning person could see the truth a mile away."

"Geez. Brutal. What did you say?"

"I asked where she could have possibly found a discerning person—those being unknown in her immediate circle."

Hank threw his head back, laughing with delight. "You're never at a loss for words, are you?"

"Rarely, but...." She paused, biting her lip for a second. "Just between us? Snappy comebacks don't make shit like that hurt any less." She sat back and shrugged, assuming a thin veneer of nonchalance. "I knew he was just slumming around with me for the novelty. I never thought we were headed to the altar, not with him being divorced and me being infertile. But I didn't think it would end like *that*."

The shock of that offhand disclosure dissolved his usual tact. Hank blurted out, "You can't have kids?"

"Nope, my uterus was removed years ago." While he was internally kicking himself and debating how best to change the subject, she tossed him a cheeky smile. "It wasn't by court order or anything." He laughed, mostly with relief that he hadn't blundered too badly. "It was about six months after Bac died." Hank made quiet murmurs of sympathy at that tragedy pile-up, and Lucia explained, "I was so stressed out, dealing with the mess he left Fidelia in." As her explanation grew more faltering, Hank inferred that this wasn't a story she often shared. "One night, um...I started hemorrhaging. And it turned out...surgery was the only remedy." Her tone sharpened as she protested, "It wasn't from a botched abortion, if that's what you're thinking."

"Why in the world would I think that?"

"My mom does. When I told her what happened, she jumped to that crazy conclusion. All because I told her I'd been spending time with this friend of Bac's, Nick Lynch, after Bac died. Nick was taking the death even worse than me and I was worried about him. In her mind that somehow translated to me not only sleeping with Lynch but getting knocked up by him and needing to...well, you know. So, she demanded to see my medical records. Like she has any right."

"Wouldn't it be easier just to show her?"

She sighed heavily and toyed with her wine glass, not meeting his eye. "It would. It's just...." She looked up at him. "She should give me the benefit of the doubt. Like with my dad. She married him believing he was an innocent baker who just happened to have mob connections, along with plenty of time and money to fly to Vegas a few times a year. She bought all that, but can't believe me?" She threw back some wine then muttered, "Pisses me off to no end."

"Did she though? Believe your father."

"As crazy as it sounds, I think so. She has *always* seen him through rose-colored glasses. She still defends him to this day." She stared out of the window, musing, "My mom is a tough lady, she jumped right back into waiting tables so she could support us after my father was sent up, but she's also painfully naive about...what he did." She gulped her wine, then said, "Enough about my family. Tell me about yours. You said you had two sisters?"

He talked about his sisters, three nieces, and two nephews at length before mentioning that his mom was a seamstress. He was surprised at Lucia's enthusiastic response. "Not many people are that excited about dressmaking."

"It's a hobby of mine." She leaned forward, confiding, "I use the sewing machines in Goldstein's shop. A perk of being down there in the basement." When Hank asked how she got started on such an incongruous hobby, Lucia explained, "I inherited my late Aunt Lidia's wardrobe. She was a bookkeeper in New York, and apparently quite the fashionista. She left behind some beautiful custom pieces. While she was tall, she wasn't quite as tall as me so I've had to retrofit most of it." She pulled lightly at the cap sleeves of her silk brocade dress. "Like this one."

"You do nice work. My mom would approve. Wait 'til I tell her about you."

"And your dad? You haven't talked about him."

Hank signaled the waitress to bring them another small carafe of wine before saying, "He died when I was twelve." Despite knowing it would raise questions he didn't usually get into on a first date, he very deliberately added, "He was murdered."

"Oh, that's awful. What happened?" Lucia smacked herself in the forehead. "Wait, that was kind of insensitive, wasn't it? You don't have to talk—"

"I don't mind. It's clear we've zoomed right past the small-talk stage. My father was a pro boxer, welterweight. Had a really promising career until Jimmy Corozzo tried to get him to take a dive." Hank studied her reaction and saw he didn't have to explain to the daughter of Sure-Shot Scafetti that he was talking about the Gambino crime family. "My dad refused."

"They killed him?"

"They sure as hell did. And no one was ever even arrested for it."

"Oh. I'm so sorry." She smiled sadly. "I can see why you have such a passion for...trying to get justice for other people."

Their pizza came and they occupied themselves with eating and staying on less emotional conversational topics. Lucia asked how a Brooklyn boy had ended up in Philly, so Hank explained that he'd earned a Benjamin Franklin Scholarship to Penn's undergrad program and had stayed on to attend Penn Carey Law.

After declining dessert and asking for the check, they sat in silence for a moment. Hank could tell

Lucia had something on her mind and decided to allow enough silence for it to come out. An old lawyer's trick, it worked perfectly. In a rush of words tumbling one after the other she said, "About your dad...how he died, I mean. Thanks for being able to separate me from my family. I know we wouldn't be here if you couldn't."

"After you told us about your family and how it affected you, any reasonable person can see that the mob hurt you almost as much as they did me. You don't have to thank me for just being fair."

"Well, it's pretty rare. A lot of people can't do it...so, bravo, Mr. Narváez."

Hank insisted on escorting her back to the office and they spent the travel time talking more about their families. As they got off the El, Lucia was telling him how the day after her high school graduation, her mom abruptly left town. "She handed me three hundred bucks, wished me luck, and said she'd let me know when she landed a waitressing job somewhere interesting. Four months later I got a postcard from Chicago."

"Wow. Did she say why?"

"She said she needed a break and a change of scenery. I'm sure she wanted to get away from Le Sorelle, and my dad's family. Which, I do not blame her for one bit."

"You've been on your own since then?"

"No, first I lived with my grandparents...."
Thinking it was time to get this out in the open, she

declared, "And then, to their horror, I moved in with Bac."

"Oh. I wondered about that."

"Yeah, he was much more than my boss."

"Was he really an FBI agent?"

"Yes, but only for a few years. The choice to leave the bureau, was not his own." Hank asked if she knew the details so Lucia admitted, "He never really said but if I had to guess, alcohol was involved. It took me a long time to realize he had a problem because he was never actually drunk, but then he was also rarely ever sober."

"He sounds like quite the character."

"He was. We didn't have much time together, but he changed my life. He left me a lot of wisdom...." With a philosophical toss of her head, she added, "...a nearly-bankrupt business, and his old hunting cabin."

"He hunted?"

"No. The only gun Bac ever owned was his snub-nose .38." With a sad smile she clarified, "I guess I should call it his drinking cabin. That's what he used it for and it was kind of falling apart. What I sold it for paid off his funeral, some of the back rent on the office, and a few of the many over-due bills, nothing else. That's why I had to choose between keeping the office or the apartment." She pointed to Overbrook Commons, now within their line of sight. "The office was necessary to Fidelia, the apartment not so much, making it a no-brainer."

They entered the office to a fervent greeting from Rocco, at least for Lucia, who explained that the dog was always stand-offish with new people. Hank accepted that explanation but exclaimed over Rocco's unexpected size. "He's a standard dachshund, the little ones are the miniatures. And as much as I hate to end the evening, he needs his walk now." She was thrilled when Hank offered to accompany her. She accepted, saying, "I really should change first," pointing at her cocktail dress and evening flats.

"Do you need me to step out?"

"Nah, I keep most of my clothes in the big bathroom next door. It's been abandoned since Goldstein's went outta business so I commandeered it for my personal use. Just like with the sewing machines. Belsky doesn't care 'cause I clean and maintain the space, so he pretends not to notice. I think his idiot son actually hasn't."

She quickly changed into jeans and a t-shirt and re-entered the office to find Hank had removed his suitcoat and tie and appeared to be surveying the room. He smiled at her, observing, "I see you're a collector."

"You mean my crystals?" Lucia walked over and pointed up to the area directly behind the desk, where there were two small windows facing Ludlow Street. Suspended by fishing line from the lintels were dozens of clear glass crystal prisms of various shapes and sizes. "I keep buying them because I think they break up the gloom in here a bit. I get so little natural light, I never lower the blinds. It's not like anyone's gonna kneel down and peep in the basement windows."

"Nice touch," Hank answered, "but I was talking about these." He waved a hand at the top of her bookcase which held a crowded assortment of plastic souvenir snow globes. He picked up the one from Miami, featuring a beach scene and over-sized pink flamingos. "Have you been to all these places?"

"I wish. Bac bought me the first one," she said, picking up the glass globe sitting on the desk, "when we went to Virginia Beach for a pool tournament. The collection just kind of grew from there. Juli and Dan bring them back from every vacation, and Belsky gives me one for Christmas every year. Some are from my mom, too, since she never really landed anywhere for long." Lucia smiled sadly. "I thought she wanted to see America but it looks like she was just killing time until my father got out of Graterford."

"What makes you say that?"

"She showed up this week—because he's out."

Hank was silent for a moment before asking, "When did that happen?"

Lucia described the circumstances of her father's release though she remained resolutely silent about his supposed death. Hank said nothing but seemed to be mulling the news over. As they left the office, Rocco charging up the stairs, Lucia said, "I guess it freaks you out...knowing my father's been released, huh?"

"It gave me pause...but it doesn't freak me out. He served his sentence, and he gets to go free. And decide what he wants to do with the rest of his life. For good or for ill. That's the way it should work—for everyone. Even Carlo Scafetti." He smiled at her. "There's a reason Lady Justice wears a blindfold."

"Oh, just like my mom does." She laughed bitterly while shaking her head. "I'm not surprised she went right back to him but...I am disappointed."

"Has she been back to Philly before this?"

"Oh yeah. Ever since she left, she's been showing up here at irregular intervals. Never any warning—then stays just long enough to visit with my dad and spend time nagging me. She'll defend me to the family but when it's just us, she has *a lot* of complaints. Change jobs, dress nicer, do something about your hair, stop living in your damn office, yadda, yadda, yadda."

"Living there does seem less than ideal. What do you do about cooking, sleeping...showers?"

"I have one of those dorm fridges for cold stuff but I don't cook. Not unless you count the canned soup and stale soft pretzels I microwave in the kitchenette. The rest is easy, I sleep on the couch and shower at the Y."

"You go to the gym every day?"

"Just about. I love my morning swim." With a shrug she finished, "Anyway, it's all just temporary."

"Everything is temporary—that don't excuse nothin'!" Lucia stared at Hank, wondering where that vehemence had come from. Hastily, he explained, "That's a line from *Moonstruck*. I'm crazy about that movie. Everything I know about Italian families, I learned from *Moonstruck*."

"In that case, buddy, have you got a lot to learn."

Reaching out a hand, he laughed, "Know anyone who's willing to teach me?"

Shifting the leash to her left hand, Lucia accepted the silent offer. They walked hand-in-hand throughout the neighborhood, ending up at the 46th street El stop, where Hank almost missed his train due to their extended good-night kiss.

CHAPTER 5

Questioning Answers

"Advances are made by answering questions. Discoveries are made by questioning answers."—Bernard Haisch

Lucia woke to the sound of Rocco barking furiously. Without opening her eyes, she said, "How 'bout you feed and walk yourself this morning? I had a late night." Despite her exhaustion, she sat up, remembering she'd promised to go see her mom first thing this morning. Suddenly the sound of knocking broke through her fog and she realized that Rocco hadn't just been asking for breakfast. "Who is it?" she called out.

"PPD. We'd like a word with you, Miss Scafetti."

"Fuck. That's all I need," Lucia muttered to Rocco. More loudly she announced, "Just a minute," and hurriedly pulled on some clothing. After stripping the sheets off the couch and tossing them in the closet, she opened the door to the sight of two men holding up police badges, introducing themselves as Lt. John Colona and Detective David Pike. Moments later they were seated in the chairs in front of her desk, with her behind it and Rocco observing from his crate.

Colona, a detective she'd heard much about but had never met, proved to be a massive man with a shock of white hair. He announced, "We're investigating the death of Frank Tumino. He was found shot to death early this morning." When Lucia simply nodded in response, Colona said, "You don't seem surprised at this news."

"He was in a dangerous line of work."

Pike asked, "And what line of work would that be?"

She studied Pike's face, as thin as the rest of him, before answering, "If you really don't know the answer to that, you should check with your colleagues in the Organized Crime Unit."

"We have reason to believe that you threatened Tumino just yesterday," Colona said. "Is that correct?"

Brushing her unruly hair out of her eyes, Lucia snorted in amusement. "Uh-oh, Gabby better hope the family never finds out she was talking to cops—especially cops that are *you*." This time it was Lucia waiting to see how Colona would react and receiving nothing but a blank look. Colona ignored the implications of her statement and demanded a direct answer. "Yes, we had words yesterday. Since I'm psychic, I'll just go ahead and answer your next question. No, I didn't kill him."

"Where were you last night between eleven PM and one AM?"

"I was on a date until about midnight. Then I was here for the rest of the night." When asked, she gave them Hank's name and contact information. "Is that all?"

Displaying no readiness to leave, Colona folded his arms. "Aren't you curious about the details of the shooting?"

"Let me test my psychic powers again—bullet to the head?"

"Very good," Colona drawled. "Specifically, one bullet through the left eye." When her head jerked up, he said, "That's how you like to kill people, isn't it?"

"Are you confusing me with my father? Have you thought about questioning him?"

"Problem is no one can seem to find Carlo—and the word on the street is he's dead."

"The word is obviously wrong."

They asked for a recounting of her time with her father since his release so Lucia gave a bare bones summary of their encounters, omitting any mention of his search for a key and scapular. Colona asked, "You're sure he was looking for money and not...say, a diamond and some rare coins?"

Looking up at the ceiling, Lucia mused, "I don't know, let me think...they sound *so much* alike." She eyed the cops, dryly declaring, "Yeah, I'm sure."

"How much money? Where did it come from?"

"He didn't say."

"Where was he going when he left Rinaldi's house?"

"He didn't say."

"Is there anything you *do* know, Miss Scafetti?" asked Pike.

"I know my father would be a much better person to ask."

Colona scoffed, "Hard to ask a dead man."

"Why are you so convinced he's dead? In the first place, you're investigating a murder committed with his MO, and in the second, there's the little issue of not finding his body."

"Carlo Scafetti is hardly the only person who can put a bullet through someone's eye," Pike countered. "As you well know."

When Lucia's only answer was a hard stare, Colona said, "Your father's enemies aren't the kind who leave corpses—I would've thought even a small-time PI would know that."

"They leave them, they just don't make them easy to find. Have you checked the docks? Tumino worked with Paulie Lugano. If Pier-Nine-Paulie offed someone recently, he'd be somewhere in the Delaware." She smiled sweetly while adding, "I assumed someone as familiar with the D'Amico crime family as yourself would know that. Maybe I was giving you too much credit."

When she made it over to Patsy's house, Lucia found her exhausted mother having a breakfast of

68

cigarettes and coffee with Patsy. "Mama, did you get any sleep last night?"

"Not enough. Then I woke up to this uproar over Frankie."

"Don't you think this means that...Dad's still alive?"

"I don't know." Angie threw up her hands. "I don't know what it means. All I know is, he ain't here and I'm not getting my hopes up." She looked over at her daughter, her face creased with concern. "You shouldn't either. It's okay to hope for the best—but you better be prepared for the worst."

Since Lucia was still unsure how she felt about her father's possible demise, she could think of no good response. With Patsy's help, she convinced her mother to try to take a nap. After downing a grappa at Patsy's insistence, Angie went upstairs to bed. As soon as she heard the bedroom door close, Lucia asked, "Did she actually sleep last night?"

"I don't know. She was still up watching TV when I went to bed last night and I found her sitting right here at the kitchen table when I got up for the early Mass."

"She was probably waiting for my dad—hoping he was gonna show up." Patsy just nodded and Lucia ventured, "I'm guessing the dinner at Carmela's is canceled."

"Even if it weren't, I don't think you'd be welcome there today."

"Why? They think I had something to do with Frankie's death?"

"Of course, they do. Not only did you threaten him, everyone knows you've always hated him."

"Why, Patsy? Why did I hate him? Am I the only one who remembers that sixteen-year-old girl he tossed out of a moving car because she wouldn't go down on him?"

"No." He glanced away, sighing heavily, before turning back to Lucia. "But that thing with Amanda Lucas.... Do we really know what happened that night? Even Gabby says the girl blamed Frankie to cover up for the guy who really hurt her. And Amanda did refuse to press charges."

"Oh yeah, the only reason for not pressing charges against a known mobster, was that she was lying. *Right*."

"Talk like that is not gonna convince people that you didn't kill Frankie."

She stared him in the eyes, biting off every word that followed. "I didn't kill him."

"*I* never thought it was you. What I can't figure out, is who did kill 'im?"

"It has to be my father. He probably outsmarted Paulie Lugano, which let's face it, is not that hard to do. Mark my words, Paulie's gonna be the next one to get it. If he's not dead already."

"It could be someone wanting us to think it was Carlo. I can't see him being alive and not letting your mom know. Angie's no actress and she's taking this really hard."

"Is she though? She seems more angry than sad."

"Anger is one of the stages of grief, Looch...just like denial."

"Meaning what?"

"Meaning, I think you cooked up this idea that it was your dad who killed Frankie, 'cause you don't wanta believe he's really dead."

"Stick to sausage making and leave the psychology to Sigmund Freud."

"It ain't Freud—I saw about the stages of grief on *The Simpsons*."

"Oh yeah, like that's so much better," she muttered as her mind wandered to another subject. "Hey, guess who's investigating Frankie's death? Colona."

"The same guy who ratted out your dad? You sure? Big guy—salt-and-pepper hair?"

"His hair's all white now but, yeah, I'm sure. John Colona—how many could there be? And he even asked about the Kimberly Star and the coins."

"Of course, he did," Patsy scoffed. "He was obsessed about them—interrogated everyone in the family, back in the day. Sounds like he hasn't changed a bit." Patsy stared at her for a second, visibly calculating the implications of this news. "I sure hope Micky never finds out his daughter was talking to that rat bastard."

Lucia tilted her head in contemplation. "Maybe Micky doesn't care. He was already one of D'Amico's lieutenants back then, I'll bet he knows the truth."

"Truth about what?"

"That Colona was never a mole. I always thought D'Amico let him turn my dad in—as payback for my dad doing the Guenther job. I don't buy that Colona sat around while my dad killed seven guys and then on the eighth one, all of a sudden remembered he was a righteous cop just because it was some fancy jewel thief who got offed."

Patsy stood up and poured himself another cup of coffee from the battered pot on the stove. He faced her, lounging against the counter. "The story always was that Colona was willing to look the other way about family business because he wanted in on those big money poker games Zio Al ran. It could be he hadn't figured out about your father's real job 'til then."

"Then he's too dumb to live." She shifted in her seat to face him. "Colona was an insider. He even went on some of those Vegas sprees with my dad and Micky and the rest." When Patsy asked where she got that idea, Lucia tried to remember the genesis of it. "I thought I heard that." She looked up at him. "He didn't?"

Shrugging, he responded, "Don't ask me. Your parents marrying put a stop to those trips before I was old enough to go."

"Okay, maybe I'm wrong about that. But I still think Colona was on D'Amico's payroll all along. And probably still is."

"Based on what? He's stayed away all these years."

"Based on the fact that he's still walking around."

"I don't know…maybe." He chuckled into his next sip of coffee. "You know, for someone who hates the family business, you've got a real head for figuring how it all works."

"Hey," she laughed. "Just because I shot down your denial theory, there's no reason to get nasty."

Late on Monday morning, Lucia heard a quick knock, and then Hank popped his head in the office door. "Have a minute?"

"Sure, come on in." She rose from behind the desk and pointed to the couch, "Have a seat."

"Thanks. I just thought you should know—"

Plopping down next to him, she finished, "That two detectives paid you a visit yesterday or this morning. Checking my *alibi* for Saturday night."

"Yeah, it was this morning. What's going on? They didn't tell me much. Just that a Frank Tumino was murdered that night, and for some reason you're a person of interest in the case." Lucia filled him in on the details, finally admitting that her father had gone missing. Hank pondered the story for a moment, before asking, "They suspect you just because you didn't get along with Tumino?"

"No, if that were the case, half of South Philly would be a suspect. It's because of how he was killed."

"One bullet through the left eye? That's your father's MO."

She sighed, brushing some stray hair out of her eyes. "And mine."

"What?"

"Six years ago, I...I killed a man."

While she was weighing his reaction, Hank evenly instructed, "Go on."

"His name was Brian Murphy. Mad-dog Murphy, they called him. He'd been running the biggest meth operation in Delaware County." She shifted slightly so she could watch Hank's face as she told the story. How it had started by her going after a bounty on a woman, Misha Kononenko, who'd disappeared after posting bail on a bad check arrest.

Hank sat back against the couch and stared at Lucia. "You did bounty-hunting?"

"I had trouble keeping the lights on at Fidelia when I first took over, so yeah, I did some bounty-hunting. But the sad thing was...." Her lips held in a tight line, Lucia shook her head at the irony. "...Kononenko was gonna be one of the last Skips I went after." Gamely trying to inject a note of levity, she said, "I'd already cornered the market on cheating husband jobs by then." The quip fell flat so she dispassionately went on to explain about finding Misha in a laundromat in Chester, apprehending her without issue, and heading back to Philadelphia.

"I knew Kononenko was connected to Murphy so I took great care to nab her quickly and quietly. Once I got her in the car, it seemed like I'd succeeded. And then...on a deserted stretch of 322, Murphy caught up with us and started blasting my car with a sawed-off shotgun. He got the gas tank and I stalled out." She swallowed, that terrible night coming into sharp focus. "He was Kononenko's boyfriend. At first, I thought he was trying to get her back but she was screaming that he was gonna kill her, gonna kill us both. Turns out, she'd been wanting to get away from him for a while. He knew if the cops got a hold of her, she'd dime him out in a New York second."

His tone softened considerably, Hank offered, "It sounds like you had no choice—but to return fire, I mean."

"Yep. When I saw him advancing on us, I...I aimed at his head. Killed him with the first shot." She knew it was unnecessary but in an act of catharsis Lucia added, "One bullet, through the left eye. And no one has ever let me forget it. My wonderful genetic gift."

"It was just a coincidence. That kind of thing is not hereditary!"

"Hell of a coincidence, ain't it? I even asked the genetics prof at CCP about it. She said she could explain about my eye color, but not *that*."

"Your eye color?"

"Yeah, both my parents have green eyes, and...." She pointed at her face. "...I got these."

After squinting at her for a moment, Hank said, "You got...hazel eyes."

"Oh, you're so gallant. Bac once said they were the color of river mud." She laughed at his look of dismay. "Bac always told the absolute truth...." Sotto voce, she concluded, "...to everyone but himself."

She watched Hank, awaiting his ultimate verdict. He was silent for a few seconds, stroking his finger across his lower lip. Finally, he said, "If everyone knows about Murphy, then someone is setting you up."

"Yes, someone is, but I can't say that's his real goal...it might be a bonus for him, though. He was pretty pissed at me." Hank asked for an explanation. "Come on, I'll tell you that story over lunch. My treat, for being such a great listener. As long as you don't mind food truck fare."

"Mind it? How do you think I survived my student years without a meal plan?" With a grin he asked, "Do you know the Snowball Truck on Spruce?"

"Of course, where else can you get Jolt around here?"

"A woman after my own heart. Let's go."

It was a rather dull surprise for Lucia when the next day, Detective Pike called her down to PPD Headquarters to make a statement about the death of Paul Lugano, found in his car, killed by a bullet to the left eye. She told Colona and Pike what she knew about the murder, which was nothing—except it was further proof that Carlo Scafetti was still alive. She learned nothing new during the interrogation except that both murders had employed the same weapon and surmised that her father had somewhere picked up a Sig Sauer P226.

Upon leaving the police station, she noticed a black BMW E38. It was a distinctive car, especially in that neighborhood. She went over to the driver's side and tapped on the tinted-glass window. When it slid down slightly, she leaned in. "Hey there, looking for me?"

Her cousin Micky eyed her impassively. "Yes, as a matter of fact, I am. Please get in."

She wanted to refuse but knew Dominic Vetere was a dangerous man—one only an idiot would trifle with. She wasn't feeling particularly idiotic that morning, so slipped into the passenger's seat, saying, "Good to see you, Mick."

"I wish I could say the same."

"You could if you lied, like I just did." Okay, maybe she *was* feeling a little bit idiotic—but Micky's pomposity was too tempting a target.

"You're making jokes? *Che cozz'?*" He moved into her personal space, growling, "Don't you realize you are in big trouble?" Lucia didn't respond but started scanning the area to see if there were other cars of a suspicious nature in evidence. Micky took that as a sign to continue. "You know, if you had just stopped at Frankie, we could've looked the other way. That *gavone* was dragging the organization down and my Gabriella is better off without him. Which she will see in time. But Paulie...." He shook his head, continuing, "He was a good soldier and D'Amico is not gonna let this go."

"D'Amico thinks *I* killed Frankie and Lugano?"

"Yeah, he does. I'm warning you, do not try and play Salvatore D'Amico for a fool." While Lucia was fighting the urge to roll her eyes at him, Micky continued, "Because you're family, I might be able to make a bargain with him and get you out of this. I need to give him something though, so you have to hand over the diamond and coins to me right—" She couldn't suppress a snort of laughter, causing Micky to snap, "You still think this is funny?"

"I shouldn't but...I do think it's funny how you all got your tongues hanging out for those damn things that are probably in some European collector's vault. And that my old man has you all chasing your tails like this. He's outsmarted everybody and is probably having a good laugh about me taking the heat for it."

"Lucia—your father is dead."

"No, he's not. The proof is staring everyone in the face. He's killing everyone they send for him."

Micky gripped the steering wheel and threw his head back against the seat. He whispered to himself, "*Managgia*, Patsy was telling the truth." He looked back at her and spoke very deliberately. "I know you don't like me, I know you don't trust me, but I think you know I am not a stupid man. You can believe me on this: Carlo Scafetti is dead. *Hai capid*?"

Doubt about her father's status creeping into her mind for the first time, Lucia stared at Micky. She started shaking her head. "No. You're wrong. These killings...it has to be him. My father isn't a stupid man, either. He's just hiding out."

"He's not. I'm sorry." He reached over and clasped her briefly on the shoulder. "I'll tell D'Amico it doesn't look like it was you. He'll trust me on this matter. I can do that for you, at least." He stared at her for a moment before asking, "And you have no idea where the diamond and coins are?"

"How could I? My father never had them, Micky." He shook his head in disgust whether at her

78

supposed naiveté or subterfuge she wasn't sure and didn't care. She categorically refused his offer to drive her back to her office and exited the car in a hurry.

During the subway ride back home, Lucia ruminated on the situation. She still believed her father was responsible for the murders, but Micky was right about one thing—she knew he was no fool. What was going on? How had her father managed to convince so many people that he was dead? She knew what Bac would say: stop assuming and start looking. And the place she needed to look was at the piers, where Lugano tended to dispose of bodies. She didn't believe she'd find much of anything. Colona and Pike had to have already been there, but it was time to see what they might have missed.

CHAPTER 6
Despite the Faults

"...you don't love because: you love despite; not for the virtues, but despite the faults."—William Faulkner, *Essays, Speeches and Public Letters*

Lucia parked at the end of Municipal Pier-Nine. All of the municipal piers, including that one, had once served as marine terminals, linking the Delaware River to the railroad yards. That method of goods transportation now being a part of history, the piers had been vacant for decades and were melancholy places. Still not sure what she was hoping—or fearing—to find, she inspected the pavement for signs of anything out of the ordinary. She'd already checked all of the other deserted piers assuming that Paulie Lugano's nickname was just that and not a designation of the only place he liked to dump off the unfortunates he'd help kill during his long and murderous life.

Bending low to examine some odd scuff marks on the ground, Lucia noticed the marks coalesced into twin tracks leading to the edge of the pier. Huh, if you were dragging a body along the ground, the feet would make marks very much like that— wouldn't they? The more she studied the scene, the more obvious it became. What the hell? How had the cops missed this?

Where the tracks ended at the pier's edge, Lucia knelt down to study some faint reddish-brown stains on the concrete. She straightened up and stared down into the choppy gray river musing—were they just rust? or could that possibly be blood? She pulled a small envelope out of her pocket and used a business card to scrape the remnants of the stains into the envelope.

While closing up the envelope, her eardrums were rocked by the sound of a bullet exploding mere inches from her feet. With no time to formulate a better plan, Lucia dove into the river to escape what she assumed was imminent death. While underwater, she quickly calculated her assailant's most likely hiding spot and decided to surface underneath the pier. The dive into the cold and murky water had her thoroughly disoriented, so she was unsure if she was actually headed in the right direction. Lucia hated to open her eyes in the mucky river but decided to risk a quick glance to try and get her bearings. If she was swimming the wrong way, out into the more turbulent river, her underwater retreat from the bullets would prove a cure far worse than the original disease.

Blinking her eyes open, an indistinct object was visible inches from her face. Some hideously deformed marine creature, was her first thought. It took her a moment to comprehend the horror of what she was actually seeing: her father's lifeless and rapidly decomposing face staring back at her. The shock of recognition froze every muscle in her body and she sank into the depths of the Delaware. The icy blackness brought her out of her stupor and Lucia mechanically began to swim, breaking the surface moments later, uncaring if the gunman was still around.

With no plan but escaping the monstrous sight of her father's bloated corpse, she swam towards the inhabited parts of the waterfront. Feeling her strength waning, Lucia knew she had to get out of the river; spotting the Philadelphia Marine Center ahead, she realized it was her best option. Despite the fact that capri pants and a t-shirt were not ideal swim garments, she doggedly accomplished the laborious journey to the Center. After hanging on limply for a minute or two in preparation for the final push, Lucia used one of the Marine Center ladders to slowly pull her wet body out of the water.

She lay gasping on the dock for several minutes, amazed that no one had appeared to offer assistance. She couldn't find her voice to call for help—not yet. Upon standing up on rubbery legs, Lucia noted there were few people around, most looking away from the sight of a fully dressed woman emerging sopping wet from the river. Probably thought she was crazy, drunk, or both.

She stumbled towards the Marine Center and entered the silent space, dripping her way to the front desk. The receptionist looked up at her approach. In a perky voice, she started, "Welcome to the Marina. What can I—Oh no, did your boat go down? Do you need help?"

Lucia drew a shaky breath. She was internally surprised by her ability to muster up a calm reply. "Yes. I need you to call 911 and report a dead body, chained underneath pier nine. Tell the operator you need both the police and the coroner."

The young girl stared at her, wide-eyed and open mouthed. "What?"

Lucia reached out a hand, dripping rivulets of water onto the desk. "Can I use your phone?"

Since a bystander had already reported someone jumping into the Delaware at Pier-Nine, the police arrived at the Marine Center in record time. The dispatcher had automatically sent an ambulance as well, so Lucia was forced to go to the nearby Jefferson University Hospital. The paramedics had been entirely unmoved by her pleas that she just needed to go home. Released from the ER two hours later, she sat in Patsy's car, groaning at the news that her mother had been called in to ID the body. "Oh my God, why would they do that to her?"

Patsy shook his head wearily. "My parents and Donna are all with her, she'll be okay. Angie is stronger than you know."

"Not strong enough for this. The fish had started on him, Patsy—she can't take seeing him like that."

"And you can?" He turned onto tenth street while growling, "What were you doing in the fucking river?"

"Oh," she said, suddenly remembering the origin of this insanely awful interlude. "Someone shot at me. Wait—did I tell that to the cops?" She paused a moment trying to remember. "Yeah. Yeah, I did." That question settled, she realized Patsy was heading in the wrong direction. "Where are you going? My office is—"

"I'm taking you to my house. I'm not gonna let you spend the night in your office. Not after all you been through."

"That's sweet, Pats, but in the first place, I need clean clothes and in the second, we gotta get Rocco." Without a word, Patsy turned onto Lombard and headed for West Philadelphia.

A few minutes later, Lucia was sitting on the couch in her office with Rocco on her lap trying to figure out how to prepare to spend the next couple of days at Patsy's. He was circling the block in his car since she'd told him it would only take her a few minutes. Lucia knew she needed to pack but was suddenly overwhelmed by the simple task. She closed her eyes in an attempt to focus and the ghastly image of her father's dead face instantly materialized. She quickly blinked her eyes open and mustered up just enough energy to call Juli.

When she announced, "My father is dead," Lucia realized it was the first time she'd said that out loud. Juli's only response was to announce that she'd be right down. After a long hug that reminded Lucia that she wasn't alone after all, Juli went to work.

Lucia was drinking the glass of orange juice Juli had forced on her, when she bustled into the office from the outside bathroom, one arm pulling Lucia's wheeled carry-on suitcase, the other full of clothing. "Your black linen dress will be good for the funeral, and your navy pencil skirt for anything else. I'll put a couple of white blouses in, too." She looked over as she placed the stack of clothing on the couch. "Feeling any better?"

"Yeah, I think the juice helped."

"I thought so. Adrenaline will only get you so far, then you crash." She put the suitcase next to the pile of clothes and started filling it as she confirmed her packing list with Lucia.

After agreeing that two pairs of shorts would be plenty, Lucia murmured, "I should have found him sooner, Juli."

"No, you shouldn't have found him at all. That's the goddamned police's job. What the hell are they playing at?"

"Yeah, you're right. But I should have realized he was dead. What's wrong with me? I'm losing my edge."

Quickly zipping up the suitcase, Juli straightened up and smiled sadly at Lucia. "Denial ain't just a river in Egypt, hun." She tossed Rocco's bag of food and blanket into an old tote bag and then escorted them both up to the street where she flagged Patsy down.

Once in the car, Lucia fell back against the seat, drained. She closed her eyes, saying, "Tell me again about those stages of grief?"

Lucia unpacked and stowed her things in Patsy's son's room and went out in the hall to check on her mom. She paused at the door to Patsy's guestroom where her mother, Donna, and Pina were all discussing which suit to bury Carlo in. Since Lucia's only input would be to ask why the hell it mattered since it was obviously going to be a closed-casket funeral, she turned around and went downstairs.

A lifelong witness, Lucia still managed to be chilled by the efficient manner with which her family handled the constant parade of incarcerations and deaths. A family of hardened soldiers, they accepted those losses as a natural consequence of the war they fought—a particularly senseless war of their own choosing. When she pressed them on why they chose it, there was never a satisfactory answer—only surprise that it was even a question. They seemed blind to the truth that it was, in fact, a choice.

Knowing Patsy and Vince had headed off together to close up the butcher shop, when the doorbell rang Lucia automatically answered it. She was more annoyed than surprised to find Detective Pike waiting on the front step. When he introduced his hulking young companion as Detective Dixon, Lucia found it impossible not to ask where Colona was. Pike answered, "Lieutenant Colona has chosen to remove himself from this arm of the investigation. For obvious reasons."

"You mean he already knows who killed my father and doesn't want to spoil the ending for the rest of you?"

Pike sighed heavily before reiterating, "May we come in?"

"I already gave you guys all the information I have, back there at the hospital."

"We'd like to speak to your mother."

"I'm not sure she's up to—"

"It's fine." Lucia whirled around to find her mother coming down the stairs. "I'll talk to them."

In spite of the dreadful sadness and horror of the day, Lucia had to smile at the way her mom handled Pike and Dixon. Angie took stonewalling to a high art—she barely admitted to knowing the deceased, her husband of thirty years, let alone answering any of their questions. As soon as they left, though, her mother had a question of her own. "What were you talking to them about? On the stoop there, as I was coming down."

"I just asked Pike where Colona was."

"John Colona? Why? Why in hell would you ask about him?"

"Because he's heading up the investigation into Frankie and Lugano's deaths, though he was more interested in grilling me about the diamond and coins than actually tracking down the murderer."

"What a surprise," Angie sneered. "That *facciadu* son-of-a-bitch. I wish I'd followed my instincts and kicked Colona right in the *cazzo* the first time I saw him, instead of making nice. A cop in a casino is always some kind of trouble."

"That was in Vegas?"

"Yeah, of course." Shrugging, Angie walked over to the easy chair and plopped down into it. "He tagged along with your dad and his cousins on that first trip to the *Flamingo*."

"I knew that," Lucia said. She glanced out the picture window at the setting sun, eyes unfocused. "How did I know that?"

"Probably 'cause you were spying on your dad and me when you were supposed to be in bed." Angie shook her head, eyeing her daughter as if the exasperation was still fresh. "We learned real quick back then to check on you before we started talking serious business."

Lucia knew her mother was referring to the sleepless nights she'd endured as a child after her father was arrested. She did not yield to her initial impulse which was to retort, "Yeah, that's how I learned my father was a paid killer." She didn't want to have that fight again—not with her mom, not on this day. Instead, she decided to test out her pet theory about Colona. "Colona was with dad and the others in Vegas more than once?"

"Yeah, a couple of times—'til Micky put a stop to it. We should've listened to Micky, me and your dad, he never trusted Colona."

"He didn't?" Lucia murmured, trying to fit this new piece of the jigsaw puzzle in with the picture she'd already constructed of the scene. "Well, I guess one snake recognizes another."

"Why are you blaming Micky? He didn't have anything to do with your father's death."

"He knew, Ma."

"Everyone knew but you."

Utterly defeated by that simple truth, Lucia changed the subject by asking what she could do to help with the funeral arrangements. Angie had a list of chores ready to go. Lucia jumped on the list immediately—grateful for any distraction from the inescapable pain of loss, pain surprising in its intensity. Before this day, she'd have put her hand on any bible and swore she no longer loved her father. Today her grief told a truth she couldn't deny: throughout the years, her stubborn heart had remained connected to Carlo Scafetti by an invisible but enduring thread.

That night, after Patsy and Angie were in bed, Lucia snuck down to the kitchen and called Hank. It was risky, calling at almost eleven PM but he'd mentioned being something of a night owl so she figured it was worth a shot. When he picked up on the second ring, she felt secure in her decision. Hank seemed relieved, having heard about her father from Juli. He gently asked if she knew what happened. She answered, "It was D'Amico, settling an old grudge, I guess," before sharing the story of finding her father's body in the river.

"Oh, Lucia. That's horrible. How the hell are you coping with...with all of that?"

"I might still be in shock? I'm not sure. And everything is gonna reach the news cycle tomorrow. I'm dreading it."

"I'm sorry. That's brutal—having to deal with publicity while you're still trying to process your father's death."

"Yeah, I'm not gonna lie, my head's spinning. I've got so many conflicting emotions. My mom says I'm feeling guilty for all those years I wouldn't see him and now I can't. That's part of it, sure, but mainly...I'm angry. Yeah, that's it. I'm mad at him. If he'd been a good man, I could at least mourn him like other people do their dads, like you did. But me, I'm stuck knowing there's at least eight families out there who think he got what he deserved. Live by the sword, and all that."

"Complicated grief, that's called." While she was silently agreeing that was a good name for it, Hank added, "Would it help to remember that he was raised in that culture? That his path was...not fully his own."

"That's a nice way to look at it—but not really true. Until him and his cousin Micky, the family had been mainly into the less violent side...you know, gambling, money-laundering, that sort of thing. Even my dad started out as just an enforcer. My mom told me that it was his ambition that moved him into contract killing. Can you imagine that? My dad thought killing people made him better than just breaking their legs."

"Do you want me to come to the funeral?"

"Thanks, but no." She'd already told Juli not to come, knowing the press would eat it up if the wife of a prominent city councilmen was at the funeral of a notorious mobster. Now she explained to Hank, "I wouldn't expose someone like you to one of these Mafia shindigs. It's real bizarro world shit." Lucia snorted in bitter amusement. "Even D'Amico will send a representative, I'm sure. That's the part I hate the most—the hypocrisy. The way they try to paint over their savagery with some stupid veneer of decency and honor."

"You've convinced me. How about I fix you dinner when you get back from your time there in Oz?"

"That sounds great. You can cook?"

"I can cook."

"Wow. And you're a fantastic listener, in the bargain." After an affectionate exchange of good-nights, Lucia hung up. She felt strengthened, better able to face the looming ordeal.

CHAPTER 7
Invisible Game

"We all come up a little short, and we go
  down hard
These days I spend my time skipping through
  the dark
Through the empires of dust, I chant your
  name
I am the hunter of invisible game"—Bruce
Springsteen, *Hunter of Invisible Game*

Late the next morning, Lucia was in Patsy's living room with Tippy Cataldo, the family's florist of choice. With Rocco on her lap to keep him quiet, she mechanically chose the flowers for her father's funeral, happy to check that task off her list. As she escorted Tippy to the door, it occurred to Lucia that the Cataldos had probably sent their kids to college at least partially on the strength of her family's frequent business—be it for the many weddings or funerals.

She went into the kitchen to find her mother, Zia Pina, and Zio Vince finishing up with the funeral director, Mario Mosti—another one who'd made a fortune off the clan. Not caring either way, she perfunctorily endorsed Angie's choice of a mahogany casket, suddenly wondering who was paying for this circus. She looked over at Patsy thinking that if it was him, she was paying him back out of her house fund for sure.

She wanted to discuss the matter with her mother but Mrs. Fanelli and her daughter from next door showed up with a huge tray of eggplant parmesan for lunch, which Patsy insisted they sit down and share with the mourners. Afterwards Lucia volunteered to do the dishes and, yielding to extensive persuasion from Pina and Lucia, Angie went upstairs to rest.

That evening when they were alone again, just the family, Lucia was about to broach the subject of money with her mother when the phone rang. She groaned, dreading the possibility that it was yet another reporter. Patsy jumped up and answered, then put his hand over the receiver. "Micky would like to be a pallbearer."

"Tell that son-of-a-bitch I'd rather French kiss a buzz saw," Lucia retorted in an undertone, "than see him at my father's funeral."

Overruling her daughter with a sharp thrust of her hand and a quelling glare, Angie announced, "Tell him, of course, Patsy." When Patsy ended the call, Angie took Lucia by the hand. "You've got to knock it off about Micky. I told you—he didn't kill your father."

"Maybe not, but I bet he sure as hell knows who did. And why."

"It's his business to know—not yours." Overpowered by Angie's devotion to *Omertà*, the Mafia Code of Silence, Lucia dropped the subject, instead asking if her mother needed help paying for the funeral. "Nah, I don't need your money. You keep it. Get yourself a nice apartment if you have so much to burn."

"Whose money *are* you using?"

"Whose money do you think? *My* money—the money I've been earning all these years. I got some saved up. What'd you think I was doing with it?"

"Besides putting it into dad's account at Graterford? I thought you were living on it."

"Goes to show what you know, Miss Private-Eye. A smart waitress can make bank."

While Zio Vince made a gallant observation that it was good-looking waitresses like Angie who made out so well, Donna and Patsy's other sister, Rosie, walked in the back door. They were accompanied by Rosie's son, Dante, who was a line cook at Le Sorelle and was carrying take-out bags from the restaurant. As he pulled out containers of soup and pasta, and a huge loaf of bread, Lucia had to admit they were eating very well these days. After they had all been served, Dante announced that Carmela had gone ahead and set the menu at the restaurant for the luncheon after the funeral—pending Angie's final approval.

Tiredly, Angie said, "It's fine. I'm sure it'll just be the same one they had for Frankie."

Reflecting that it could almost be the same *food* they had for Frankie, Lucia tried to recall when the family had last endured two funerals this close together. She was glad she hadn't spoken the thought out loud when she remembered it was when Donna's husband had died in the same suspicious car accident as Zia Carmela's husband, Al. That thought nudged her into remembering that they would soon be facing a third funeral.

Lucia stopped eating long enough to ask who had informed her grandfather about his son's death. Vince, Pina, and Angie all exchanged a rapid-fire series of conspiratorial glances before Pina said, "No one. We decided we're not gonna tell Antonio."

"What? You *have* to. This is his son we're talking about—he has a right to know."

Loudly Vince proclaimed, "No. I've known Tony longer than anyone, and I know what he would want. To die in peace, that's what he wants. That's what we all want."

"Funny how my grandfather happens to want exactly what you want him to, huh, Zio?"

Throwing his hand up towards the ceiling, Vince glared at his great-niece. "*Gabbadost'*—you never listen to anyone."

"Really? I'm the only hard-head here?" However good that point was, Lucia was very much alone in this quarrel. Even Patsy stood against her, as

96

everyone fired back that there was no point in telling Tony, who was near death and couldn't take the shock. "You can't treat him like he's already gone. It's disrespectful!" The argument raged over dinner until Lucia said she was going to tell him and no one could stop her. "I'm his only living blood relative now. *I* get to decide." She'd always thought the Italian-American obsession with who was related to whom "by blood" was stupid, but she wasn't one to pass up a chance to use it in her favor.

Pina stood up from the table with a scraping sound. "Okay! Okay, let it be on your head...." she stridently announced, pointing her finger at Lucia. "Let it be on your head if this kills him."

"Fine. Let it be on my head." Lucia rolled her eyes. "Just one more thing I'll burn in Hell for."

Lucia hated the smell of nursing homes—a mixture of urine, antiseptic, and despair. She walked down the hall towards her grandfather's room with a heavy heart and a doubting mind. She couldn't imagine not telling her grandfather that her father was dead, but she also wondered if the family was right—that she should let him die in peace, never knowing his son had predeceased him.

For several minutes she sat by Antonio's bedside, holding his hand, watching him breathe laboriously. When his eyes fluttered open, Lucia seized the opportunity. Bending down close to his ear, she said, "*Nonno*, my dad is dead." He turned and blinked at her, shaking his head weakly. "Yes, I'm sorry, it's true. Your son is gone."

"How," he coughed. He tried again, "How...did...." Trailing off, breathing heavily, Antonio closed his eyes again.

"He was murdered. He had some...enemies waiting for him when he got out of Graterford and...and they killed him." With her sadness beginning to overwhelm her, blinded by tears, she could say no more. Hearing her grandfather choking and wheezing, Lucia looked up and saw he was crying, too.

She tried giving him a sip of water from the cup on his bedside table, putting the straw to his lips but he refused. Between coughs he was mumbling words she could barely distinguish. Bending low, Lucia heard him repeating, "*Colpa mia.*"

"No, it wasn't your fault. It was D'Amico. You couldn't have stopped it."

Antonio tossed his head feverishly, his mumbling growing more agitated and confused. Between coughs and longs spells of labored breathing he gasped out a series of seemingly disconnected words and phrases, mixing English and Italian. She recognized that Antonio was talking about her father but was unsure of his meaning. "*Mio figlio...innocent.*" That phrase Lucia got—her grandfather still thought his son innocent of the crimes he'd openly admitted to. Patting his hand, she quietly shushed him but Antonio continued his ramblings.

"Should...have...*fermato...lasciato*...assassin...*cattiv*

a...loon...." He repeated the word "loon" again—or had it been "the loon"?

Initially, Lucia thought that perhaps her grandfather was trying to say he'd been crazy to let his son associate with murderers but then wondered if he was talking about a particular *assassino* called the Loon. A thought struck her. "Did my dad learn the trade from someone called the Loon?"

Antonio started weeping in response, saying no more, and breathing erratically. He seemed to be alternating between fast, shallow breaths, then slow, heavier breathing, then moments when she wasn't sure he was breathing at all. Alarmed, she rang for the nurse. The nurse soon appeared and started checking her grandfather's vitals, asking Lucia to leave the room.

When the nurse emerged, she told Lucia that her grandfather was experiencing Cheyne-Stokes respirations, which was a sign of impending death. She'd employed a gentle fan blowing towards him to offer some temporary relief but his time was short. Lucia crept back in the room, kissed Antonio on the cheek and said good-bye. She wasn't sure if he knew she was there.

The next day as they were dressing for Carlo's funeral, the family received word from the nursing home that his father was now completely unresponsive. Angie seemed indifferent to the news though Pina wasn't above issuing an "I told you so" to Lucia. Patsy reminded everyone that they'd been warned Antonio could slip into an oblivious state at any moment while Lucia, doubting her actions but unable to wish she'd done differently, stayed silent. On the day of his burial, she didn't want to get into the fact that Antonio might have shared with her an invaluable insight into her father's past. Her main focus today had to be on supporting her mother through the ordeal.

An hour later in the vestibule of St. Rita's, Lucia found that the Pre-Mass ritual was proving far less trying than she'd feared. She watched her mother greet mourners unmolested thanks to the vigilance of Micky, his younger brother, Ray, and Rosie's husband, Carmine. The trio stood guard at the doors, keeping press and other gawkers from entering. Carmine, one of Micky's enforcers, was a natural at the job, and although Ray was merely an accountant in D'Amico's organization, due to his bulky height and forbidding mien he made as talented a watchdog as his more lethal family members.

Moments later, Lucia did spot the unwelcome sight of an over-teased, over-bleached, Aqua-Netted helmet of hair moving her way. She stepped into the path of Patsy's ex-wife, blocking her progress. In a low tone, she asked, "What are you doing here, Annette?"

Annette gestured toward Patsy who was in conversation with his teenage son. "I brought Patrick to the funeral."

"What are you *still* doing here, Annette?"

Balancing on teetering heels that brought her to within striking distance of Lucia's eyeline, Annette declared, "I took a half-day, so I'm staying."

"I didn't know they gave half-days in hell. Does Satan provide demons with Dental, too?"

"Why don't you knock it off, Chichi? You're not the only one who ever needed to get outta this family."

"Here's a news flash for you—screwing the UPS guy in your husband's house was not the only way to get out of this family."

Eyes narrowed in barely restrained wrath, Annette ordered, "Move. I'm gonna go offer your mom my condolences on *her* loss."

Lucia did step aside but murmured, "Keep it short, she has enough grief to deal with today."

Leaving their small circle of teenage and young adult children behind, Rosie and Donna came over to Lucia almost immediately afterwards. Rosie glanced back at Annette, asking in a whisper, "What were you two talking about?"

"Her amazing hair-do."

Donna smiled briefly. "Yeah, back when they split up, I wasn't gonna keep doing it but Patsy said it was okay, I should." She leaned in adding, "I charge her full price, though. And then some."

"Worth every penny." Lucia was vaguely aware that she was using such malicious sarcasm as an ineffective shield against the pain of the day, but she also figured life, fate, God, whoever—should give her this one.

The requiem Mass proceeded without incident, leaving Lucia alone with her thoughts—some utterly unwelcome companions. Like with Antonio, she was conflicted over her final exchanges with her father, but also knew she'd probably do nothing different given the chance. So, why was she so shattered? By the time they filed out of church, Lucia had reached the conclusion that she was grieving the death of hope. A hope she'd subconsciously nurtured for years: that her father would reform, repent, atone, and in some measure become the man she'd idolized as a child. A man she could again love without guilt or restraint. Mourning that unfulfilled dream was proving tougher than mourning the man who'd engendered it.

The misery of the day was not solely due to bereavement. At the gravesite in Saint Aloysius cemetery, Zia Carmela very deliberately maneuvered to stand next to Lucia, she assumed to finally offer her condolences. Alas, she had given the old bat too much credit. As they were leaving, Carmela pointed to the space near Carlo, next to Sofia, that would shortly be occupied by Lucia's grandfather. "Soon they'll all be together. The whole family. Except for Lidia." Carmela paused to catch Lucia's eye. "She's buried up in New York *among strangers*...." Another fateful pause ensued before she finished, "...because she rejected her family." Lucia toyed with the idea of faux-innocently asking her great-aunt what she was getting at but saw her mother watching them and so let it go.

The paramount ordeal of all transpired at the luncheon. Up until then she'd managed to avoid talking to the D'Amico scion who'd been sent as the representative of the organization. While others had exclaimed at the respect shown by the old man in sending his elder son, there were few people, other than Sal himself, who Lucia would not have rather seen. When she spied the scarecrow-like figure of Vinnie D'Amico heading her way, Lucia glanced skyward and enjoined Heaven that she better be getting time off purgatory for enduring this endless day.

Hank answered the door wearing a white apron and a wide smile. While he and Lucia shared a passionate kiss, she dropped the leash allowing Rocco to charge ahead and start dashing about, exploring the bright, orderly apartment. When they broke apart, Lucia held up a slim brown paper-bag. "I brought a red— you said beef, right?"

"Correct."

"Then why do you look disappointed?"

His smile turned shy as he admitted, "I'm not disappointed. It's just...see, when you asked about bringing Rocco, I thought you meant you wanted to...well, to be honest—I was hoping you might also be bringing an overnight bag."

She kissed him again, then whispered in his ear, "I left it in the car in case we weren't on the same page." He beckoned her into the kitchen, throwing a provocative glance over his shoulder and assuring her they were of one mind on their after-dinner plans. Leaning over the stove, she enthused, "That smells great. What is it?"

"*Carne frita* with *arroz con habichuelas*."

Lucia tilted her head. "*Carne frita* must be fried meat, since it sounds almost the same in Italian but you're gonna have to translate the rest—I only got a C in Spanish."

Laughing, Hank explained, "Rice and beans. My mom made it all the time. Still does."

While opening the bottle of wine, Lucia shared the details of her father's funeral. Hank set out two wine glasses, observing, "It sounds as bad as you said it would be."

"Oh, it was so much worse. Patsy's bitch of an ex-wife showed up. As did Vinnie D'Amico. The worst D'Amico of all."

"Really?"

"Okay, not the worst person—that's the old man, for sure, may he someday rot in hell. Vinnie, though, is the most annoying."

"How so?"

"His voice alone is a crime against humanity. When he laughs, cats stop fighting in the alley to ask what that horrible noise was. And when it comes to trying to have a conversation with him, he can't find the point with a flashlight and two maps."

"What did you have to talk about?"

"Besides the phony condolences? He wanted to let me know that the bullets from the pier matched the ones that killed Tumino and Lugano. Yes, I learned that from Vinnie D'Amico—not the PPD. I

don't know what that says about Colona and Pike."
She stopped to grimace. "Wait, yes, I do. Anyway, he
said if I had any leads on who it was that shot at me,
then the so-called 'Organization' would be happy to
take the problem off my hands. Meaning neither the
cops nor the mob has any idea who this guy is. Which
is pretty impressive."

"You sound almost admiring."

"I wouldn't go that far. If I ever meet up with the
Loon, he's not gonna find an admirer. Far from it."

"Wait—the Loon?" As Hank served up dinner,
she told him about her last encounter with her
grandfather. "You're going after an assassin? I don't
like the sounds of that."

"Eh, I don't think this guy is James Bond. My
grandfather was probably saying *assassino* which is
Italian for murderer. I really think he meant a
hitman. I've been asking around but so far no one's
ever heard of a hitman called the Loon. I even sent
an email to Rockingham, asking him to check the
DA's organized crime database."

"What about your mom? Would she know your
father's...um, associates?"

"I doubt it, she always says my dad never talked
about his work. Also, she'd freak if she knew I was
looking into this. She's been very adamant that this
whole thing is *not my business*."

"Then why are you looking into it? Why is
finding this Loon guy so important to you?"

"Because not only did he turn my father into a
hitman, it's obvious he's back here in Philly. And
while I'm not upset that he killed Frankie and

Lugano, he also took a potshot at me. Which everyone seems to be forgetting." She took a bite then continued, "Call me sensitive, but I take offense to that sort of thing."

"You think he's trying to avenge your father?"

She shook her head. "Nah, there's a lot less of that sort of thing than the movies would have you believe. With the mob, it's always about power and money. This time, I believe it's the money my father had hidden away somewhere."

"That makes sense, except...how would this other hitman know about that?"

"That's a good question. And the answer might be something I've wondered about for a long time— where someone like my father ever heard of a dude like Klaus Guenther, let alone what he'd stolen, and when he'd be passing through Philadelphia. Though why the Loon wouldn't just take Guenther out himself, I haven't yet figured out."

"Maybe he was in prison at the time."

"That's an excellent theory." Laughing, she added, "That narrows it down to every hitman who was in prison in 1976."

Hank stood up. "You don't have to solve this tonight. Now—ready for dessert?"

"You bet." She looked towards the sink. "Shouldn't we do the dishes first?"

Grinning broadly, he said, "I meant ice cream."

"Oh." Lucia closed her eyes, her face flushed with red. "Smooth, I am not."

"Not smooth, but eager." Hank stopped behind her chair and put his head next to hers, whispering throatily, "I like that."

CHAPTER 8
The Existence of Dragons

"People who deny the existence of dragons are often eaten by dragons. From within."—Ursula K. Le Guin, *The Wave in the Mind: Talks and Essays on the Writer, the Reader and the Imagination*

After her very enjoyable night with Hank, Lucia gifted herself with an enjoyable morning playing hooky, feeling she deserved it after the week she'd had. Hank went off to work leaving her still in her bathrobe. She treated herself to a leisurely shower, then she and Rocco explored Hank's neighborhood. After finally dropping Rocco at the office, she grabbed a coffee and doughnut with Juli and then headed off to one of her favorite places—Adelson's Fabrics on 4th Street in Old City.

Adelson's was right on Philadelphia's Fabric Row, full of fabulous fabrics and unique trim items.

The place was currently run by Grace Nagai, a veritable guru of sewing and dressmaking. Grace had left a message that a specialty fabric Lucia had ordered was in; additionally, Lucia needed to consult with Grace on her latest project. She was remaking her Aunt Lidia's cashmere coat into a long jacket and couldn't get the hem right.

Grace was busy when Lucia arrived so she lost herself in the wonderful world of dream sewing projects. An hour later, Grace found her studying a gorgeous cream-colored silk. "Thinking about wedding gowns?"

"No!" Lucia yelped, having not heard Grace coming up behind her. "It's just really pretty and has a unique sheen and I was wondering how much it cost and what it felt like, that's all."

"Okay, calm down; it was a joke."

"And I'm nowhere near talented enough to sew a wedding gown. Not that I need one. Nope."

"Methinks the lady doth protest too much."

"Hey, that is not nice, Gracie," Lucia laughed. "Go call someone else a lady."

"Come on—show me the coat."

After a short time studying the garment, Grace said, "Yes, I see the problem. The original hem...you said it was ripped along the bottom?" Lucia nodded. "I'm sure it had hem weights. The new hem will need them, too, or it won't lay right."

"Hem weights?"

"Yes, you sew them into the hem, and they weight it down so it lays against the body properly and doesn't curl at the ends." When Lucia asked where she would get something like that, Grace offered to see if they had any in the storeroom. "First I'll get the fabric for Rocco's bed, then I'll go downstairs and root around."

The mention of Rocco prodded Lucia's memory. She looked at her watch and did some quick calculations; she would not make it back in time to give him his customary lunchtime walk. Since she was picking up fabric to fix the bed he'd chewed up, very expensive fabric that could supposedly stand up to dachshund teeth, she was tempted to say he could wait. But Rocco was not above doing his business on the carpet to let Lucia know what he thought about being kept waiting. Yep, not a good idea. Matter decided, she asked Grace to borrow the phone and called Alex Harris.

Years earlier, Lucia had caught Alex trying to break into one of the upstairs offices in Overbrook Commons late one night. After scaring the hell out of the teenager, she'd kindly offered some advice on the limitations of his chosen profession of burglary. To her surprise he took it and now supported himself through a series of diverse enterprises. She helped out by employing him frequently as courier, gofer, and, since Rocco tolerated Alex fairly well, occasional dog-walker. Alex promised he'd swing by in a few minutes. She told him that Juli had a key to the office and could let him in.

Almost an hour later, Lucia got back to the office to find Alex and Rocco still out on their walk. She didn't think much of it since her mind was on the sewing projects ahead. Grace hadn't been able to

111

locate any hem weights but said some people used washers and Lucia decided that was her best bet. She was planning a trip to the hardware store while carrying all of the new fabric over to Goldstein's shop when she heard Alex running down the steps calling her name over and over. As soon as he saw Lucia, Alex exclaimed, "He took Rocco, I'm so sorry, he had a gun, I didn't know what to do!"

"What? Slow down, who did what to Rocco?"

She ushered the dazed and panting young man into the office and made him sit on the couch, then told him to take a deep breath. Alex obeyed, then hurriedly explained, "I was walking Rocco back here, we were on 47th and Chestnut when this guy stuck a gun in my ribs and said he was taking the dog. Then he grabbed Rocco, jumped in his car and was gone. I chased him as far as I could but he got away."

Her immediate thought was that it had to be the same person who'd grabbed Rocco at the dog show but that theory didn't hold up to further scrutiny. The dog had been neutered since then and was therefore useless as breeding stock. Lucia turned to Alex. "Did you get the license plate?"

"Um, it definitely started with F, I...and then C...or it could have been a G, then one, and maybe seven...." He shook his head. "I'm not sure. It all happened so fast."

"How about the guy—what did he look like?"

"Short, stocky, needed a shave. He looked...."

"What?"

Brushing a shaky hand across his forehead, Alex glanced off to the side and then back up at her. "I know this is gonna sound crazy but he looked sorta like this guy that sells hot merch outta his trunk on Pattison after Phillies games."

Knowing about his checkered past, Lucia asked, "You've just seen this guy, or you supplied him with merchandise back in the day?"

Alex took a deep breath, then sheepishly admitted, "I might've brushed up against him once or twice."

"Do you remember his name?"

"I'm not sure I ever even knew his whole name...Benny something, maybe? Sorry, that was like five years ago."

"Do you know anyone who would know his name?"

"Yeah, I might."

"Good." She reached out a hand and pulled him to his feet. "Let's get busy."

While Alex was checking his connections for a lead on the kidnapper, Lucia received a call from the man himself. "Hey, Scafetti, I got your dog. If you ever wanta see him alive again, you're gonna have to play ball. Are we clear?"

"Who is this?"

"You don't need my name, you just need to listen very carefully. I want that diamond and those coins your old man stole and I want them today. Are you gonna cooperate or do I gotta start mailing you parts of your dog? Oh, but right now, he wants to say hello."

Lucia heard a muffled yelp of pain. With great effort, she tamped down the white-hot fury surging through her veins. "I don't have the items you want nearby. I will get them but I need time. I also need you to hear this, you're only getting them if my dog is alive *and well*. If he's hurt, I will hurt you back. Measure for measure." Alex entered the office and Lucia motioned for him to be quiet.

"You don't threaten me, bitch, I'm the one holding all the cards. You got four hours. You know the gas station between Penrose and Pattison?"

"I'll find it."

"Be there at six and bring the diamond and coins. I'll have your fucking dog with me but you're only getting him after I get the stuff. Look for a light blue Sedan Deville. If you're thinking of trying anything stupid, just remember—it ain't even a crime to kill a dog." He emitted a nails-on-chalkboard laugh. "I think I'd just have to pay a fine." The line went dead.

She slammed the phone down, then collected herself. Lucia looked up at Alex. "You get a name?"

"Manny Griffin."

"Good. Now I have something to work with."

That evening, while waiting for Griffin at the gas station, Lucia practiced the deep breathing exercises she'd learned in an "Exam Stress-Buster" session at CCP. She saw the Cadillac pull into the station and park in such a way that Griffin could exit the parking lot quickly. The plate did not match the partial Alex had gotten when Griffin took Rocco so Lucia figured the car had been stolen. She recognized that from their present location Griffin could have it on either I-76 or I-95 in minutes and silently gave him kudos for a solid plan. She got out and approached the car with extreme caution.

Griffin barked, "Get in the back." He was wearing a hoodie pulled tight about his face and had his hand in his pocket, on his gun she assumed. Rocco, his mouth duct-taped shut, was lying next to Griffin. When she was in the rear seat, he looked at her, using the rear-view mirror. "Put the stuff on the front seat and get out. Get back in your car and wait. Once I check the goods, and if they're right, I'll let him outta the car." He gave his signature ugly laugh. "I assume he'll head over to you—but that's your problem."

"I don't have the stuff." Lucia leaned forward. "But you're gonna give me Rocco and let me walk away. Right now."

"And why would I do that?"

"Because I assume you'd like to see your daughter again."

"What kind a' bullshit is this? You don't know my daughter—you don't even know who I am!"

"Deirdre, isn't that her name?" Lucia asked, her voice iced with menace. "Deirdre Griffin. Nice kid, little mousy but sweet. Works at *The Quickstop* there on Frankford, right?"

His eyes wide and breathing shallow, Griffin yelled, "What the fuck are you trying to pull? You're bluffing."

Nodding towards the station, Lucia said, "Why don't you go in there, call your wife, see if Deirdre ever made it home from work. She always gets home at five on the dot. Ain't that right?"

Seeming to calm down slightly, Griffin said, "Oh, I see what your game is." He shoved Rocco to the floor and pulled a cell phone out of his pocket, sneering, "I don't have to go in there. I can call my wife from right here." He stared at her through narrowed eyes.

"Please do." Lucia watched him pull up a small antenna on the phone with his teeth and make the call with his left hand, his right hand never leaving his gun. She made a mental note to see how much those cell phone things cost. Micky certainly seemed to love the one he had. Lucia had previously dismissed them as expensive toys, but she now grudgingly admitted they could be damn useful.

Though the call had started quietly enough, Griffin was now shouting at his wife, "She didn't call or nothing?" By the time he'd hung up, he was white-faced and trembling. He turned and looked at Lucia, "What did you do? Where is my daughter?"

"Did you really think you were gonna pull this shit on a *Scafetti* and get away with it? My family can make your daughter disappear...and we won't even pay a fine."

"No, don't hurt her. Please. She didn't do nothing to you. Colona said you hardly talk to your family even—"

"Colona? He put you up to this?!"

"Yes, I mean, no! Not this. He...he's asking around, seeing if anyone knows anything about you trying to move the diamond and coins. Told me to keep an ear to the ground, said he'd give me a cut of the proceeds if I brought him anything good. This plan seemed...like a short-cut to the loot. I didn't wanta hurt your dog, really. Just let Deirdre go. Please."

"I'm taking my dog now and heading to his vet. When they say he's okay...*if* they say he's okay, then I call my cousins and they'll let your daughter go. Understand? Now, put that fucking gun away." After he obeyed, she slid into the front seat and gently lifted Rocco up. When she had him tucked safely under her right arm, she reached over with her left, grabbed Griffin's hand that was still holding the phone, and slammed it full force into the dashboard. She got out while he was still howling in pain, pausing only long enough to snarl, "Rocco says, that's payback, bitch." Unsure if she'd broken his phone or his hand, Lucia hoped it was both.

When she had Rocco in her car, Lucia cut his mouth free with her pocket knife. She hugged him, crooning, "You're all right, you're all right. I'm sorry you had to go through that." She petted and held him until he'd stopped trembling, saying, "Okay, let's get you to the vet and they'll get that shit off your nose. Then, I gotta call Alex."

Lucia was walking down Locust Street when she spotted Rockingham heading towards her. She waved the takeout bag from Abner's to let him know the lunch she'd promised him had been procured. With his long stride he caught up to her quickly.

He looked down at the bag and said, "I hope this lunch isn't to thank me for looking into that 'Loon thing' for you, because there's nothing in our database."

"Nope, like I said, I don't want anything from you. I have some very interesting information *for you.*"

"And that would be...?" She glanced around at the passers-by, suggesting they find a spot to eat that was both shady and private, before getting into that. Davis agreed and bent down to say hello to Rocco. The dog responded by backing away and moving behind Lucia. "I see he's still my biggest fan."

"Don't take it personally. You know Rocco doesn't like most people."

When they started walking, Davis pointed at the dog, trotting ahead of them. "Does he like *Enrique*?"

She ignored the way he over-pronounced the name and shrugged. "They're still working it out—and he goes by Hank, by the way."

"Have you told Hank you're having lunch with your ex-boyfriend?"

"I don't see why he'd care." She pulled Rocco away from the discarded remains of a soft pretzel, remarking, "Why the interest in Narváez? You're surprised someone that good-looking is into me?"

He glared at her before answering, "I'll gamely ignore the unflattering implication there and just say I didn't think he was *your* type. He's a little...."

"Short? That doesn't bother me."

"Actually, I was going to say callow, but yes, that, too."

"Callow!?"

"Meaning young and inexp—"

"I know what it means, Davis. I just can't believe you were pompous enough to say it. Hank is *my age*. I'm done dating older men. It's like with smoking—"

"—bad for you?"

"I gave it up for Lent and then found I didn't miss it." After a beat she added, in a sardonic echo, "But now that you mention it, yeah, that, too."

They spotted a deserted bench on Locust Walk and sat down. When Lucia took out three paper-wrapped sandwiches, Davis said, "I'm not *that* hungry."

She handed Rockingham a cheesesteak, then opened and pulled a chunk off the extra one, which she tossed to the ecstatic dachshund. "This one's for Rocco."

"You're letting him have a cheesesteak?"

"It's only a half. The poor boy had a rough week."

"Why? Did you give him a bath? Or did he have to actually interact with another dog?"

"He was held hostage and had his mouth duct-taped shut by some moronic, small-time hood." When Davis laughed in response, Lucia insisted, "I'm not joking. This loser, Manny Griffin, grabbed him to get me to give up the whereabouts of the South African coins and diamond that my father supposedly had. The same stupid rumor that got him killed."

"Good God, are you serious?" When she nodded, he asked, "Have you told the police?"

"No, because they're the ones behind it. At least one of them is." He started to protest so she said,

"Hear me out." While they ate, she filled him in on the whole story. Lucia finished by telling him she'd confirmed that Griffin was an informant for Colona and waited breathlessly for his reaction.

For a long minute, Davis made no response other than taking another bite of his cheesesteak. Finally, he swallowed and gave her a penetrating stare. "Why would Griffin tell you about being an informant for Colona? That's a risky thing to put out there—if it were true."

"It's true! He blurted it out when he thought I'd kidnapped his daughter as revenge for him taking Rocco."

Rockingham scrubbed a hand across his lower jaw. "I hate that I have to ask you this but...*did* you kidnap his daughter?"

"No, I just told him that so he'd let Rocco go."

"And he believed you, because...?"

"Because she was late getting home from work." To stop the cross-examination, she immediately explained, "Which I arranged for, by having this good-looking young guy 'bump into her' and ask her out for coffee."

"I don't know whether to be impressed or appalled." She grinned and waggled her eyebrows at him. In response, he shook his head in exasperated bemusement. "Why are you telling me this?"

"I thought the head of that Police Corruption Task Force I read about in the Inquirer would be interested in this news about Colona."

"They didn't print the names of the task force members let alone revealing who was heading it up."

"That is one unconvincing non-denial." She slurped some soda and waited him out for a minute, finally realizing that silence wasn't going to break down a seasoned prosecutor. "Come on, I know it's you. With your political ambitions, this task force has your fingerprints all over it. And...if the task force is going by the usual MO, you're working your way up the chain to try to get to the big fish. Think how much faster it would be if you started with someone like Colona."

Davis removed his round tortoiseshell-framed glasses and rubbed his eyes briefly before returning them to his face. "Look, you're right about the task force—but this thing with Colona, I don't know. You're talking about the hero who caught Sure-Shot Scafetti. There's nothing incriminating about him asking Griffin about the diamond and coins. That sounds like part of his legitimate investigation into your father's death. You only have Griffin's word that there was anything nefarious about it. You can't believe everything some dim-witted dog-napper belches out, Lucy-Lou."

His patronizing tone grated even more than the nickname. She took a deep breath, chanting Bac's mantra to herself: *Lose your temper, Lose your focus, Lose your life.* Exhaling, she embarked on an alternate approach. "Did you know Colona was friendly with my family for *years* before he turned my dad in? I'm talking almost twelve years."

"And that means what, exactly? In case you've forgotten, your family runs a very popular restaurant, butcher shop and formerly, bakery."

121

Knowing that calling Rockingham arrogant and naive wouldn't get her anywhere, Lucia checked that impulse. "Let me ask you this, that so-called quiet release the DA arranged for my father—would Colona have known about that?"

After a moment's hesitation Rockingham admitted, "As the arresting officer, yes, he would have been informed."

"Uh-huh. Kind of closes the loop on how D'Amico found out so fast about my dad getting out, doesn't it?"

"Or," Davis drawled, "a more reasonable supposition would be that D'Amico learned about it from a member of your notoriously criminal family already in his employ."

"Nope. Objection. The only ones who knew weren't the blabbing types."

"Sorry. Based on your family's well-known and well-documented proclivities, I'm going to overrule that objection. I know you love...at least some of them, but they are much more suspect in this matter than Colona." When she thumped her hand down in disgust, his tone softened. "I would think you of all people would object to mere guilt by association. And that's all you have on Colona. That...and perhaps a deep-seated prejudice against the man who brought down your father."

"It is neither of those things. It's a mountain of circumstantial evidence pointing to a clear conclusion."

"Nice try, but that's called 'citing facts not in evidence'. Bring me something better than hearsay and conjecture on Colona—and I'll take a look at it. Swearsies."

Wondering how she could have ever fallen for a guy who could unironically use that term, Lucia stood up. "Okay, then. Thanks for nothing." When Rockingham glowered in response, she said, "Oh, lighten up, Got-Rocks, it was a joke." She looked down at the dog currently straining at the leash—in the wrong direction, naturally. "No, we gotta go home, Rocco. I've got work to do."

Together they walked towards 38th Street, where Davis was most likely to quickly hail a taxi. As she said good-bye, he belayed her with a hand on her arm. In an undertone he said, "For my own peace of mind, I have to know how you figured out about me running the task force."

"If you're worried other people are gonna figure it out, too, don't be. When I read about it, I just knew." She shrugged. "Intuition like that being one of my unique talents. Like holding my breath...and blow-jobs." Cocking her head, Lucia mused, "Which is kind of the same talent now that I think about it."

He closed his eyes briefly, as if in pain. "Do you have to be so—"

"Vulgar? Yeah, I do. It's right there in the hard-boiled detective's handbook."

"Is there a chapter in that book about gathering hard evidence? I would suggest you re-read it."

"Don't need to." The light changed and she crossed, calling back, "I wrote it."

CHAPTER 9
A World of Thieves

"In a closed society where everybody's guilty, the only crime is getting caught. In a world of thieves, the only final sin is stupidity."—Hunter S. Thompson, *Fear and Loathing in Las Vegas*

Lucia had insisted it was her turn to make dinner—as long as Hank was willing to loan her his kitchen. He was happy to oblige and as she poured the sauce over the pasta that night, Hank breathed in the aroma wafting from the dish. "That smells wonderful. Though, I always thought it was Lobster Fra Diavolo—I didn't know you could make it with shrimp."

"You can, when lobster is out of your budget and more work than you want to deal with anyway," Lucia laughed. "Just don't tell my Zia Carmela what I did to her recipe."

"My lips are sealed."

"Good, that means I get to eat all of this." Lucia was elated at the way Hank laughed at her lame quip. She wanted to shout, "He likes me—he really likes me!" but instead served up both the pasta and the tale of her frustrating experience with Rockingham earlier that day.

Since her conscience forbade her from including the information about the Police Corruption Task Force, Hank found the ADA's disinterest in Colona's purported connection to Rocco's misadventure unsurprising. "You'd probably have been better off just telling him how little effort Colona seems to be putting in on the murder investigations."

"Why? So he could condescendingly tell me I don't understand police procedure?" She gave a snort of bitter laughter. "He actually thinks Colona asking around about the diamond and coins is part of his so-called 'legitimate investigation'." Sighing, Lucia said, "Looks like I have to dig more into Colona's past with my family. There's something there, I just know it."

"I guess asking your mom what she remembers is out of the question?"

"We did talk a little bit about it before the funeral. She confirmed that Colona was friends with my dad and his cousins but said Micky didn't trust him." Lucia paused, scratching the side of her head. "That bit of news has me even more confused. If I'm right that Colona had an in with D'Amico himself, Micky not trusting him just doesn't add up."

"Maybe ask her why she thinks Micky didn't trust Colona."

"I'd like to but the subject of Colona *really* upsets her and I hate to burden her more right now. She seems...I don't know...lost. Patsy says she's been spending a lot of time wandering around the city alone, visiting the places she used to go with my father. She was so focused on waiting for him to get outta Graterford, then on getting him buried and now that's all over and she's...stuck in neutral, not knowing what to do next. I asked her what her plans are and she said she's waiting for a sign."

"A sign from God?"

Throwing out a hand, Lucia elaborated, "From God, from the universe, from my father, she couldn't say."

After reflecting on that pronouncement for a moment, Hank said, "I can see how frustrating that is for you but...I think you need to be patient with her. Your mom's been on a real emotional roller coaster of late."

After downing a forkful of shrimp, Lucia nodded. "You're right. I guess it's gonna take her some time to come up with a new plan for the rest of her life." She sighed heavily. "I'm glad she has Patsy looking after her." With a fond smile, she observed, "He's such a mother hen. In a way, they could be good for each other."

"You mean your mom gets emotional support from Patsy while looking after her gives him something new to focus on?"

"Yeah...but not just that. When I see them together, I kind of wish...." With a shrug Lucia trailed off, embarrassed to give voice to the thought.

"What?"

"I know it's too soon but, in the future...it would be nice if they could...you know, get together." She peered at Hank from beneath her lashes. "That's a weird thing to be thinking, right?"

"No, not really. I understand how you'd want two of the people you love most to find happiness with each other." Hank tilted his head in thought. "But somewhere I got the idea that Patsy is a lot younger than your mom, no?"

Shaking her head, Lucia said, "Only ten years. Which is nothing considering that's six less than there was between me and Bac."

He quirked an eyebrow, his lips twisted in a mock grimace. "Yeah, I'm afraid that's not quite the slam dunk argument you think you're making."

"Oh, not you, too." She drew a deep breath, before asserting, "I know how it maybe looked from the outside, but...we weren't like that. *Bac* wasn't like that. Whatever problems there were, he didn't take advantage of me. Bac wasn't capable of taking advantage of anyone." Lucia tossed her hair over her shoulder, smiling faintly. "That's one of the reasons he was such a lousy businessman."

Hank gave the tiniest huff of laughter, then slipped into a more somber mood as he asked, "How did he die? You never said."

"Car accident. His friend, Nick Lynch—the one I told you about on our first date?" Hank nodded, so

Lucia continued, "Lynch bought this beautiful brand-new Corvette. Bac loved Corvettes—he had one himself for years. They decided to have a guy's weekend at the cabin and Lynch let Bac drive. He missed a turn...and drove right into a tree. Bac died almost instantly. Lynch survived—probably because he was wearing his seatbelt, while Bac...wasn't." Hank made murmurs of sincere sympathy but Lucia's mind had already drifted back to their earlier subject. "You know what? I should ask Lynch if he knew Colona back in the day. He was Chester's chief of police in the late 70s. Maybe they crossed paths."

"Sounds like a good plan." His smile turned mischievous as Hank said, "Speaking of good plans— I hope you're planning on spending the night again."

"Sorry...." She nodded towards the dog watching them from the rug by the sink. "But Rocco has been really jumpy since his...ordeal, so spending the night in a strange place is not a great idea." She graced Hank with a playful smile of her own. "However, I was planning to stay until after dessert. And I don't mean ice cream."

"Now, that's a great plan."

The next day Lucia was feeling drained after a morning spent delivering bad news to two emotional clients. Just once she'd like to be able to say to a client something like, "Nope, your spouse isn't cheating. In fact, they're planning a huge, happy surprise for you. All is well in your marriage." Fantasy, fantasy—it had never happened and the more rational part of her realized it never would. By the time a client hired a PI to follow their spouse around, they'd already amassed enough indirect evidence to know the truth.

In her present mood, Lucia was dismayed to spot a teary young woman waiting outside the office door as she returned from her client rounds. She wondered how bad the story was if this one was crying already. Reaching the bottom step, Lucia called out, "Hi, are you here for Fidelia Investigations? I'm Lucia Scafetti."

When the rail-thin girl turned around, Lucia saw she was younger than she'd initially thought, no more than nineteen or twenty. The girl brushed the lank, straw-colored hair out of her eyes and glared at Lucia for a moment. "Well, I hope you're fucking happy and proud of yourself, Lucia Scafetti. My father ain't been home for days." With a heaving sob, she finished, "He's probably dead."

Key in hand, Lucia tilted her head in intense scrutiny, trying to place this possibly unhinged individual. Over the noise Rocco had started to make, she asked, "I'm sorry—have we met?"

"I'm Deirdre Griffin. You used me to get to my dad." Her pale face twisted into a mask of scorn, she weepily snarled, "Remember?"

Wordlessly, Lucia unlocked the door and held up one finger, signaling for Deirdre to wait. After Rocco was secured in his crate, Lucia asked Griffin to come inside. Deirdre complied, stopping to stare into the crate. She pointed at the dog, sniffling, "Was he worth it? My dad's life, I mean."

Lucia clamped down on the instinctive response that to her, Rocco most certainly was. Gesturing towards one of the guest chairs, she silently told Deirdre to sit down. When they were both seated, Lucia handed her a couple of tissues from the box she kept on her desk, then leaned forward to address the weepy girl. "Why do you think your father is dead?"

Dabbing at her eyes, Deirdre said, "'Cause that's what everyone's saying."

"Have you reported his disappearance to the police?"

"My mom did. They haven't done nothing to find him. They don't give a shit."

"I hear that," Lucia muttered. More loudly, she asked, "What is it you want from me?"

"I wanted you to know—that's all. I wanted you to know that all that poking around you did to find out who he was and who he worked with...it probably got him killed. That's what my mom says." Running out of steam, Deirdre seemed to visibly deflate. She wiped her nose with her tissues before sobbing out, "I know he's not...a boy scout or anything. But he never hurt no one. He wouldn't've hurt your dog." When Lucia couldn't stop a huff of disbelief from escaping at that assertion, the girl insisted, "Not hurt him for real." While Lucia was wondering if it was her place to break the truth to this forlorn kid, Deirdre quietly added, "No matter what he did, he's my dad and I still love him."

"Yeah...I understand," Lucia said—and, damn, did she ever. "How long has your father been missing? When was the last time you saw him?"

After a fresh flood of tears, Deirdre choked out, "Wednesday. Two days after you busted up his hand. All 'cause he took your dog for a few hours."

"No. Because he hurt my dog and threatened to kill him...." Lucia paused briefly to emphasize what followed. "...unless I gave him some things I didn't even have."

"You coulda just told him you didn't have those things. He would've understood. He's not a bad man—not deep down. And your dog come out of it all just fine."

"No thanks to your father." Seeing this exchange was now headed nowhere productive, Lucia stood up to indicate the tête-à-tête was at an end. She walked over to the door and opened it, announcing, "I'll look into your father's disappearance—see what I can find out."

Her shoulders slumped in sullen defiance, Deirdre hesitated but eventually rose and walked over to the door. She peered doubtfully up into Lucia's face, asking, "Why? Why would you help me? 'Cause you feel guilty?"

Believing the girl deserved the truth, Lucia gave it to her—part of it anyway. "No, I don't feel guilty, but I do know what it's like to...to miss your father."

When Deirdre left, Lucia closed the door and leaned against it, sorrowfully reflecting that yet another person had apparently died in pursuit of Klaus Guenther's stolen treasure. She suddenly wondered if the Kimberly Star—wherever it was—had some kind of curse on it. She let Rocco out saying, "That damn thing sure has been unlucky for us, hasn't it?" Deciding she couldn't do anything about a possibly hexed diamond, Lucia instead focused her energies on determining the fate of Manny Griffin. She started by calling Alex Harris for the name of someone who might have an insight into Griffin's disappearance.

An hour later, Lucia was talking to Charlie Scribner in his ancient thrift shop in the Frankford section of Philadelphia. Charlie seemed even older than his store and his hacking cough and wheezing breaths made Lucia glad she hadn't put off her visit to see him. "Yeah," he panted out. "I heard about Manny. Damn shame—but kinda expected."

"Why do you say that, Mr. Scribner?"

"The news about him working for Colona spread through the community like wildfire."

"The community? What community would that be?"

With a picket-fence grin, he answered, "Mine. The community of folks who deal in second-hand merchandise...the kind you don't ask too many questions about."

"Anyone in your community particularly interested in the fact that Griffin was an informant for Colona?"

"There might be. Even though the news shouldn't't've come as no big surprise."

"Why is that?"

"Well," he drawled, "that's a long story and I'm a busy man."

She glanced around the deserted shop, before saying, "Yeah, I can see that. Is there something I could do to...purchase some of your time?" While Scribner was still considering the matter, Lucia pointed to a small cardboard box of dusty crystals, evidently remnants from a busted chandelier. "How much for the crystals?"

"Depends on the size—three dollars for the small ones and seven-fifty for the big ones. If you wanta take the whole box, I'll let you have it for...twenty-five."

"That seems mighty steep for seven or eight pieces of glass. I'll give you ten dollars for the box—and that long story about Manny Griffin."

"Make it fifteen and you got yourself a deal." Lucia agreed and while he was laboriously wrapping the crystals, one by one, in yellowed sheets of newspaper, Charlie shared the story of Manny Griffin and his former partner, Ted Kieffer. "They was doing a real brisk business there in Society Hill for years."

"Break-ins?"

"Yep. Then they got caught. Kieffer was a kid, had to rely on a public defender while Manny somewheres found the money for his own lawyer. The goods were found in Kieffer's car with no real link to Manny so Manny's lawyer insisted on separate trials. It worked; Manny got probation while Kieffer got sent up for three years." He paused to catch her eye before continuing, "I always did think Manny's deal seemed a little too good to be true, ya' know?"

"So, Griffin rolled over on Kieffer and Kieffer did time while Griffin walked?"

"Sure looks that way. Kieffer got out two years ago a lot worse for the wear."

"How so?"

"He got in a lotta fights on the inside. Broke his leg one time. Prison doc didn't set it right or something and...." Scribner shrugged, "He's never been the same, I hear. He sure ain't pulling no more second-story jobs."

"Did he ever try to confront Griffin before the recent revelation?"

"Search me—but if I'd've been in Kieffer's shoes, I sure would've."

"Uh-huh. Any idea where I could find Kieffer?"

"Nope." He gave her a cagey, gap-toothed smile. "Not unless you see something else ya'd like to buy."

"I don't suppose you have any hem weights?"

"What the hell is that?"

"It's for sewing. You sew them into a hem."

"Nope, never heard of nothing like that. You sew, huh? Maybe you'd like some buttons. Those I got."

He pointed to a shelf where Lucia found a small plastic case of vintage buttons. Most unremarkable but there were six silver ones with beautiful glass cabochon inserts. She wouldn't mind adding those to her collection. Lucia walked back to the counter and tossed the case on it. "Okay. I'll take these. Five dollars."

"Ten." She argued him down to seven and Scribner threw them in the bag with the crystals, advising, "Try McKinley's Bar, there on Griscom. Kieffer's brother-in-law owns the place. I think Kieffer does odd jobs for 'im."

McKinley's turned out to be about what Lucia expected—small, dim, grimy, and extremely unfriendly. Even though he had confirmed he was the owner, the bartender claimed to have never heard of a Ted Kieffer, his apparent brother-in-law. While she was formulating her follow-up question, out of the corner of her eye Lucia noticed the man who'd been playing a solo game of pool slip out a back door. He moved quickly, though he was hindered by a noticeable limp.

She left, pretending to accept the fact that Kieffer wasn't around, then made tracks for the alley behind the bar. Lucia rounded the corner to find the alley led to a brick wall and was completely empty. She turned to leave and the man she'd been chasing jumped down from the fire escape—blocking her only exit and armed with an impressive knife. He advanced on her, growling, "Who are you? What the hell do you want?!"

Lucia backed away slowly, though the move put her deeper in the alley, it still seemed the most advisable course of action. "I'm a private investigator. I just want to talk to you about Manny Griffin."

"I knew it," he yelled, walking towards her while brandishing the knife in a threatening gesture. Lucia retreated until her back was literally against the wall. "Choots sent you—didn't he?"

"What? No. Who or what is Choots?"

Kieffer growled, "Stop playing dumb," while pointing the knife at her throat. "Choots Griffin is Manny's brother. I know all about him telling *everyone* he's gonna get me. Saying I'm responsible for Manny going missing."

"Uh, no. I swear, I didn't even know Griffin had a brother." She took a deep breath then explained, "I promised Deirdre, Manny's daughter, that I'd see what I could find out." Aware that Kieffer stood between her and her only escape route, Lucia considered her options. She could rush this guy and most likely escape unscathed but that would also mean getting no information from him. It was worth attempting de-escalation first. She held her hands out and in a soothing tone said, "How 'bout we talk over a game of pool?"

"Fuck off."

Ignoring his belligerence, Lucia gave a light laugh. "I've played solo pool myself a few times. It really sucks—doesn't it?" Sweat trickled down her spine while Kieffer continued to glare at her, still holding the knife inches from her throat. "Look, I'm no fan of Griffin, either. He kidnapped my dog. I'm the one who dug up the info about him and Colona in the first place. I'm not looking for vengeance or even justice for the guy. But he has a kid who deserves to at least know what happened to him."

"Just leave me alone, huh? I don't know nothing 'bout Griffin."

"Come on, one game of pool? You win, I leave with no questions asked; I win—we talk."

Kieffer's demeanor changed suddenly. His knife hand fell to his side, while he nodded and chuckled, "You got a deal, lady."

Lucia had planned to lay off a bit so as not to humiliate Kieffer but found she actually needed to dig deep just to beat him. When she pocketed the eight-ball, he said, "Damn, Scafetti, you're good."

"So are you."

"Yeah, I tried the pro circuit for a while. It's a lot harder when *everyone* you go up against is crazy good—and knows all the tricks."

Lucia nodded, admitting, "Tell me about it. I tried it, too." She smiled at him. "You want to play another—while we talk?" Halfway into the second game Kieffer loosened up enough to admit that he'd heard the news about Griffin being one of Colona's informants. "Were you surprised?"

"Nah. That's the thing—Manny told me everything when I went to see 'im after getting out. That's why it's so stupid everyone thinking it was me who went after 'im now."

"Why did Griffin come clean to you?"

"He felt kind of bad, I think." Kieffer put the six-ball away before continuing, "Not just for diming me out but for getting mixed up with Colona in the first place. He said he'd've been better off doing time with me—at least that's got an end to it."

"Meaning what?"

"Meaning once you start snitching for Colona—he owns you. Forever. He says jump, you better say

'How high, sir?' or he'll frame you for something…or even…put you on a one-way ferry ride."

"Griffin told you that?"

"He sure as hell did." Kieffer missed his next shot, turning play over to Lucia. As she studied the table he said, "I bet that's why Manny went after those goods he thought you had. Probably saw it as his ticket outta hell."

Lucia leaned down, aiming for the eleven-ball. "Only once Colona found out, it turned out to be Griffin's ticket on that ferry."

"That would be my bet." After Kieffer beat her in a very close game, Lucia thanked him for his help and went to leave. She was almost at the door when she heard Kieffer yell, "Scafetti, wait a minute."

She glanced back to find Kieffer motioning her over, so she trotted back to the pool table and waited while Kieffer looked around, obviously wary of eavesdroppers. "What is it?"

Once he was assured of privacy, Kieffer whispered, "You probably already figured this out but just in case…everybody in Philly who's, you know, in the game, has heard about that diamond and those coins. You need to watch your back."

"Heard about them from Colona?"

"From him or someone he's asked about it."

As concerning as that news was, Lucia shelved it while she considered her next move in locating Manny Griffin. That ferry ride comment told her to look in New Jersey—among the unidentified dead. She headed back to the office to call Camden County's Medical Examiner, Dr. Geraldine Foltz.

She'd spoken to the ME several times in her search for that missing girl, Billie Hansell. Foltz wasn't immediately available but did return the call several hours later.

When Lucia explained her problem, Foltz wearily sighed, "I've got at least a dozen unidentified corpses right now that roughly fit Griffin's description. Can you narrow it down any?"

"How many of them have a broken hand?"

After a slight pause, Foltz said, "One. Killed by a bullet to the head. Who should I contact about IDing the body?"

CHAPTER 10
Every Lock Contains a Secret

"Every key belongs to a lock, and every lock contains a secret."—H.S. Crow, *Lunora and the Monster King*

Hank was giving Lucia a much-appreciated after-sex back-rub while she shared the sad story of her previous day spent in search of Manny Griffin. When he finished, she glanced over her shoulder, saying, "That was fantastic. I feel so much better now. Just what the doctor ordered." She smiled. "*All* of that, I mean, in case I wasn't clear."

They both sat up, propped against their respective pillows, Hank still pondering the story. "You really think Colona killed Griffin?"

"I do. I also think he's gonna get away with it based on the fact that I let the PPD know that I was the one who located the body and, so far, no one has even bothered to follow up."

"You gonna tell Rockingham?"

"I talked to him this afternoon. He shrugged it off as all just more hearsay and conjecture. He even said that it's more likely that Kieffer killed Griffin and fed me that story to throw me off his scent."

"What did you say to that?"

"What could I say? That I'm the one who talked to Kieffer and his story had the ring of truth to it? He'd've laughed in my face. Rockingham's already dismissed my intuition and I don't have anything concrete right now." She ran her hands through her hair, saying, "Still, I'd put folding money on Colona being behind Griffin's murder. Even if he wasn't the one who pulled the trigger, I'll bet he put someone up to it."

After nodding along with her assertions, Hank offered, "As pissed as I was about Griffin pulling that stunt with Rocco, he didn't deserve to die."

"I know."

"At least you got some closure for his family. How'd they take the news?"

"Badly—total state of denial at first. I wasn't surprised, though. Having been in their shoes, I'm sure they were still holding out hope he was okay. Griffin's wife was even arguing about it being useless, driving all the way to Jersey when it couldn't possibly be her husband in that morgue—until I told her about the broken hand."

"How did you know about that?"

"Um...I knew...because I was the one who broke it. The day I got Rocco back."

Hank stared at her wide-eyed for a moment before asking, "What? Why did you have to do that? I thought he believed the story about his daughter."

"He did. The hand was...." Lucia hesitated over the word "payback," thinking it would make Hank see her in a bad light, though she silently admitted to herself it might be an accurate assessment. "It was insurance. I wanted Griffin to know that if he came after me or Rocco again, he was in for a world of hurt." She soothed her conscience with the thought that wasn't a wholly inaccurate statement—she had done it at least partially as a warning.

"And now Kieffer thinks there's a bunch of other Griffins out there, planning their moves. To get at some shit you don't even have." Shaking his head, Hank said, "You know what? It's too bad you don't actually know where the diamond and coins are."

"Why?" Lucia laughed. "Are you sick of practicing law? Thinking I could cash out and make a fortune?"

"No," he chuckled in return. "If you had them, then you could hand them over to the authorities and get all these thugs off your back."

"Hand them over to which authorities?" She shrugged, admitting, "I don't have a scorecard for the good guys and bad guys in the PPD. I could be handing them over to someone who's just gonna give them to Colona or make off with the goods themselves."

"So? Once you handed them over that would no longer be your problem—right?"

"Yeah, that's one way to look at it. Thing is, though, I don't have them." She laughed while leaning over to kiss Hank's neck, muttering, "I'll just have to use my brilliant detective skills to find another way to get these guys off my back."

"Good." Hank smiled wickedly, while tracing his hand up and down her spine. "I don't want anyone on your back but me."

Leaning into Hank's touch, Lucia sighed, "We keep this up and I'm gonna get revved up again."

"How is that a bad thing? We have time for another round before you gotta get Rocco back home—right?"

She kissed him, murmuring, "Plenty of time."

Lucia got back to her office very late but still too keyed up from that extended lovemaking session with Hank to sleep. Deciding to work until she was tired enough to sleep, she sat cross-legged on the couch, Rocco snoozing beside her, cataloguing everything she knew, or suspected, about Colona. Once finished, she reviewed the list which nearly filled the page of the legal pad, before doodling a couple of stars next to: *He thinks I have the Kimberly Star and the Kruger Double-Nine Ponds.*

Of course, D'Amico maintained the same delusion since Vinnie—in his usual roundabout way—had asked at her father's funeral if she didn't want to unburden herself of such valuable and hard to fence goods. Counting Griffin, that made three people who thought she had them. Her grandmother used to say, "If two people say you're sick, lay down." Lucia wasn't fully convinced of that bit of wisdom but thought maybe it was time to at least take her temperature.

Could she have something like that without knowing it? No. What could she conceivably have? The key, maybe. The one her father had needed to unlock the money that he'd hidden away—perhaps the stolen goods, too. She was skeptical about that last part but there was only one way to find out—locate that key. It wasn't in the mink, Carlo himself had torn that coat apart. But the truth she hadn't told anyone was that she'd worn that mink long before her dad had gotten to it. Lucia forced herself to do something she'd been avoiding for eight months—minutely recall the events of the wedding she'd attended with Rockingham.

She ran through a mental checklist. Nothing significant had happened in the church, then at the reception she'd checked the coat along with everyone else in their party, didn't see it again until...oh yeah. After Amelia Rockingham had scorched her good, Lucia had volunteered to get the coats as a way to buy some time to fully compose herself. That memory prompted Lucia to recall dabbing her eyes with a handkerchief in the cloakroom. Where had she gotten that handkerchief? From the coat? That was the most reasonable conjecture, so, what had she done with it?

Jumping up, Lucia ran out into the hall bathroom and searched the smaller Ikea wardrobe she'd installed there. Buried in a dark corner, she found the prize—the vintage evening bag which she'd been so thrilled to find for the wedding, the one that now held only bad memories. She clicked it open and found an embroidered handkerchief wadded up in the corner. It did indeed look like one of her grandmother's.

One good shake of the cloth and a green scapular, the cord wrapped tightly around the plastic covering, tumbled into her lap. Upon closer examination, she found a small brass key tucked inside the plastic. Even though there was no danger of being observed in the windowless bathroom, Lucia instinctively glanced around as she removed it. Okay, she had the key—that was step one. The question remained, though, the key to what? It was unlike any key she'd seen before—too small to be for a door or a safety deposit box or anything mundane like that. On its face was etched a symbol that looked like three hearts in a circle and the number 260. Some sleuthing was in order.

Conscious of possibly being under scrutiny by multiple parties, Lucia took the key, along with all the ones she could find that used to belong to Bac to a locksmith who'd helped her before. Since Bac had been an inveterate packrat, she dumped twenty-seven keys on Tristan Kern's dusty counter at Fairmount Lock and Safe.

"What the hell is this?" Tristan barked.

"Missing person's case. I need IDs on all of these keys so I can figure out which ones the guy might have taken and what he left behind."

"I'm not doing this for free."

"No shit. How much were you thinking?" When Tristan said he wanted twenty-dollars, Lucia agreed and slapped down a five-dollar deposit. "Any idea how long this will take?"

"It'll take how long it takes. I'll call you."

"You're a peach."

"Watch your mouth, kid. You try getting one of them young yahoos in the business to do this for you. Unless they're grinding a new key or jimmying open a car door, stuff a monkey could do, they don't know their ass from a hole in the ground." Since Tristan had spoken nothing but the truth, Lucia thanked him politely and left the shop.

When she got back to her neighborhood, she decided to run some errands before going back to the office. While price-checking lipsticks in the drug store, Lucia noticed the same guy that she'd just seen in the grocery store. Taking her purchases to the checkout line, she used the reflections in the windows to watch him do the same. Oh yeah, he was tailing her. A cop for sure—despite the casual clothing, he had that same severe haircut they all have, those shiny black shoes, that nice loose shirt to conceal the gun and handcuffs. She debated whether to ignore him or to have a little fun losing him. As tempting as the latter idea was, she had a client coming to the office in forty minutes, so she let the cop follow her back. As Lucia and her shadow reached the front steps of Overbook Commons, she turned and tipped an imaginary cap at the man. With a smile she called out, "Morning, officer."

Lucia was thrilled and not all that surprised when Kern called her the next day to let her know he'd identified all of the keys. She smiled to herself; the old man just could not resist a puzzle. Before leaving for Kern's shop, she pulled on some baggy jeans and a baggier shirt she'd inherited from Bac and tucked her braided hair into a beat-up straw fedora she'd found at the Goodwill. It was one of her go-to disguises; a six-foot tall woman people tended to notice and remember, whereas a six-foot tall schlubby man?—not so much.

She crisscrossed the block a few times to ensure her disguise worked; it seemed to have, but just to be sure, she decided to drive her car to the locksmith and follow a circuitous route. She parked blocks away and made a careful survey of her surroundings, once assured she was alone, Lucia hurried to Kern's shop. Tristan didn't even bat an eye when she walked into his shop in her disguise. She guessed Kern either figured that was her customary casual attire or just didn't give a damn what she was up to.

After paying the remainder of his fee, she started to examine the small white tags he'd attached to each key. The IDs were scrawled on the tags in pencil. She was careful to show much more interest in the key to Bac's first apartment, the random motel key, and the one to the trunk of a Corvette that had met its maker in 1987, than to the small brass key.

She finally picked it up and peered at the label. "What's this say? What's a 'Mousedear'?"

"Can't you read? That says 'Mausoleum'."

"Oh. Nothing for me there."

"Yeah," Tristan laughed. "I don't think you're gonna find this guy in one of them nooks they use for ashes."

"If I do, he's got bigger problems than a wife that wants to track him down." She paused briefly, her mind working furiously. "Do you have a phone book I can use?" She held up the motel key. "I want to see if I can set up a meeting with the manager at this place."

He pointed back to the desk which was even dustier than his counter. "Sure, knock yourself out."

Lucia had not been able to find a Yellow Page ad for a cemetery or mausoleum featuring the same three hearts in a circle logo as was on the key. Oh well, it had been worth a shot. She returned to her office, thinking, *Okay, I gotta do this the hard way.* She called every funeral home in the city, making notes of which ones offered storage for cremains—a word she'd just learned but quickly came to loathe. The next two days proved exhausting; Lucia spent her time dodging her police tail and as soon as she was sure the coast was clear, visiting funeral homes, posing as a grieving relative. When she made time out of those activities to visit with her mother, it occurred to Lucia it wasn't really that much of an act.

After crossing the last funeral home off her list, Lucia sat, staring at the paper, wondering what to do next. None of the places in Philadelphia had cremation niches that required keys like the one in her pocket—most of them didn't have niches that opened and closed at all. Now what? *Start over—at the beginning*, Bac's voice said in her mind, as clear as if he'd been standing beside her.

Exhaling heavily, she retraced her mental steps. First, she'd found the key with the scapular in her grandmother's handkerchief. Was that the beginning—or would that have been when she first heard about the key? Yes, that was it, when her dad had asked her about it. He was the one who'd known what the key was for, he was heading out to use it, or rather to subvert needing it, the last time she saw him alive.

She sat up straight, a memory from that morning striking her: he took Patsy's car, which they'd later found abandoned on Oregon Avenue. D'Amico's thugs had caught up with him as he was headed...somewhere. To the Schuylkill or to I-95? If so—he was headed out of the city. That was now the most logical assumption available to her. Lucia sighed wearily and started over, using a pencil to methodically draw ever-widening circles around the city on a paper map. She then neatly listed all of the funeral homes in each zone. Time to start "interviewing" these places again.

On the second day of this grind, it looked as if she'd hit paydirt. One non-denominational cemetery outside of the city limits had cremation niches that opened with a key. At the receptionist's urging, Lucia agreed to call back when the funeral director was available, but she intended to proceed to the place immediately. She needed this to be a solo trip—both on the way there, and upon arrival.

Lucia's destination, the Bellwood Cemetery, was in Bensalem, unfamiliar territory, requiring her to dig her book of maps out of the trunk of the Chevelle before proceeding to it. While still in the city, she took note of the tail she'd picked up. She muttered, "Get a life, asshole," while deftly weaving through traffic, using every nearby panel truck and monster SUV as a screen to hide her position from her pursuer. She carefully stayed with the flow of traffic until she spotted a golden opportunity. As soon as the Chevelle was hidden by a plumber's van, Lucia made an illegal turn, went against traffic for a short portion of Logan's Circle and by the time she was on Vine Street was fairly sure she'd lost him. After driving a few lazy loops around Old City just to be sure, Lucia finally headed for I-95 unencumbered.

Her main focus for the rest of the drive was to ensure she wasn't being followed again so Lucia didn't spend too much time wondering what she'd find at the cemetery. The first thing of interest she found was a sign for the "Cremation Niches" pointing to an unassuming stone building. The sign featured the same three-heart logo as was on the key. Bingo.

It didn't take long to locate the glass-fronted nook marked 260, with a brass urn housed within. Lucia had to crouch down to read the small metal plaque on the bottom of the niche. Her heart lurched and mouth went dry upon seeing the name engraved there: L. Scafetti. She whispered, "*Che cozz'*?" torn between the equally horrifying possibilities of an implied death threat or a morbid prophecy. Suddenly fearful of having walked into a trap, Lucia whirled around and surveyed the room, wishing she'd brought her weapon. But the cool softly lit space echoed with vacant silence.

She steadied her nerves, pulled the key out of her pocket, and searched for the lock—determined to see what the hell was in that urn and what it signified. The lock was tricky to locate but she finally found it above that macabre plaque. It took a few tries to unlatch the glass door, though Lucia was unsure if that was from disuse or because these niches weren't meant to be opened on a regular basis.

After lifting the urn from its niche, Lucia took a deep breath and looked inside, only to be greeted by the sight of an innocuous green Hallmark envelope stiff with age. A quick peek inside the envelope revealed a card—and many hundred-dollar bills. Instinctively, Lucia jammed the envelope back in the urn and slammed the lid on. She'd been fairly confident of finding her father's money one way or another—but had been wholly unprepared to find it in a funeral urn marked with her name.

Feeling an urgent need for privacy, she raced to the single stall bathroom near the entrance and locked herself in. Upon counting the bills, Lucia realized she was holding $25,000. Hoping for further insight, she scanned the card, which proved to be a condolence missive from her Aunt Lidia's roommate, Molly O'Connor, to Lucia's grandparents. As comprehension dawned, twin surges of relief and embarrassment engulfed her—L. Scafetti was Lidia Scafetti. But what the hell was Lidia doing in an urn in Bensalem?

Reading the entire card was most enlightening: Molly apologized for having Lidia cremated against her parents' wishes but said she felt compelled to carry out Lidia's final directive. As she read on, Lucia chortled to herself, "Aunt Lidia, you devil, you," since it was clear that Lidia and Molly had been more than roommates. Rather than a lonely spinster with a narrow life, her aunt had evidently been a kickass lesbian with an awesome wardrobe.

Leaning against the door, Lucia contemplated this revelation, slowly assembling a hypothesis. Her grandparents must have secreted Lidia's remains out here in the 'burbs to hide the fact that she was not only gay but had been cremated back when the Roman Catholic Church didn't allow the practice. Hugging the urn to her chest, Lucia ruminated on how much she wished she'd known this fascinating rebel of an aunt. She lifted the lid of the urn, intending to tell what remained there of Lidia about her longings—when she thought she spied something metallic in the ashes. Lucia shook it gently in order to see the contents better and almost dropped the urn as she breathed, "Holy fucking shit."

CHAPTER 11
The Very Heart of Danger

"...they seem to forget 'that there is safety in the very heart of danger.'"—Vincent van Gogh, Letter to Theo van Gogh. Etten, Thursday, 10 or Friday, 11 November 1881

Lucia was still performing her deep breathing exercises to calm herself down when she noticed a State Trooper's car on the shoulder of I-95. She'd only entered the highway moments before and hadn't had time to kick the Chevelle into high gear, so she barely gave it a second thought, even when the car moved onto the roadway behind her—until she heard the siren and saw the flashing lights. Still, she told herself it was a coincidence, it had to be—there was no reason to pull her over, then the cop moved directly behind her with the siren blaring. Lucia put her blinker on and pulled the car over, muttering, "What in the hell is this, now."

She watched in the rearview mirror for a few interminable minutes while the cop was on his radio. She kept telling herself it was a mistake, he'd made some kind of mistake, and would soon realize it. However, the young man, and damn, was he young, walked up to the car. She exhaled before forcing out a calmly puzzled, "Is there a problem, Officer?"

"License and registration, ma'am."

"I hope this isn't gonna take long," she said, pulling out the requested items. "I gotta pick up my kids from the sitter." He made no response but took her documents back to his vehicle. Bac had taught her how to drive so as to evade capture and she was fairly sure that in the Chevelle SS 454, she could outrun this green State Trooper—but weighed the many downsides of doing so. Like, number one, the police would then have a solid reason for arresting her later. Nope, running wasn't an option—or should be considered only as a last resort.

Finally, the cop came back, leaned into the window, and handed over her cards. "Ma'am, I'm afraid I'm going to have to hold you here."

"What's going on, Officer? Like I said my kids are—"

"There's some kind of...open search warrant out on this car, ma'am."

"A search warrant for what?"

"It's a PPD matter, I'm not clear on what it's for. You probably know better than me. If not, they'll explain when they get here."

Lucia took note of the shiny wedding band on the officer's hand and made a quick decision.

Slamming her hand against the dash, she wailed, "That louse! That dirty, rotten no-good ex-husband of mine." Whipping up some fake tears to go with the story, she continued, "I let him borrow this car. What the hell did he use it for? He swore to me he had a job interview. And I believed him, I was stupid enough to believe him."

"Oh, I see."

She sniffled, asking "Can't *you* search the car? Then I won't have to wait for the PPD." Over his protests she explained, "If I'm late, my sitter—she'll put my kids out on the street, she will, she's done it before. She's not great, but that's all I can afford, you know?" She gestured at her wallet still on the seat beside her. "You saw where I live, West Philly—you know what it's like there? You know what could happen to two little kids on the street, don't you?" She could see the young cop wavering and went for the throat. With tears now running down her cheeks, she blubbered, "You got kids?"

Shifting his weight from foot to foot and staring off at the horizon, the trooper muttered, "My wife and I, we've only been married a few months, so no, not yet."

"But you want 'em right?" He nodded. "Well, when you have some, I hope to Almighty God they never have to stand out on a street corner with rapists and murderers circling them, wondering why their momma deserted them."

He looked back at his Police cruiser, then at her. "You give your permission for me to search this vehicle?"

157

"Yes. Yes, sir, I do."

"Could you exit the vehicle, ma'am?"

"Oh, thank you—thank you so much! God bless you." She got out of the car quickly, knowing she was in a desperate race against Colona and his goons who were probably on their way to this location already. When the cop saw Lidia's urn on the floor, Lucia explained, "That's my mom. I had to go pick her up today. They kicked her out, those bastards, because I missed a few payments on the mausoleum, there. Can you believe it?"

While reluctantly lifting the lid, he said, "That's a shame."

She had to give him credit, the young officer did a thorough search of the car. As the minutes ticked by, Lucia sweated each one of them, hearing distant sirens in every whistle of the wind or whine of passing tractor-trailers. She knew the only thing saving her right now was that this particular alert had been directed to a very specific subset of the PPD.

When the search was concluded, Lucia could see the cop wavering, wondering if he'd neglected anything. Fortunately, the only thing he'd missed was the secret compartment that had been installed in the car by the Chevelle's original owner. You couldn't really blame the young man for that lapse— this particular compartment was located behind the backseat which had been rigged with a set of hydraulic cylinders. The only way to make the seat slide forward and reveal the compartment was by simultaneously pressing and holding the switches for the door locks and the windows.

Lucia knew more experienced cops—like Colona and Pike—would probably take note of those hydraulic cylinders and was therefore desperate to exit the scene before those individuals showed up. Finally, the state trooper was satisfied with his search and told Lucia she was free to go.

After thanking him profusely for his kindness, she hurriedly got in the car, reiterating that she had to get to her children. She drove away, observing the police cruiser in the rearview mirror. When he passed her, Lucia took the next exit off the highway. Using back roads all the way, she made it home to the city with no further interference.

On high alert, she parked a few blocks away and made a careful approach on foot to Overbrook Commons. What she found was unsurprising, considering her recent run of bad luck. Colona himself was loitering out front. She did a quick reconnaissance of the back alley and saw that both Pikc and Dixon were stationed there. Silently wishing all sorts of misfortune upon her tormentors, Lucia considered her options. Inspiration struck and she got back in the car, heading for the nearest drug store where she purchased the largest box of tampons they carried.

Ten minutes later, Lucia walked briskly towards the front of her building, swinging the plastic bag, pretending to be lost in thought. She flattered herself that she made a credible show of being startled when Colona barked, "Where you been, Scafetti?"

"I've been working on a case, Lieutenant." Rather than answering her, Lucia saw his attention was riveted on the bag in her hand. "You should try it some time."

"A case, huh?" He looked her up and down before remarking, "In Bucks County?"

"How did you know I was in Bucks County?"

With an evil smirk, Colona said, "I'm psychic."

"Yeah? Why don't you use your psychic powers to tell me how much I'm gonna win when I sue the city for unlawful police detention?"

"What detention? We're just having a friendly chat here."

"This is obviously some new definition of the word 'friendly'."

"How 'bout you stop stalling and give me a peek in that bag?"

"How 'bout you get out of my way since you don't have a legitimate warrant and I'm in a hurry."

"And why are you in such an all-fired up hurry?"

She pulled the box of tampons out, holding it aloft and announcing, "Because I'm experiencing a bit of a personal crisis at the moment. And if you don't let me go, *right now*, I'll never be able to wear these jeans in public again."

Lucia wanted to laugh when Colona hurriedly stepped back, his nose wrinkled and upper lip curled in disgust. "Get outta here," he snarled.

"With pleasure."

When safely in her office Lucia greeted Rocco, while drawing the shade on the door and locking it, throwing the deadbolt for good measure. Now, she told herself, she needed to calm down and think. First close those goddamned blinds on the windows, then think. She spent twenty minutes in profound deliberation, then Lucia got busy. She didn't get much sleep that night but when she finally closed her eyes, she was breathing easily for the first time in many hours.

Early the next morning Hank bumped into Lucia in the kitchenette. She had a travel mug and was wearing a suit so he assumed she had an appointment and graciously allowed her access to the coffee carafe before him. He took the opportunity to ask, "Hey, when I was coming in this morning, I noticed the blinds on your office windows were drawn. Is everything okay?"

"Oh yeah," she drawled. "I forgot to open them. I closed them last night because...." She smiled, dropping her voice to a conspiratorial whisper. "I'm being tailed these days."

"Really?" He supposed this was one of the realities of being a private investigator but wondered how she could be so cavalier. "Do you think you're in danger?"

"Nah, it's a cop."

"Are you sure? Maybe he's one of those guys Kieffer warned you about?"

"I'm sure. This guy could only be more obvious if he had one of those windbreakers with PPD on the back in big white letters. Colona even has some bogus alert out for whenever my car leaves the city—

looks like he wants to make sure I'm not trying to fence the Kimberly Star in Bucks County."

Though Colona's move sounded alarming, her merry laugh calmed his fears somewhat. Afterall, she'd been doing this job since before she could legally vote so he was inclined to bow to her wisdom on which matters were concerning and which could be shrugged off. Waving a hand at her attire, Hank asked, "Headed somewhere important?"

"Just into Center City for a brochure drop, trolling for new clients at some law offices."

"That reminds me! Max and I got a referral from someone we went to law school with—her firm has more business than they can handle. I asked Maddie if they're looking for a PI and she said she'd be willing to hear your pitch. If she likes what you have to say, she'll talk to the partners about hiring you on." He pulled out his wallet and handed over one of Maddie's business cards. "All you gotta do is turn on the charm."

"Wow, thanks. You're wonderful!" She studied the card, running a finger lightly over the fancy gold embossing at the top, flaunting the firm's portentous name of Fritz, Fritz, and Bailey. "I'll go call her right now." While Hank filled his own coffee mug, Lucia asked, "Could you loan me some of your charm before I go?"

"Nonsense." Hank looked around; upon noting the coast was clear he kissed her, murmuring, "You have charm in abundance."

Lucia got back from her tour of Center City law offices not overly hopeful that she'd picked up any new business. She was almost positive most of her brochures went in the trash can as soon as her back was turned—but hey, you've got to take your shot, right? She was more optimistic about the meeting she'd set up with Hank's friend Madeline Forrester for later that afternoon. She traded her dress shoes for sneakers and got to work returning some calls, intending to practice her sales pitch after walking Rocco and having lunch.

As she was re-donning her dress shoes in preparation for heading out, there was a knock at the door. Assuming it was a potential client, Lucia muttered to herself, "It never rains but it pours." She told Rocco to shut up then opened the door to find a soberly clad woman and man standing on the threshold with two uniformed police officers flanking them. Some internal cursing ensued while she debated whether they were planning to bring her in and expected a fight or were a search squad. The latter seemed more likely. "Can I help you?"

The steel-haired woman and the other detective held up their badges. She announced, "Ms. Scafetti, I'm Lieutenant Daniels, and this is Detective Quint, Officers Clay, and Vazquez. May we come in?"

"What's the magic words?"

Quint, the youngest of the group by far, volunteered, "May we please come in?"

She and Daniels both stared at Quint as Daniels removed a folded piece of paper from her breast pocket. "We have a warrant."

"There we go," Lucia said, studying the paper. After reading it over thoroughly, she granted, "Well, this seems legit—unlike that bullshit you guys tried to pull last night."

Quint responded by looking uncertainly at Daniels, but none of the others reacted at all. Sighing, Lucia pointed behind her. "Give me a minute to corral my dog." After allowing them all into the office, she asked, "Is this going to take long? I'm supposed to meet with a potential client in twenty-five minutes."

Daniels smiled thinly. "Oh, that's too bad. Looks like you're going to be late."

"In that case, give me one more second." While the four officers glared at her, Lucia called Maddie Forrester and with profuse apologies managed to reschedule her appointment for the next day. When she finished the call, Lucia looked at the pair of detectives seated across from her and the officers standing back near the door. "Now, what's this all about?"

"We're with the Organized Crime Unit," Daniels said. "And we'd like to talk to you about the driving force behind the deaths of your father, Paul Lugano, and Frank Tumino." While studying Lucia, Daniels added, "There is also the possibly related murder of Manfred Griffin."

"You mean someone's actually looking into Griffin's murder? I'm impressed."

Daniels' icy smile made its second appearance. "You're easily impressed, then."

"Not really. What happened to Colona, Pike, and Dixon?"

"They're still assigned to the original investigation. Our unit's particular interest is in the...larger implications of this recent spate of activity." There was a pause where it seemed Daniels was once again gauging Lucia's reaction. Seeing there was none, she explained, "We're looking to avoid a mob war."

"Either you're new at this or you should know that three or even four deaths hardly constitute a war."

"That's how it starts—isn't it?"

"No. It starts with two factions. Last I heard, D'Amico was still firmly in control."

"Four million dollars is a lot of incentive for a new faction to arise."

"Four million—where are you getting that figure? My dad killed Klaus Guenther—not Bill Gates."

"Now, who's playing dumb? The Kimberly Star is worth more than three million, the Kruger Double-Nine Ponds go for about fifty-thousand each, and there was rumored to be what? Ten or twelve of them."

"There, you said it yourself—*rumor*. Guenther must've already fenced the diamond and coins before he landed in the US. If not, my father didn't get them. Nothing like that stays hidden for twenty-years."

"You don't mind if we search your office spaces, do you?"

"Yeah, I do but that warrant of yours says otherwise. Especially if I want to keep my PI license."

"Correct," Daniels said, rising from her seat. "Let's start by you taking that padlock off that bathroom in the hall."

Her voice dripping with insincere sweetness, Lucia asked, "I guess my car is already done since it was searched last night? You do know about that farce—right?"

"Whatever search you're referring to was not performed by our unit, so yes, as indicated on the warrant, we will be searching your vehicle as well."

"Too bad. Seems a shame to waste that nice young man's time."

Her poker face intact, Daniels retorted, "You can give your car keys to Officer Vazquez." Lucia did so, informing Vazquez her car was on the street, one block down.

The remaining three officers spread out, not only turning the bathroom upside down and inside out but thoroughly searching Goldstein's deserted shop. Daniels examined the contents of the acrylic thread organizer on top of the sewing machine Lucia favored the most. When finished, she looked around, obviously seeking anything she might have missed. "Does Milo Belsky know you make use of this space?"

"I think so."

"You think so?"

With a slight chuckle, Lucia explained, "It's easier to get forgiveness than permission."

166

Gracing her with a withering stare, Daniels warned, "Not always."

Vasquez entered the room holding out Lucia's keys. "Interesting after-market feature you have there in that Chevelle, Ms. Scafetti."

"The back-seat compartment?" Shrugging, Lucia said, "It's for groceries."

She followed Daniels and Vasquez back into the chaotic office which the other two officers were still tearing apart, serenaded by Rocco's snarling and growling from his crate. After lifting him out, at Clay's insistence so the cop could examine the interior of the crate, Lucia petted the dog, murmuring soothingly that it was almost over— though it didn't seem quite true.

Lucia groaned internally, thinking of how long it was going to take her to put the office to rights, while watching Officer Clay move on to inspect the brass funeral urn on the bookcase. "That's my aunt." He lifted the lid and gingerly peered inside while shaking the contents. "I'm sure she's now had more cops peek up her skirt dead than she ever did alive."

Clay quickly put the urn back, looking slightly abashed. "We're almost done here."

"I'm sorry I don't have a teddy bear for you guys to rip open like when your colleagues searched my parent's house, but I've outgrown them."

Daniels, who was surveying the room, answered without even looking back at Lucia, "We'll muddle through without one."

"You're a trooper."

Vazquez had been rifling through the desk and announced, "Lieutenant, look at this. Concealed beneath the desk." She was holding up Bac's pistol which Lucia kept hidden under the center drawer.

Daniels murmured, "Interesting." She turned to face Lucia. "Do you have a permit for that?" After Lucia put Rocco back in his crate and produced her gun permits, Daniels looked around the disheveled office. She pointed at the hinged painting hanging opposite the filing cabinet. "What's in the safe?"

"My camera, my Glock, case notes and client paperwork, some cash." Lucia crossed the room and snapped her fingers. "Oh yeah! And a four-million-dollar diamond."

"Knock it off. How much cash?"

She opened the safe responding, "A couple hundred. I use it for bribes. That's about the going rate, isn't it?"

Daniels examined the contents, declaring, "I do not find you at all amusing, Scafetti."

"Few do. I think my true genius won't be appreciated until after my death."

"If you're trying to keep the diamond and coins hidden from both *us* and D'Amico, that might come much sooner than you think."

Watching Daniels study her stack of legal pads with a puzzled frown, Lucia smiled to herself, thankful that she made all her notes in the shorthand she'd learned in high school. "Careful, Lieutenant—that sounded more like a threat than a warning."

After thrusting the items back in the safe, Daniels turned and gave Lucia a long, measured look. "Only a person with a guilty conscience confuses the two."

"Good point—but I don't think I'm the one who has them confused."

Daniels had no response other than offering her business card to Lucia. "If you think of anything *useful* we should know, give me a call."

Lucia took the card, nodding in feigned agreement before ushering them all out. As they were walking down the hall, Lucia called after them, "I assume it's one of your guys who's been following me around. You should know, he is *really* obvious. Do better!"

Since her afternoon schedule had been screwed up by the PPD's Organized Crime Unit, after reassembling her office, Lucia decided it was as good a time as any to go out in search of Bac's old friend, Nick "Chief" Lynch. Baccaro had met Nick while he was still Chief of Police in Chester and had called him that even after Nick left the force, and that's how Lucia thought of him, too. Besides a love for sports cars, Chief also shared Bac's love for booze so Lucia started the search in one of the many dive bars she knew Chief and Bac had frequented. She finally found him in the third one, sitting at the bar watching the highlights of last night's Phillies win over the Rockies on a grainy black-and-white TV.

She slid onto the cracked vinyl stool next to him. "Hey, Chief, how's life treating you these days?"

"Lucy! Where the hell you been keeping yourself?"

"Been keeping myself busy."

"You still running Fidelia?"

"Oh yeah. Got it turning a steady profit these days."

"Damn. How the hell'd you do that?" Chief downed the last of his whiskey, shaking his head. "Bac must be turning over in his grave."

Snorting with mild amusement, Lucia admitted, "He *would* be wondering where all of his training went wrong." She got herself a beer and Chief a refill and then regaled him with the latest on Fidelia's rising prospects.

"Bac was right about you. He said you'd be a better PI than him someday and look at you now."

"I'm not a better PI, I'm a better businessman, um, woman, whatever."

"You still miss him—don't you?"

Lucia squinted across the room, seeing the bar had started to fill up with the after-work crowd. "How can I—when he lives in my head?"

"Too bad that's the only place he lives."

Chief finished his drink in a gulp, still she assumed, trying to drown his guilt after all these years. Lucia signaled the bartender to bring him another. "It wasn't your fault, Chief. Not your fault he died, and not your fault you lived."

Looking entirely unconvinced, Chief nodded glumly. "Since you are such a sharp hand at business, I don't think you hunted me down to waste an afternoon offering your grief counseling services." He swiveled to face her. "What is it you're looking for today?"

"Information."

"I see." Chief glanced around, before jerking his head towards the dingy booths in the back. "Should we go somewhere more private?"

"Probably for the best." They decamped to the back booth; once seated she asked, "When you were still in blue, did you ever run into a Philly cop named John Colona?"

"Ain't he the guy that busted your dad?" She nodded and Chief said, "Oh shit. I heard about what happened to your old man. Sorry for...for your loss." Lucia mechanically thanked him. "Is that what this is about?"

"Sort of. Colona's running the investigation but he ain't running it too hard. He's more focused on finding buried treasure than a murderer."

"Buried treasure?"

"It's another long story. The question I have for you is, did you ever hear that Colona's dirty?"

"Sure did. Way back before he became a hero for bringing down Sure-Shot Scafetti, there were always rumors to that effect. Especially about him maybe being on D'Amico's payroll."

"I figured. Anything else? Have you ever heard about him having anyone killed?"

"Nah, can't say I heard anything that bad, but considering what I do know about him, it's not completely out of the question."

"Like what?"

Stroking the stubble on his chin, Chief said, "Not only was he known for keeping very questionable company back in the day, but he also got caught in an Internal Affairs sting. He was going out of his way to bust young hookers and then letting 'em off with a warning—as long as they obliged him."

"Gross. I guess Colona got away with it?"

"Well, Rizzo saved his job but Colona was demoted back down to sergeant. Quite a comedown for a guy who was one of the youngest detectives ever and thought he was gonna be commissioner someday. Drove him crazy if anyone mentioned it. That's when he picked up the nickname 'Cuckoo' Colona."

Lucia whispered to herself, "Cuckoo—like looney. The Loon."

"What?"

"Nothing." Lucia took a long swig of beer as she pondered the implications. She turned towards Chief, asking, "Do you happen to know if ol' 'Cuckoo' Colona is a good shot?"

"No idea."

"Anybody you could ask?"

He held up his glass. "Buy me another and I'll think on it."

"Deal."

Chief had barely started on his drink when he looked up suddenly and snapped his fingers. "Patty Kourosh."

Lucia cocked her head at him. "Who's that?"

"She's an ex-Philly-cop. She's who you can get more info on Colona from."

"Why her?"

"Because she had some kind of beef with Colona. Not sure exactly what happened but I heard he's the reason she's an ex-cop."

"You know even ex-cops tend to close ranks, Chief. You sure she's gonna be willing to talk to me?"

After taking a long sip, he shrugged. "I think so. It won't hurt to ask. Offer to help her out with her business. She set herself up as a PI after leaving the PPD and I bet she could use some of your expertise."

"Seeing how long it took me to start turning even a miniscule profit with Fidelia, my honest advice would be to find another line of work."

Chuckling, Chief raised his eyebrows at her. "Maybe don't be *that* honest."

Chapter 12
To Turn and Face the Flames

"Family dysfunction rolls down from generation to generation, like a fire in the woods, taking down everything in its path until one person in one generation has the courage to turn and face the flames."—Terry Real

The next day Lucia was getting ready to leave for her delayed meeting with Madeline Forrester when she heard a quick double knock on the door followed by her mother saying, "Lucia, are you home?"

She opened the door to find her mom decked out in a linen pantsuit and smiling broadly. She looked Lucia up and down. "Oh, don't you look nice. Let's go. We can kill some time window-shopping before lunch."

Since the noise of Rocco's barking made conversation impossible, Lucia stepped out into the hall. "I don't have any time to kill. I have a meeting in a half an hour. Were we supposed to go for lunch?"

Rolling her eyes, Angie groused, "What? I have to make an appointment to have lunch with my own daughter?"

"Unfortunately, yeah, you kind of do," Lucia sighed. "I'm trying to run a business here." Over the sound of Angie muttering her opinions on Lucia's choice of business, she extended an olive branch. "If you come back at one PM, we can go to lunch then."

"How 'bout I just hang out here?" Angie offered. "You got magazines in there, right?"

"Yeah, but I'm going to be gone for over an hour."

"And your poor dog is gonna be alone all that time?"

"He's used to it." Anxious to get going, Lucia said, "Okay, sure, if you want to wait and keep Rocco company, that sounds great." She fished out her office key. "Here, take my key in case you get bored with my magazine selection." She leaned over and kissed Angie on the cheek. "I really gotta run, Ma."

Ninety minutes later Lucia was humming a happy tune as she skipped down the stairs towards her office. Her happy mood abruptly evaporated at the sight of Lydia's funeral urn sitting outside in the hall.

When she bent down to pick it up, the rumbling commotion emanating from the office transformed her irritation into concern. She hastily swung the door open, calling out, "Mama, are you—" Her query was arrested by the sight of her mother rearranging her guest chairs across from the leather couch which now stood in the middle of the room. Putting the urn down on the floor behind her, Lucia demanded, "What the hell?"

Angie turned to her with a proud smile. "Doesn't it look nice? So much cozier." Her smile turned to a frown upon spying the urn. "What are you doing with that thing? It's bad luck. Get rid of it."

"I can't—not yet. It's a...it's from a case of mine. It's a person who has no one else in the world and so it falls to me to decide what to do with them."

"So? Take it to the cemetery, or to the river or...I don't know, to the dump. Anywhere but here."

"In the first place, that's disrespectful, and in the second, you know I don't believe in curses. For now, this can hang out on my bookcase until I make up my mind what to do with it."

Waving a hand at her, Angie retorted, "Okay, don't listen to me—you never do. But don't say I didn't warn you." With a sigh she added, "Like this family needs more bad luck." Plopping down on the couch, she spread her arms across the back. "Now, what's wrong with the room? Are you saying it doesn't look homier this way?"

"It doesn't matter." Rubbing her forehead wearily, Lucia explained, "Yes, this is my home but first and foremost it's a place of business. And we need to put everything back the way it was before."

Looking crestfallen, Angie protested, "I was trying to do something nice for you."

Lucia suspected her mother's frantic activity had much more to do with a burst of manic grief than altruism so treaded lightly. "I appreciate that, really, but I need it the way it was." She looked around calculating how much work there was to be done. "How did you even move all of this by yourself?"

"Your boyfriend helped me. And that tall friend of his." Whipping around in shock, Lucia demanded an explanation. "He came looking for you and heard the noise, I guess. He burst in here ready to save the day." Angie laughed. "He's good looking but *so* suspicious. He wouldn't believe I was your mother until I showed him that picture of us at your graduation." Angie pointed to the picture on the bookshelf which was now located under the windows.

As Lucia put the office back to rights with Angie contributing little but long-suffering sighs, Lucia explained that Hank's suspicion had a righteous cause: the recent spate of police harassment she'd endured.

Upon hearing about the police squad searching the office, Angie said, "Those sons of bitches. They tore poor Patsy's home apart, too."

"What? When was this?"

"Yesterday." Her arms folded tight against her body, Angie continued, "It's all Colona's doing. That *facciadu* bastard has it in for us."

"What's the story there, Ma? What happened between dad and him?"

"I told you what happened. He made nice for years and at the first opportunity, he betrayed your poor father. *Disgraziat'*." She pointed a finger at Lucia. "You stay away from him; he's nothing but grief for anyone named Scafetti. Hear me? If he bothers you anymore, let me know and...and I'll have it taken care of."

Knowing that meant getting Micky, if not Sal D'Amico himself, involved, Lucia had no intention of following her mother's orders. She kept that resolution to herself, allowing her mother to wax long about her hatred for Colona without interruption.

Angie stopped her diatribe only when she noticed Lucia arranging Lydia's urn on the bookcase. "For the last time, you're asking for the *maliocch* keeping that thing here. Don't we have enough trouble right now without you inviting more into our lives?"

Since there was no winning that argument, and the room once again resembled an office, Lucia distracted her mother by proposing they partake of a cuisine she knew Angie was especially fond of. "Ready for lunch, Ma? How about Mexican?"

"Is there any *decent* Mexican around here? I don't eat that Taco Bell shit."

"I know. Marguerite's on 40th is very authentic. They even have chicken mole."

"This I gotta see—lead on."

Angie ended up being impressed with the food and even more impressed with Lucia offering to pay, though she insisted on taking care of it. She and Lucia parted ways at Overbrook. Lucia waited for almost half an hour before heading in what she assumed was the same general direction in which her mother had gone—to South Philadelphia. Since there was no doubt that Angie would thoroughly disapprove of them, Lucia needed to ensure her mother remained ignorant of her plans for the afternoon—tracking down the witnesses to the Tumino and Lugano murders.

Later that night, Lucia rang the doorbell to Hank's apartment with her elbow since she was juggling a pizza box, an overnight bag, a small plaid blanket, and Rocco's leash. Thankfully, Hank was expecting her and answered the door quickly. He took the pizza box from her, asking, "Pietros?"

"Ha, I wish. I picked it up at Drexel Pizza. You said they're good, right?"

Hank agreed that her choice was fine and placed the box on the table, already set for two. He dashed into the kitchen and brought back two icy bottles of beer, asking, "Do you like Thai food?"

"Getting sick of Italian food already?"

Laughingly, he protested, "No, how would that even be possible? I asked about Thai food because

Max suggested a group dinner with you, me, him, and Wally at Manu's. Dan and Juli, too, if they're available." At her puzzled look, Hank clarified, "Manu's is the Thai place there on 42nd and Walnut. What do you think?"

"Sounds great. I've never had Thai food but I'd love to try it. Who is this Wally guy?"

"Someone Max met at the gym. A doctor. His mom will be thrilled."

After they'd both taken their places at the table, Lucia smiled widely at Hank. "Speaking of Max and mothers, I understand you guys met my mom today. She said you're very cute but *also* very suspicious."

Ducking his head sheepishly, Hank responded, "Sorry about that. I thought it was prudent to be sure—after you told me about being followed, and the cops searching your office. And your mom doesn't look anything like you—"

"Yeah, she's petite and gorgeous."

"And you're tall and gorgeous." Lucia silently took the compliment, thinking that if he really believed that, it must be love, or at the very least infatuation. "Anyway, when I heard the commotion in your office I had to see if you needed help. So, I peek in and find this strange woman dragging the furniture around. That's when I went and got Max. Then somehow...we got roped into helping her even though I was pretty sure you'd object to her little project." Hank shrugged, looking helpless. "I'm sorry."

"No problem. I know there's no arguing with my mom. She's a force of nature."

"I'll say. When I said I had to go, she ordered me to take that funeral urn you have and get rid of it. I guess you saw I stuck it in the hall."

"Yeah, thanks for not throwing it in the Delaware like my mom would have wanted."

"Is it...uh, was it someone close to you?"

For a long moment, the thought of unburdening herself to Hank was tempting, but that would unleash an array of questions—questions Lucia wasn't ready to answer, maybe wasn't even yet able to answer. In the end, Lucia gave him the same story as she had to her mother.

Hank offered, "It happens. I've heard of lawyers who end up with their clients' ashes." He then changed the subject by asking for more details on Lucia's meeting with Forrester.

"Maddie is going to talk to the partners. I won't be the only PI they use, but it looks like I'll at least be put on their list. With a busy firm like theirs, that's a lot more than I could've hoped for a few weeks ago."

Talking of Maddie reminded Lucia that she'd wanted to ask Hank about the case he and Max had gotten from her firm. He told her about the work they'd already done for the client, who was suffering from retaliation after reporting her landlord to Licenses & Inspections.

They cleaned up the after-dinner mess in companiable silence and then Hank proposed having their coffee in the living room. She agreed and while they drank it, Lucia told Hank that she'd spent her afternoon tracking down and interviewing the woman who'd found Paul Lugano's body.

Frowning deeply, Hank shook his head. "If the PPD catches you interfering in an active investigation, you're gonna end up with your ass in a sling."

"That's the problem—it turns out the investigation is even less active than I thought before. About on par with the non-investigation into Griffin's murder. No detective on the case has even questioned this woman. No one at all has talked to her since she gave her report to the uniforms who took the call."

"What?"

"I know—right? When I went to talk to her, she thought I was a cop at first and said it was about time the detectives got in on it."

"What did you learn?"

"Based on what she told me, it sounds like Paulie's killer was in the car with him—and he never even drew his weapon."

"He knew his assailant?"

"Sure sounds that way. Meaning the Loon was someone familiar to Lugano."

"What about Tumino?"

"Harder to say. His was a real execution-style killing." She rolled her shoulders to ease some of the tension away. "Ugh, let's talk about something else." She gave him her most flirtatious smile. "Or not talk at all."

"Great idea. You look like someone who could use a shoulder rub."

"And you are a brilliant and insightful man."

They were still cuddling on the couch a while later. "Since you brought your bag, and his blanket," Hank said, "I assume Rocco's recovered enough to spend the night here?"

"I think so. He's been a lot better and he does love the fact that when we stay here, he gets cornflakes for breakfast instead of dog food—so, it's worth a shot. The proof is in the pudding, though."

He nudged her down on the couch with a wicked smile. "Then let's get cooking." Happy to oblige, Lucia started unbuttoning his shirt.

A few days later, Lucia slid into a booth at Bob's Diner in the Roxborough section of Philadelphia. She assumed the pretty, fortyish woman across from her was Kourosh, since Patty said she'd be wearing a red t-shirt. "Kourosh?" she said, "I'm Lucia Scafetti."

Reaching a hand across the Formica tabletop, Kourosh returned the greeting. "Nice to meet you."

"Do you mind if we start by discussing Colona— then we can go over your business plan and I'll offer my advice?"

"Oh, I don't have a...business plan. Do I need one?"

"The bad news is yes, you do. The good news is that's an easy enough thing to fix." As their waitress showed up to take their orders, she gave Patty an encouraging smile. They both wanted Cokes and Patty asked for a bowl of chili. Lucia couldn't imagine getting anything hot to eat on such a sticky-hot afternoon so ordered a turkey club. When they were alone again, Lucia leaned towards Kourosh. "Now, about Colona—what happened between you two?"

"Nothing. That was his problem with me."

"Oh, I see. I take it he sexually harassed you?"

"Did he ever. Me and at least a dozen other women. I was the only one stupid enough to file a complaint, though."

"He retaliated?"

"Not overtly. He's too smart for that. But I got moved to Records for, as my captain put it, 'my own comfort'."

"I'm sorry, that sucks."

"More than you know. Records is where careers go to die. I stuck it out for a year, hoping if I played nice, I could get a transfer somewhere better—no dice."

Shaking her head at the injustice, Lucia asked, "So, Colona is a slimy predator—what else? Have you ever heard about him mistreating informants? Maybe even having them killed?"

"Wow, no." Kourosh sat back against the seat in surprise. "Nothing that bad. Not having them killed."

"What then?"

"I have heard about him knocking them around a lot." She leaned forward, her arms resting on the tabletop. "Unfortunately, that kind of thing isn't all that unusual with...with some cops of that generation."

"Anything else?"

"Just that he keeps them on a very tight leash. He doesn't like any other cop talking to his snitches or even knowing their names."

"Is *that* unusual?"

"Among detectives on the same squad? Yeah."

"Any idea if he's in bed with D'Amico—or ever was?"

"Can't say that I ever heard that. He likes to gamble, I know that. Supposedly he spends all his vacation time in Atlantic City. And he's got a nasty temper. It drives him crazy whenever anyone gets promoted above him. He's sixty-three and it's finally dawning on him that lieutenant is as high up as he's ever gonna get."

"Lynch said Colona's nickname is 'Cuckoo Colona.' Have you ever heard that?"

"Yeah, I've heard that one whispered behind his back a few times. It sure fits him when he's boiling mad."

"Do you know what the story is about how he busted my father?"

"Not the official story but...." Patty drew a deep breath, obviously weighing how to tell the tale nicely.

"Go ahead—it can't be worse than the shit the other girls used to say to me at Goretti."

"Goretti?"

"Saint Maria Goretti—my high school."

"Oh, right. Anyway, the story is Colona played your family for a bunch of suckers. He hung around them, letting them think he was cool with their...um, activities until he figured out who D'Amico's hotshot hitman was, and then he reeled him in."

186

With a snort of humorless laughter, Lucia scoffed, "Sure took him long enough. Was he going for the world record as an infiltrator?"

"True—but no one minded after the conviction came down. That arrest got him his re-promotion to lieutenant."

"That was eighteen-years ago and he's still a lieutenant. Something tells me your top brass may not have totally bought into Colona's story."

"Maybe, maybe not. There's a lot of competition for those captain slots."

"How many of them brought down Sure-Shot Scafetti?"

"Good point."

Their food arrived and caused a lull in the conversation. Lucia ate while trying to synthesize everything she'd learned about Colona's relationship with her family into a cogent theory. "Do you happen to know if Colona's a good shot?"

"He's never had an OIS but he sure loves to brag about how many times he won the sharpshooter's medal 'back in his day'." Lucia was slotting that piece of the puzzle in—it fit very nicely indeed, as Patty asked, "Okay—my turn?" When she nodded, Kourosh blurted, "What's a business plan and how the hell did you figure all of that kind of stuff out?"

"When I started working at Fidelia, my boss suggested I take some courses in Criminology. Seemed like a good idea, so I signed up at the community college. Later, when I took the business over, my accountant convinced me that I needed to learn how to actually make money a hell of a lot more than I needed to study Criminal Psychology. That's when I switched to taking business courses."

"Oh, no. Do I need to go back to college?"

Lucia smiled at Patty's wide-eyed dismay. "You don't need an associate's degree like I got but it wouldn't hurt to maybe take a course or two. But I can give you the highlights right here." She spent some time sharing the business acumen she'd acquired and making suggestions for Patty, who was furiously scribbling away, taking notes. "If there's anything I forgot, or you need to talk through an idea," Lucia said, "give me a call. Hang onto that card I gave you. Or—I'm in the book. You're in the Yellow Pages, too, right?"

Laughing, Patty protested, "Yes, that much I figured out on my own." She tucked a strand of her straight dark hair behind an ear and ventured, "Can I ask you something? Something kind of personal?"

"Um...sure."

"Leaving the force...it was hard for me. It still is. Like breaking up with my family." She stared into Lucia's eyes. "How did you manage to do it? Break away from your family, I mean."

"I didn't fully break away, but I'm not gonna pretend I don't know what you're getting at." When the waitress appeared to offer them drink refills, Lucia stared out at the parking lot for a moment, trying to think how best to summarize her journey. Leaning forward, she started, "I think it was because of my dad." She held up a hand, saying, "Not like what you think I mean. You see, unlike the rest of the guys in the family, he insisted I be kept in the dark—

meaning he let me grow up thinking he was a baker. The other kids, they grew up knowing, at least a little bit, about what their dads did. Thinking it was...you know, normal. Not me. That's why the truth knocked me back so hard."

"How did you find out? When your dad was arrested?"

"No, much later, during the trial. I was up late one night and heard my dad's lawyer telling him and my mom that the DA might use the weapon to connect him to the seven other unsolved murders. I was sitting up on the staircase, waiting for my dad to tell Gus that he was innocent, that he'd never killed anyone. That he couldn't. But instead..." Lucia paused and swallowed, the memory still stinging after all those years, "...instead, they all started discussing...strategies. And then it hit me. He'd done it. Not only one murder—but eight of them."

"God, that must have been awful."

"Yeah, it was." Lucia gulped some soda before reminiscing, "You know, before that night? I'd even managed to create a false memory that my father was home with me the night Guenther was killed. I kept trying to get them to let me testify on his behalf. No wonder they laughed it off every time I said that." She downed the rest of her soda in an effort to wash away the lump in her throat.

"But you were just a kid—you didn't strike out on your own then, did you?"

"No, no way. My mom had a long talk with me. Explained that it wasn't what I was thinking. Ten years old and I got the 'It's just business' and 'Those men had it coming' speeches. I tried to swallow that bullshit, I tried being the dutiful daughter—supporting my dad, visiting him in prison with her and then later, my grandmother. But there was this part of me, deep down inside, that never bought it. And as I grew up and started seeing the...all of the carnage and collateral damage around me, that Lucia, the rebellious one, got stronger and stronger."

Smiling, Patty ventured, "And now she's the dominant one."

"Yep. But that dutiful one—she's a stubborn bitch. I can't quite kill her off." Lucia chuckled. "That's what I inherited from my mom—not the beauty or the gracefulness, but that dutiful side. She is the stereotypical Mafia wife."

"Did she grow up with it—like you did?"

"No, her family is a whole 'nother flavor of dysfunction. The 'everyone hates everyone else' estrangement flavor. I guess that's why she took to the '*La Famiglia*' thing like a starving woman to a banquet." Lucia shook her head. "Did you find anything useful in that train wreck of an explanation?"

"Yep. I need to start nurturing the rebellious Patty and starve the hell out of the dutiful one." She gathered up her notes and shoved them in her bag, asking, "How about you? Learn anything good about Colona?"

"Oh, yes. Very useful information. In fact—let me get the check to thank you."

"Seeing as you're the one who knows how to make money, I'll let you do that." The two women left the diner, agreeing to keep in touch.

Lucia went home and took out the legal pad with the heading, 'John Colona,' and added the new information. Reading it over, she felt there was an extremely strong possibility that she'd identified him as the Loon. However, she was eternally aware of Bac's chief decree—'Never fall so in love with a theory that you stop investigating other possibilities. Always look for contradictory evidence." Throughout her career, it had proved to be great advice—but where to look for it in this case? She put the legal pad away, intending to mull the subject over later.

When she pulled out her notes for the next night's computer class, an idea struck her. Her classmate, Andre Bradley, had introduced her to Usenet—a massive collection of electronic bulletin boards on every subject under the sun. She'd been equal parts repelled and intrigued to find there was a 'True Crime' group that fixated on people like her dad, as well as serial killers and others of that type. Lucia decided to stay after class tomorrow and see if anyone in the alt.true-crime Usenet group knew of Mafia-style killings committed with her father's MO, that were of either more recent vintage or predated his first kill.

Maybe Colona wasn't the Loon. Maybe the Loon had been out there all those years, racking up body counts and had dipped into Philly recently to score

Klaus Guenther's stolen goods. Only further investigation could rule that theory out.

CHAPTER 13
The True Mystery

"The true mystery of the world is the visible, not the invisible...."—Oscar Wilde, *The Picture of Dorian Gray*

The next night on the way to her computer class, Lucia spotted her not-so-friendly neighborhood police stalker on the El. When she switched from the Market-Frankford to the Broad-Street line, he faithfully followed. She studied him in the reflective windows of the subway car, wondering if he intended to take a seat next to her in class. He did follow her to the business center but dropped off as she entered the building. Knowing she intended to stay late and use the computers for her personal project she mentally instructed him to go grab a coffee as he had a long wait ahead of him.

It took Lucia a little while to remember how to navigate the Usenet groups but once she did, she found the True Crime group easily enough. The members posted many enthusiastic suggestions in answer to her query. However, none of the killers they proposed as possibilities fit the profile that she'd described so none of the responses were particularly helpful. One user, who seemed as fascinated with hitmen as she'd once been with comic book superheroes, did volunteer to do some checking through his substantial files. The fact that he even had such files made Lucia fervently hope that she'd never meet this guy, Hugo, in person.

Though the idea of staying a little longer and checking out the Usenet sewing group was tempting, it was getting late and Rocco needed his walk. All the way home, Lucia continually and meticulously scoured her surroundings for signs of her police shadow but didn't see him anywhere. The relief was short-lived when she got to the steps leading down to her office and spied a most unwelcome sight waiting outside the door. She'd thought finding her father there was as bad as it could get but seeing Colona's white hair peeking out of the shadows proved her wrong.

When she reached the bottom of the steps, he straightened up and gave her an insolent smile. "You're late."

"I wasn't aware we had an appointment, Lieutenant."

"Yeah, there's a lot of things you're not aware of. Like I know you been hiding things you got no business hiding and snooping into things you got no business snooping into."

"The only thing I'm hiding is how sick I am of you boneheads in blue harassing me for that stupid diamond and those coins. Go ahead, send in another search squad. They'll find the same thing the first one did—*nothing*. As for snooping, tell me, exactly what is it that I'm accused of snooping into?"

"My informants, for starters—and what's worse, my cases."

"Okay, you got me there, but I thought *someone* should investigate those crimes."

"Investigate? Is that what you call witness intimidation?"

"Those witnesses seemed more relieved than intimidated, to me. Relieved that someone was actually trying to solve the murders. You know—like *you're* supposed to be doing."

He stepped close enough to her that she could feel his moist breath on her cheek. "You really think I give a shit who killed any of those low-life scumbags? You think *that*, is what this is all about?"

Refusing to flinch away, she calmly replied, "No, I'm coming to the conclusion that you already know who killed them. But in case I'm wrong, and because the city is paying you to give a shit, you should at least look into it, rather than...." She shrugged, "How *are* you filling your time? Playing poker or forcing yourself on unwilling women?"

"What the fuck are you babbling about?"

"In the first place, that you need to make some minimum pretense of doing actual police work, and in the second, stop chasing after fool's gold, and for good measure, get the hell out of my personal space."

"What?" His lip curled in a sneer, he continued, "You think I'm interested in a gorilla like you? Don't flatter yourself."

"That's a relief, since I wouldn't fuck you with a rented vagina."

His face reddening, he shot back, "Your mom sure didn't feel that way. And she was actually worth getting close to back in the day. Yeah, she was a looker—unlike you."

Lucia guessed Colona was trying to provoke her, if so, he had grossly underestimated how often she'd heard that same sentiment, always couched less crudely but nonetheless recognizable. "Oh, are you one of those guys?" she cooed. "You think the waitress is into you when she really only wants your money?" She gave a light laugh. "Do you also believe the stripper really likes you and the hooker when she says it's the biggest one she's ever seen?" Her voice grew even more acerbically mocking as she added, "You do, don't you?"

He shoved her against the wall, snarling, "Shut up, you fucking dipshit, before I make you sorry you were ever born." The noise woke Rocco and he began barking furiously. Pointing a finger at her, Colona yelled over the din, "You listen up good, I took your old man down, and I can do the same to you. If you don't wanta end up in his old cell doing time for double-homicide, then you'll give me that diamond and those coins. They're mine. I paid for 'em and no two-bit, trigger-happy PI is gonna—"

"You paid for them?!" Lucia stared at Colona, swiftly integrating this unexpected gift of information. Nodding, she slowly repeated, "Oh, you paid for them."

"Yeah...with...with all my hard work," he stuttered, stepping backwards. "All my hard work on the Guenther case. That's what I meant."

"Of course. What else could you mean?" Lucia moved towards the door saying very deliberately, "If there's nothing else, Lieutenant, I need to get my dog. His barking tends to draw...." She paused to stare at him. "...a lot of attention."

He turned on his heel, striding away but tossing over his shoulder, "This ain't over, bitch."

"It sure isn't."

Once in her office, Lucia took one moment to greet Rocco before crossing the room to the safe. She swiftly opened it and withdrew her gun and shoulder holster. She stripped off her shirt and donned the gun. The next time she was confronted by Colona or one of his goons, she was going to be armed. Feeling a sense of relief that she didn't want to examine too closely, she watched as Colona's feet moved past her office windows. At least he was really gone.

She looked down at Rocco, asking, "Did you hear what that dickwad said about your grandma? I don't believe it—do you?" She pondered the distasteful notion for a moment, before announcing to the ether, "If it's true, Ma, I may have to kill you and then myself."

Later, after Rocco's walk, the dog snoozed in his bed while Lucia sat at the desk adding the new information to her Colona notes. She felt like the picture was really coming together. Colona—the so-called Loon—had at some point taught her father how to shoot, allowing him to become Sure-Shot Scafetti. Later he'd hired Carlo to take out Guenther, a high value target known to him through police channels. That's what the twenty-five grand was—Carlo's fee for the murder of Klaus Guenther. Or at least part of it, she mused, knowing the upfront fee was often only a down payment. If so, Colona had paid very well indeed for something he never got. No wonder the fucker was so obsessed.

Pondering his killing of Frankie and Lugano, she decided that maybe that wasn't solely an attempt to set her up. Maybe when they couldn't produce any information about the diamond and coins, Colona assumed they were holding out on him. Using his skill with a gun, he not only got rid of them but did it in such a way as to throw all of the suspicion on her. Double duty murders, as it were.

Suddenly the beautiful theory she was constructing ran into an ugly fact, causing her to bang her head on the desk. Rocco woke at the sound, and stared at Lucia, trying to figure out what had caused her distress. She looked down at the dog, saying, "If I inherited my shooting ability from my father, would that mean my father is actually...him? No. Please God, no." She stood up and started pacing, thinking aloud by talking through this horrific idea with Rocco, who was not much of a conversationalist but was an excellent listener.

"No. He only said that to piss me off. My mother has better taste than that." A moment passed and she continued, "But she did say that thing about 'making nice' with him. But...nah, she wouldn't've cheated on my dad plus everyone says I look exactly like Lidia. Right?" She looked down at Rocco, as if waiting for his assent. He offered nothing but a head tilt so her thoughts crowded into the vacuum—carrying additional doubts. "On the other hand, by my calculation she was already pregnant when they got married and Colona has brown eyes, and would brown plus green give you...?" Lucia trailed off pointing at her own eyes.

In an effort to lay this nagging fear to rest, Lucia went over to the closet and dug through the upper shelf until she found her grandmother's photo album. She paged through it until she found the picture she wanted. It was one taken at her baptism with her godparents. There it was, showing a surprisingly tiny Lucia in Lidia's arms, a beaming sixteen-year-old Patsy standing beside her. Lidia looked just as happy as Patsy and exhibited no visible signs of the leukemia which would take her life just one year later. She held the book up to Rocco, as if he was the one who needed convincing. "Look, it's true. I'm the picture of Lidia."

Feeling somewhat comforted, she scanned the other photos, stopping at the ones from the christening celebration which had been held at Le Sorelle. "That son-of-a-bitch. He was at my baptism." She closed the book and looked over at the dog who seemed supremely bored by this discourse at this point. "You are one cold, black-hearted bastard, aren't you, Colona? No wonder you fit right in with that crowd. But which way did you fit—who was playing who back then?"

She laughed as Rocco turned and showed his butt, letting her know he wanted the light off and chatter to stop. "All right, I know you need your beauty sleep. And I need to think. Bac always said, 'When in doubt, keep digging.'" She went off to prepare for bed, wondering what further wrinkle the Usenet true-crime groupies could possibly add to this mystery.

Lucia and Hank were strolling up Walnut Street at a leisurely pace, heading back to her office after the group dinner at the Thai restaurant. He reached for her hand and she turned and smiled at him. "That was really great, wasn't it?"

Hank asked, "You talking about the food or the company?"

"Both. The company especially—though I am gonna have to have some more of that Pad Kra...what was it, again?"

"Just say, stir-fried pork with basil."

"I'm gonna have to have more of that stir-fried pork with basil again real soon."

Slipping an arm around her waist, he replied, "I'm glad to hear you enjoyed yourself tonight. I was thinking maybe you weren't having such a good time."

"Why would you think that?"

"You were pretty quiet."

"I didn't have that much to add to the conversation." With a shrug, she explained, "Wally is a fascinating guy and it was good to hear he thinks these new HIV therapies might turn the tide, but what am I gonna contribute to that discussion?"

"What about Dan's idea of a city-wide needle exchange program? I thought you'd have something to say there."

"I didn't want to be a downer and say that while it's a fantastic idea, I'm skeptical he can get it to pass."

Hank squeezed her side. "You sure the reason you're so quiet has nothing to do with the fact that you're armed? And have been constantly for the past couple of days?"

"I was wondering how long it was gonna take for you to say something."

"Well, now I'm saying something. What's going on?"

Sighing, she rolled the tension from her shoulders. "I had a kind of...run in with Colona the other night."

"He threatened you?"

"Um, yeah, kinda. Nothing overt. He's pissed I'm snooping around the Tumino-Lugano murders...." She sighed. "I will pause here for the well-deserved, 'I told you so.'"

"Consider it said."

"So, he made some vague noise about taking me down like he had my father, which is nonsense since, hello, I'm not a hitman."

"Do you think he's threatening to frame you for those murders?"

"It sure sounds like it; he even alluded to trying to charge me with witness intimidation for talking to the woman who'd found Lugano's body." She felt Hank tense up so rushed to assure him, "Even someone as desperate as Colona has to know that's a reach. Not only do I have an alibi for the most probable time of Frankie's death, but there's nothing to tie me to those murders except the bullet through the eye thing."

"Which is weak, even as circumstantial evidence."

"Exactly. Plus, actually charging me would really throw a spotlight on the crimes he most likely committed himself. I think he's mainly trying to scare me. He still thinks I know where the diamond and coins are, which in a way is good."

"How the hell is that good?"

"Because it keeps him chasing after that nonsense rather than figuring out that I'm spending my time digging up his past."

"And what have you found so far?"

"A lot of ugly shit...but not enough to take back to Rockingham. Not yet. Let me see what those Usenet folks have for me when I go back to class tomorrow night."

"The what folks now?"

"Usenet, it's a computer thing." Grinning widely, she announced, "I may not have figured out web pages yet but I am way past only knowing how to use e-mail. I'm nearly a bona-fide computer nerd…" She dropped her voice and stage-whispered, "I am on 'The Net.'"

Turning to stare at her, Hank raised his eyebrows. "The net?"

"You know, 'The Net'," Lucia answered, in a lilting tone, letting him know she was only half-serious. "It's that movie with the chick from 'Speed' about super-secret computer stuff. You haven't seen the ads for it? They're everywhere."

"Keep this up and people with a net will be coming for you," Hank laughed.

"Be nice or I'm not inviting you up to make out on the couch in my office."

Holding his hands up in mock surrender, Hank said, "I take it all back." He pulled her in for a kiss, whispering, "I hope we're not gonna stop at making out."

"You're in luck," she murmured, as they broke apart. "Since I was hoping the same thing."

Normally Lucia found her computer classes interesting since she was learning about the heretofore unknown but intriguing world of the internet. Tonight's class focused on something called 'hypertext markup language' and she diligently took detailed notes but her mind was constantly drifting away to the computer lab and the true crime Usenet group. Once released, she reluctantly turned down Andre's invite to grab a beer with him and his new girlfriend and dashed over to the lab. Once there, she hurriedly logged on to the first available computer.

While the computer booted up, Lucia pondered what she was hoping to find. Obviously, something that would confirm Colona as the Loon would be ideal—but that was precisely what this group was unlikely to provide. As she began scanning the board, she found that most of the posts were entirely unhelpful; many were merely people asking if she was related to Carlo Scafetti since her CCP e-mail displayed her last name. Finally, she saw a long post from Hugo, entitled 'Copy-Cat Sure-Shots.' Here was gold—though gold that poked huge holes in her pet theory.

Hugo had posted about ten killings where the victim was shot dead by a bullet to the left eye, all of them outside of Philadelphia. He expounded for several paragraphs on why these were likely copycat murders, either ignoring or ignorant of the fact that two of the killings preceded her father's first known contract. Lucia thanked Hugo for the information but made no comment on his manifesto, since she had no interest in educating morbidly obsessed individuals on the very great difference between contract and serial killers. The latter were often obsessed with style and fame, so copycat murders were not unknown amongst them. The former's only obsessions were efficiency and profit, neither of which was augmented by copying the style of another hitman.

Speaking of efficiency, Lucia's initial impulse had been to print out Hugo's list but she was paranoid about another search, legal or otherwise, of her office. She didn't want anyone finding her notes and getting tipped off to her discoveries. To prevent that possibility, she laboriously copied the list out, confident that it rendered her notes safe from everyone but an elderly stenographer. The ancient nun who'd taught the business track at her high school had still favored Gregg Shorthand Simplified, a system of shorthand which had fallen out of general use in the 60s.

Lucia spent the trip home absorbed in thoughts of those ten murders: eight, all located west of the Mississippi, committed well after her father's incarceration—plus two before he purportedly started killing for D'Amico. Tantalizingly, those two had occurred in Las Vegas. Patsy had said her parents' marriage put an end to the family Vegas trips. Perhaps the truth was that her father had been merely using those trips as cover for his first two assignments as a hitman. It made sense—a couple of trips to stake out the victims and get the lay of the land, then one trip each to take care of "business."

She wondered if Colona had perhaps assisted in those kills but quickly discarded the theory. In the first place, her mom said Micky had put a stop to Colona's participation early on and in the second, there were those eight more recent killings. Nonetheless, her stubborn mind refused to give up entirely on Colona as the Loon. After all, Colona didn't have to be present for those Vegas murders and maybe he was freelancing outside of Philadelphia on a regular basis. Lucia had to admit it was unlikely—but not impossible. Not with all of those murders committed so far away. And not with his taste for high-stake gambling possibly requiring an alternate source of income to keep the party going. She wracked her brain for someone who could shed some light on those hits but her contacts in that arena were all strictly local.

As she walked Rocco that night, Lucia tossed her favored theories around in her mind, admitting that none was perfect or even fully coherent, but sensing she was getting close. Close wasn't good enough, though, and she wondered where the missing puzzle piece could be found. This stage of investigation—where she could feel the answer dangling just out of reach, was equal parts invigorating and infuriating, but truly addictive. She was eternally glad that Baccaro had introduced her to what she regarded as her true calling in life, but sorry he'd left so much for her to learn on her own. She looked up at the stars, barely visible against the city lights, murmuring, "What would you do now, Bac?" The version of Bac which did live on in her mind gave an answer. Lucia nodded, sighing, "Okay, yeah, but a double scotch isn't gonna help me out at all."

CHAPTER 14
Born for Trouble

"For affliction does not come from the dust, Nor does trouble sprout from the ground, For man is born for trouble, As sparks fly upward."—Job 5:6-7

Knowing his time was short, Lucia had been visiting her grandfather on a more regular basis since he'd slipped into a coma. The hospice nurse had explained that dying people are often able to hear and understand voices, emphasizing that hearing is one of the last senses to be lost prior to death. In response, Lucia spent her visits monologuing on as many cheery and mundane topics as she could come up with at the time.

Lucia rarely ran into other family members at the nursing home, since they favored early morning visits while she usually showed up after the dinner hour. Due to these conflicting schedules, she was surprised one night to walk into her grandfather's room and find her Uncle Vince holding Antonio's hand and reminiscing aloud about the old days. She listened, smiling faintly, while Vince retold the story of Tony introducing Vince to Pina.

At the first break in his narrative, she greeted her great-uncle and asked why he was there so late. Vince looked up and smiled back. "I couldn't make it this morning with Pina so I came tonight." She sat down next to him as he continued, "Patsy said you always visit this late—why?"

"For me, it's easier to come after work."

Vince's mouth twisted at the mention of her work, causing Lucia to silently pray he wasn't planning to trot out his usual critique of her job. She was relieved when all he asked was, "And your mother? You make time for her, too?"

"Yes, I've been seeing her as often as I can."

"Good. She needs you—she carries so much pain right now. She needs us all." He leaned toward her. "You now see clear the value of family—yes?"

What she saw was the standard lecture coming at her like a runaway freight train. Lucia sighed and stiffened her spine. Her fight or flight reflex was useless—neither being an option at her grandfather's bedside. She was going to have to sit there and take it. "Yes, I see the value of family. I always have, Zio."

"I hope so. I hope you know it's not too late. You can always embrace your family. We want that. You can still come back to us."

"I didn't realize I'd gone anywhere."

"We know, Lucia, we know you stand apart. We all see the judgment in your eyes. You *schieve* us as criminals. Even now, you're thinking, 'This man launders money for the Mafia—what right has *he* to lecture me?'"

She reached over and patted Vince's hand. "I do not *schieve* you." It was the best dodge she could come up with against an accusation that was nearly prescient in its accuracy.

Vincent Rinaldi might not have been an honest man, but he was an astute one so he saw right through her subterfuge. "Your business—is it so much better than mine? You carry a gun—what other woman in this family needs to carry a gun? You get in between man and wife, making trouble in marriages and tearing them apart. You spy on ordinary people under orders from insurance companies and lawyers. What common criminal has ever stolen as much as those crooks?" Unable to agree, unwilling to disagree, Lucia made a non-committal sound which she hoped Vince took as concurrence. "You are my son's *figliocce*—that gives me the right to speak plain with you, yes?"

"Yes, of course." That first part was at least true, she was Patsy's goddaughter.

"I see the life you've chosen and I want to weep." He started counting off what she lacked on his fingers. "You've got no husband, no children, no home even." More head-shaking ensued as he continued, "When I think what you could have had. Rosie tells me Albie Zarelli still asks about you. His own sister says so."

Oh dear God, not Albert Zarelli—the boy Rosie had fixed her up with in high school. Back then the family eyed up any tall boy with the thought, 'This one is perfect for Lucia.' It didn't matter if he had the brains and personality of a concussed monkey—exhibit Albie—she was forced to endure at least one date to appease her supposedly well-meaning relatives. Though she had to admit that the fact that she dated Albie for over a year proved how limited her choices were back then. When she returned her attention to her great-uncle, he was retelling the story of her leaving Albert sitting in a restaurant after his senior prom. That anecdote never got old for any of the family.

"I got called to work."

He scoffed, "Work, at that time of night. We should have known then you were no secretary." Vince shook his finger at her. "Albie is a steady man; he would have married you—unlike that Baccaro louse you threw him away for. With Albie you could have had a good life."

Rather than pointing out she wasn't looking to marry *anyone* at age seventeen or eighteen, she deflected, "Didn't he leave Philly a few years ago?"

"Yes, he's in Reno working for D'Amico's friend, Gary Luzerne." Shrugging, Vince expounded, "There's more opportunity out there right now but I know he intends to come back to Philadelphia someday."

Suddenly, a light broke through the gloom of this interminable exchange. "Reno, huh?" Lucia glanced at her great-uncle, her mind working furiously. "Is he still making book, or what?"

"He does a little book making, a little of this, a little of that. He does very well for himself."

"I should give him a call."

Vince sat up straight and stared at her. "You want to make jokes at me? I'm trying to help you and I get repaid in disrespect—"

"No, Zio! I'm serious. I'd love to talk to Albie."

What she wanted to talk to Albie about, Vince didn't need to know, she rationalized. Lucia supposed she should feel some regret at her skillful duplicity—especially considering how happy she'd made Vince, who immediately promised to get Zarelli's phone number from his sister, Sharon. She should feel guilty, but she didn't —at least not much.

Albert Zarelli returned Lucia's phone message within a few hours. Her question of whether it was a sign of boredom or nostalgia on his part, was answered when he spent the first twenty minutes of the call telling her how great his life was and how many beautiful women he was dating. Apparently, her rejection still stung a little after a dozen years. Other than a few faux-appreciative noises, she made no interruptions to his payback monologue. In light of her motivation for calling him, he deserved as much.

It must have dawned on Albert at some point that he'd been monopolizing the conversation since he interrupted himself to ask, "So, hey, you're still doing that private-eye stuff, right? That's what Sharon told me. You went to college for it and everything, is what she said. That's crazy. You gotta go to school to learn to peek in windows and stuff?"

"Well, not quite. Though speaking of that—"

"Oh God, I forgot! You're in mourning for your old man right now. What a jerk I am. Damn it, I should've said something right off the bat, I meant to, but I was so surprised to be talking to you after all these years and I out and out forgot. I'm real sorry for your loss and all. Yeah, Sharon told me what they did to him. That was rough. What a shame, I hope you'll forgive my language, but that was a fucking shame."

"Thanks, yeah, it was awful."

"How's your mom doing? She doing okay? Hey, no offense, but is she still hella fine? Forgive me for saying so, but I saw her like six years ago and she was still a stone-cold fox. I mean, 'specially for her age, and all. I gotta tell you, I hope you'll excuse me telling on myself like this, but more than once when we was dating, one of my friends would say, 'Albie, you should go after the mother' and I'd laugh and say, 'Yeah, I really should'." Since the most Lucia could muster up in response was a half-hearted chuckle, Albie rushed to say, "I never meant it though. That's just how guys talk when we get together. You shouldn't take me serious, you know. You was my first, and I was your first, and that's always gonna be special."

Lucia caught herself before blurting out, "We had sex?" Was he referencing those dozens of hand jobs? With effort she dredged up the memory of an unfortunate encounter in the backseat of Albie's father's Buick LeSabre. "Yeah, that really was a *magical* night," she glibly lied, still uncertain whether that fumbling experience counted as sex—had she even taken her panties off? Oh well, not her concern right now.

"Yeah, we had some good times, back then, for sure." He laughed and then abruptly stopped, apparently recalling the primary subject. "But how is she though, really? Your mother?"

"She's doing...as well as can be expected."

"That's good, that's good. Tell her I said hello and extend my condolences to her. I'm not hitting on her long distance or nothing. Like I said, I'm seeing these two different women now—and the blackjack dealer is a major babe, so, my sincere condolences to your mom."

"I will tell her you said so." Lucia sighed internally, thinking the number of lies she was racking up on this call alone must have completely erased any good will she'd built up with God at her father's funeral.

"Do you know what happened with your dad? I mean, the man just got outta Graterford—ain't that right? He just got out, no time to even catch his breath and they whack him. Dump him right in the fucking river."

"We're not sure what happened but it's connected to Frankie's death for sure that's why I'm—"

"Oh yeah, Frankie Tumino got it, too. 'Nother goddamned shame. He was a good guy, real dependable, and all. Not an up-and-comer like me, didn't have the brains for it, excuse me for saying so, but a good foot soldier, you know." Lucia was able to provide her verbal assent to at least part of that stream of bombast and with great effort eventually refocused Albert's attention on the connection between Frankie's death and that of her father. "What're you saying? You think the same guy did 'em both?"

"No, but the guy who killed Frankie knows why my father was killed." That statement was a straight up truth in Lucia's mind—perhaps the first she'd been able to provide in this entire conversation. "So, I'm trying to track him down. Near as I can make out, he's not a local but he kills the same way as my old man did—one bullet through the left eye. You ever hear of a pro working out your way who had that MO?"

"Nah, not here in Reno. No one in Luzerne's organization—"

"This guy would be a free-lancer, not strictly outta Reno. I think he did a job there back in '92. Shortly after you got out there? You never heard about it?"

"Oh, the specialist!"

"The Specialist? That's his handle? Not something like the Loon?"

"The loon? Nah." He stopped to wheeze out a laugh, before continuing, "Excuse me for saying so, Chichi, but that sounds like it came outta one of those comic books you used to read. The specialist is what Gary called this guy when they brought him in. More like a title than a handle. You know, like, 'Hey, we need the specialist on this.' And they had to bust a gut to get him. He works very irregular-like, real down low, too, through an agent. Not even Gary knows his real name."

"Why? Does he maybe have a straight-job on the side?"

"Nah, I never heard of any of these guys doing that. You'll pardon the expression but that's kinda stupid. A guy like this, he makes real money; he don't need no side gigs. If you were in the know like me, you'd understand. This specialist, he can get to people other pros can't. I don't know why; I never heard no more about him. It seems crazy to bring a guy like that in to kill Frankie. Like, you don't need Randall Cunningham to beat some Pee-Wee football team, you know. You sure it's him?"

Figuring a smoke-screen was in order to prevent Albert from discussing the matter with Gary Luzerne, or even worse, his own big-mouthed sister, Lucia agreed, "Yeah, you're right, that doesn't make sense. Must not be our guy. I gotta give you props, Albie, you do know your stuff." Lucia signed off with one last massive lie about looking Albie up if she was ever in Reno or getting together with him the next time he was in Philly.

As soon as she was off the phone, Lucia pulled out her set of notepads. She hesitated for a moment, unsure whether to start a new one for the so-called 'Specialist' or add the information from Albie to

Colona's file. After a second, she did start a fresh file but did so recognizing that nothing Zarelli had told her, completely ruled out Colona as the primary suspect.

Lucia's latest weeping client had barely left the office when Juli knocked and popped her head in the door. "Hey, girl—you up for a water ice break?"

"Am I ever!" Jumping up, Lucia trotted over and pulled her friend in for a quick hug. "Where you been hiding out, stranger? If it wasn't for that dinner with the guys, I would've thought you moved outta Overbrook."

"Yeah, I've been busy as hell."

Lucia checked her wallet to make sure she had money, told Rocco to be good, then left the office with Juli. "Busy at work or home?"

"Both." They walked up the steps and out into the hot sunshine, Juli offering her explanation. "One of my major clients is being audited by the IRS and with Lily and Tess home from camp, we've got a pile of laundry a show horse couldn't jump." After a slight pause, she added, "Speaking of the kids—there's this 'Neighborhood Outreach' thing on August 11th that Dan wants me to attend with him." She tilted her head towards Lucia. "You up for some babysitting?"

"Of course. Tell the girls we're on for HBO and Trivial Pursuit that night. Oh yeah, and ask them if they want fries or onion rings with their cheesesteaks." Before Juli could reply, Lucia waved a hand at her. "Ah, never mind, I'll just get both."

"Considering this is a free service you offer, you don't have to bring dinner, too."

"Free service," Lucia scoffed. "Why would you pay me to have fun with your kids?" With a grin she proclaimed, "Besides, most babysitters don't bring their pain-in-the-ass dog. Get ready to be cleaning dog hairs off the cushions on the porch for a week."

"I'm ready," Juli chuckled, shaking her head, before venturing, "I know how much Rocco loves our porch, but I'm sure he'd do fine in an apartment for a little while. You don't *have* to keep saving every penny for that house."

"Nah, I can stick it out. You know how I am once I set my mind on something."

"I do—and I worry that tunnel vision of yours is going to get you in trouble someday."

"I don't think of it as tunnel vision. Bac always called it being 'goal-oriented' and 'resolute'."

"Yeah? Bac also called bourbon and Doritos breakfast." Since that was absolutely true Lucia had no answer other than a knowing chuckle. "Speaking of you and trouble, who was the sobbing woman leaving your office just now? Another wife who got bad news?"

"A fiancée who got bad news. Her mom was the one who hired me. The wedding is in three weeks." Lucia rubbed her forehead. "Or would've been in three weeks."

"Yikes, you do see the worst of humanity."

"There are many days I regret focusing on this segment of the business back when I took over Fidelia."

"Really? I still remember how excited you were when those 'Is He Cheating on You?' flyers, started yielding results."

Lucia laughed, also recalling her enthusiasm at having steady work in those days. "Okay, I admit nabbing cheaters does beat bounty hunting—and bankruptcy."

"I've always wondered—do any of those guys ever try and have a go at you? You know—after you blow up their lives?"

"In the first place, they're the ones who blew up their lives and in the second, yeah, a few have tried it."

"And?"

"And they found out they shouldn't mess with someone like me."

"That's not why you're presently armed, is it?"

They had reached the water ice truck so rather than answering directly, Lucia muttered, "I have got to get a less obvious holster."

They strolled back to the office building slowly, though eating their water ices quickly, knowing the sun would turn them into juice in minutes. When they reached a deserted stretch of sidewalk, Juli elbowed Lucia gently. "So? The gun?" As succinctly as possible, Lucia gave her the same explanation she'd given Hank. "Okay, say you're right about Colona. Why is this your job? What's worth the risk of taking on a powerful and ruthless crooked cop?"

"My mom is worth it, Juli. She deserves the truth about why the hell her husband was killed just as she was getting him back. It might bring her some peace of mind—help her get unstuck so she can do more than wander around the damn city daydreaming about the supposed good times with my dad."

"Are you sure *you're* not the one who's stuck—the one who can't move on?"

After a long silence, Lucia was forced to admit, "No, I'm not sure."

Having reached the shade of the few trees on Fallon Street, across from Overbrook, they stopped, taking the opportunity to discard their empty paper cups and sticky plastic spoons in the trash. Lucia also took a moment for further introspection. When her thoughts were fully assembled, she shared them with Juli. "I think Colona did my dad wrong, not only arresting him for the Guenther murder that he might have played a part in but something more fundamental than that. I need to figure it out. It's the last thing I can do for him." She shook her head, admitting, "I could be wrong—maybe it's my guilt for rejecting my dad all those years, maybe I want to believe he's better than he was but—I am so close to the answer. I'm not gonna stop, now. I can't."

Juli grasped her by both arms and stared up into her face. "I can surely see that. No use preaching to the deaf so just promise me you'll be careful. Very careful."

"I promise. I'm not wearing this gun because it does so much for my figure." Glad to see Juli manage a genuine laugh, Lucia said, "Now, come on, I gotta grab my stuff and get over to Fritz, Fritz, and Bailey. They have their first case for me."

"That's great! Congratulations. See, your hard work *is* starting to pay off. You and Fidelia are definitely heading towards a brighter future."

That night while Lucia walked Rocco, her mind was focused on her new skip-tracing assignment from the Center City law firm. A witness in a high-profile hit-and-run had disappeared and it was now Lucia's job to find her. She planned to spend her dinner hour brainstorming strategies and decided to treat herself to a hoagie. She dropped Rocco off in the office and headed off to the Lee's Hoagie House a few blocks away.

Lucia approached the office door with her dinner in hand, lost in thought. Before she could fit her key in the lock, the unusual silence suddenly pierced her awareness. Rocco's customary welcoming barks were notable in their absence. A fissure of alarm shot up her spine. Was he just asleep or was something very wrong in that office? She dropped the bag of food on the threshold, drew her gun, and quietly slipped into the room, which was ominously unlocked. "Rocco?" she whispered into the darkness. There was no response, but she thought she heard a rustle of movement. Lucia reached for the light and flipped it on—and found herself staring into the face of a burly man, pointing his own gun directly at her forehead.

"If you're looking for that stupid dog of yours, he's cowering behind the couch there. You better be quiet like him, or you're gonna wind up very dead." He stuck his free hand out. "First things first, gimme that."

Handing her weapon over, Lucia asked, "Who are you and what do you want?"

"None a' your fucking business who I am. What I want is that diamond and them coins you got." He stared her down, before adding, "You got 'em, don't you?" When she didn't answer, he growled, "Admit it!"

In an effort to keep the situation from boiling over, Lucia nodded slowly. "Yeah, I do. And they're right here in this office."

"Great. Hand 'em over. I'm leaving wit' them or wit' your corpse. Your choice."

Lucia drew a deep breath. "Okay, you can have them." She pointed at the painting hanging on the wall near the desk. "I need to get to the safe."

"I already opened it. They ain't in there."

"It's got a false back."

"Well, ain't you the tricky bitch?" He stood back, clearing her path, and gestured at the safe with his gun. "Show me—but don't try anyt'ing."

Moving cautiously, aware of the gun trained on her, Lucia walked to the safe and threw open the door which had been slightly ajar. She pretended to fumble inside for a moment. "It's stuck." She glanced at the desk and said evenly, "I'm just gonna get the letter opener to help me pry it back. That's all."

"You better be telling the truth. One wrong move, and I start blasting."

Lucia overtly reached for the letter opener, veering off at the last second to make a swift grab for the glass snow globe and hurling it at the intruder. Two shots rang out as she dove under the desk. One second later a resounding thud rattled the room, accompanied by the gunman's yelp of pain. Knowing his fall had bought her but a momentary reprieve, she scrabbled for Bac's gun.

A sudden wave of nausea and dizziness assaulted her, thwarting her efforts to remove the pistol from its hiding spot. She became dimly aware of a searing pain in her side. When Lucia grabbed her abdomen, her shirt squelched in her fingers with a wet stickiness, telegraphing dire news: she was bleeding profusely, and probably didn't have long before she passed out.

Her consciousness narrowing to the sound of her heart pounding in her ears, Lucia's only thought was to bid farewell to the world with the Catholic prayer, *An Act of Contrition*. She mumbled, "Oh my God, I am heartily sorry for...." At that moment, that was all she had of the official prayer. Weakly she continued, "...you know, for everything, sorry for everything, God," before blacking out.

Chapter 15

Neither Wrong nor Right

**"And further still at an unearthly height,
One luminary clock against the sky
Proclaimed the time was neither wrong nor
right.**

**I have been one acquainted with the
night."—Robert Frost, *Acquainted with the
Night***

Lucia's first sensation upon regaining consciousness
was of bright light and cold. Without opening her
eyes, she slurred, "Tha's good. Not ver' Hell like."

A sunny female voice asked, "What was that?"

"Juli?" She looked up into the warm brown eyes
of her friend and smiled. "I'm alive?"

After throwing back her head in delighted
laughter, Juli answered, "Yes, it seems God does
watch out for babies, fools, and drunks."

"If that last part was true, Bac would surely still be here," Lucia murmured. She unwisely tried to sit up, and immediately fell back in exhausted agony. Her eyes closed in pain, she asked, "Where am I? And how did I survive that...um...I got shot. Didn't I?"

"You most certainly did. Your mom explained all of this to you in recovery—remember? You even told her to call that law firm and explain why you were going to be late on that skip-tracing assignment." Since the last thing Lucia clearly recalled was the sensation of bleeding out under her desk, she shook her head at Juli. "You don't remember *any* of that?"

"No...not at all." Lucia attempted to assemble her scattered memories into a cohesive whole but as she reached for them, they skittered away from her. She pulled one down and hung onto it. "Wait, my mom was talking to me in...in the dream I was having. That happened? She's really here?"

"Your cousin Patsy took her down to the cafeteria to get a bite to eat and some coffee a little while ago but yeah, she's still here. They both are."

"How's my mom...uh, taking this?"

"She threatened to kill you if you died, then she said this is the bad luck she warned you about from the urn you have in your office. Patsy, on the other hand, tried to donate his spleen since yours was being removed. They had to explain to him twice that you can live without a spleen."

Lucia sighed, "That all sounds about right," as she glanced around in an effort to determine her surroundings. Nothing looked familiar. "My brain feels like it's full of cotton balls so can you fill in the blanks for me? For starters—where am I exactly? And what the hell happened to my spleen?"

"You're at HUP, recovering from abdominal surgery. You needed surgery because that bullet nicked your spleen. And you survived that only because Old Man Belsky was working late and heard the gunshots. While that was nothing unusual in that neighborhood, that guy who shot you was also screaming bloody murder, so he called the cops."

"The guy who shot me was screaming?"

"Yeah, because Rocco attacked him."

"He did?" A cold fear seized her, causing Lucia to flash her eyes open. "Is he okay?"

"Uh, no, he died there in the office."

Rolling over in anguish, tears squeezed out from the eyes she'd clenched shut in an automatic response to the wave of sorrow. Lucia muttered, "Oh, my poor boy." She heard the door open but didn't look up.

"What's wrong?" At the sound of his voice, she glanced up to see Hank standing next to Juli. "Should I get the nurse?"

Juli said, "I told her about Rocco and she started crying. I think it might be the drugs."

Hank sat down on the bed and gently took Lucia's hand. "Nothing's been decided yet. I'll represent him at the hearing, and even if that goes badly, there's a lot of steps before...before they do anything drastic."

"What hearing?"

"The Animal Control Hearing," Hank explained. "I've been looking into it and it's always step one when a dog has...uh...caused grievous bodily harm."

A nurse stuck her head in the door. "Ms. Scafetti's family is back and they want to see her. You'll have to leave. Only two visitors at a time."

"Could you ask them to wait one more minute, please," Juli responded. "We're filling her in on some things that happened last night." The nurse agreed and closed the door.

Lucia swiped a hand across her clammy brow, pleading, "Uh, could we start over—from the beginning? I'm kind of lost. That asshole killed Rocco and there's still gonna be a hearing?"

Chuckling with apparent relief, Juli shook her head vigorously. "No, no, Rocco is alive. The asshole is dead. Because Rocco killed him."

"Killed him! Are you...are you serious? How?"

Hank said, "In the usual manner that...um, that dogs kill." Since Lucia's only response was to stare up at him, speechless with bewilderment, he elaborated, "As best they can figure, you beaned the gunman with that snow globe and Rocco took advantage of him being down and disoriented. He literally went right for the throat. Seems like the little guy was completely savage in defense of you. I understand it was pretty horrific. One of the paramedics almost threw up at the scene."

"Wow." She looked up at her companions beaming with a mixture of pride and relief. "See, he was a good, brave dog all along. Can I see him? Is he here?" As Hank explained that Rocco was being held at Animal Control, the last few minutes of the conversation came into sharp focus for Lucia. "Wait, what was that about the hearing maybe going badly? They wouldn't...they can't put him to sleep, right?"

After glancing nervously at Juli, Hank reluctantly acknowledged, "It has been known to happen when a dog who kills is judged to be a danger to society."

"But Rocco isn't! He did it to save me. He's a *hero*."

"He certainly is to me. When this is all over, I'm gonna buy him a porterhouse steak from Ruth's Chris. And like I said, this hearing is standard procedure." He leaned over and kissed her on the cheek. "Max and I are both gonna be there. You have nothing to worry about. Except getting better." Hank left the room, pausing only to say he'd be back later.

Juli went to follow him out but Lucia called her back. "Honey, your mom and cousin are waiting. I'll be back later today."

"Did Hank tell you how often these things end badly for the dog? A dog like Rocco with a history of biting?" When she demurred about the exact figure, Lucia insisted, "Juli, tell me."

"More often than not, he said." She patted Lucia's arm, adding, in a chipper tone, "But those dogs didn't have two Ivy League lawyers representing them—did they? Now get some rest and don't worry."

Juli caught up with Hank at the elevator. When he offered to walk her to her car, she gratefully accepted, feeling exhausted both physically and emotionally.

"Will you be okay to drive home? How long have you been here?" he asked.

"I'll be fine. I got here just a few minutes before you did."

As they boarded the elevator, Hank ran his hands through his tousled mop of hair, giving his scalp a slight scratch. "Who called you? Not Lucia's family?"

"No, Belsky did, right after he called the cops." When Hank thanked her for letting him know about the shooting, she acknowledged his gratitude with a wave of her hand. "No problem. I knew Lucia would want you here." After a moment she thought to say, "Thank *you* for looking into the thing with Rocco—I wouldn't have known where to even start with that mess."

"I'm happy to take that worry off of Lucia—and you."

Mindful of her last exchange with Lucia, Juli asked, "Do you think there is a chance Animal Control will have him put down?"

Hank pulled himself up to his full height before answering. "If I can twice argue murder in the second down to manslaughter, which I have done," he stressed, "then I'm sure I can get a heroic dog off with a suspended sentence."

Shaking her head, she gave a huff of tired laughter. "That dog. I remember when she took him from that client of hers. She was barely clearing expenses then, living on peanut butter sandwiches and off-brand canned soup. I tried to persuade her that the last thing she needed was another mouth to feed. She told me, 'But Juli, he's so beautiful, and he *needs* me.' Over the years, I've watched the trouble he's caused for her and that bad deal looked more like a disastrous one. Now, it seems like that crazy deal really paid off for her in the end."

They'd reached the parking garage, and Hank followed her to her car, observing, "Sounds like you've been a good friend to her for a long time."

Stopping, keys in hand, Juli nodded, thinking back. "Not as long as I should have been."

"What do you mean?"

"When Baccaro brought her on board, I was appalled. Hearing her last name, I assumed the worst—that he was getting mixed up with the mob." She rubbed at the back of her neck before continuing, "When it became clear they were a couple, I was a different brand of appalled. After that, I tended to avoid them both. It wasn't that hard. Bac had always been a pain-in-the-ass client, anyway. The kind who'd bring in a shoebox of balled up receipts and expect me to wave my magic wand and turn it into a coherent tax return."

"What changed your mind?"

"When Baccaro died I expected Lucia to just disappear. But she actually went to work and closed out every pending case Fidelia had, then asked for my help with the billing and invoices. I was impressed. Until she did disappear without paying me a dime. For months. I figured I was right about her, until I wasn't."

"What happened? Where did she go?"

"I didn't know until much later. When she came back and finally paid me, I found out she'd been in the Poconos, cleaning up Bac's cabin and selling it off. She took that money and plowed it right back into the business. I saw how determined she was to make a go of it, and how badly she needed a decent mentor for once in her life, so I stepped up."

"She was lucky. Lucky to have you in her corner, Juli."

Juli got into her car, saying, "Don't worry—over the years, she's paid off that bill, too. With interest." With a faint smile at the bittersweet memory, she leaned out the window towards Hank. "Last year, when my mom was dying, Lucia picked the girls up from school anytime Dan and I couldn't make it. I'd always come home to a clean house and dinner, ready on the stove, too." She pulled out of the parking space, calling out, "I'll see you tomorrow. Or later today, I mean."

As soon as Juli had left Lucia's room, Angie and Patsy burst in, showering her with hugs and kisses and peppering her with questions. Weakly, Lucia explained, "I don't remember much. I don't even remember talking to you guys in the recovery room. I'm so tired and everything is still kind of fuzzy."

"Can you remember who shot you?" Her mom tenderly brushed the hair back from Lucia's face, reiterating, "Who was it that did this to you?"

"I don't know, I didn't recognize the guy. I've never seen him before. All I know is, he wanted that diamond and those coins."

"That fucking asshole." In a tone she'd never heard him use before, Patsy said, "They're not gonna get away with this. Whoever it was. I'll call Micky—"

"No!" Angie put a firm hand on Patsy's shoulder. "That's not what Lucia wants." She smiled down at her daughter. "She's never wanted to do things that way."

Patsy frowned before confirming, "Is that right? You don't want the family's help on this?"

"What could they do? What if D'Amico is the one behind this?"

"He's not," Patsy said. "Lucia...Sal's no saint, but...but he would've taken other steps first. As a courtesy to the family."

Angie agreed, "He's right. This came from outside the organization. I'd bet on it. Or someone inside went rogue." She shrugged, admitting, "It happens."

"Then the family still can't do anything," Lucia said. "The man who shot me is dead and we don't know who he was or who sent him. Not yet." Her mom started to protest, so she added, "I'm not gonna do anything about finding out. I couldn't even if I wanted to." This time she added the "yet" silently.

Patsy stalked away from the bed, pacing furiously, and ranting out vows of vengeance, finishing with, "There's gotta be something we can do!"

"There might be...." Lucia hesitated, then, her doubts vanquished, she finished, "Yeah, I think there is."

Smiling for the first time that visit, Patsy walked back and leaned over Lucia. "What? Tell me. Tell me what you need."

Feeling much stronger and more in command of her faculties, the next day Lucia listened as Hank told her about visiting Rocco at Animal Control. "They're treating him okay. Really, they are."

"I bet he's super depressed, though. I wonder if he even knows that I'm still alive."

"Considering that they had to forcibly remove him from the ambulance, I think so."

Wincing, Lucia asked, "How forcibly? He didn't bite the paramedics, did he?"

"Yeah," Hank sighed. "He sure as hell made a credible attempt."

"How do you know all of this? Were you there?"

Easing himself into the bedside chair, he shook his head. "No. It's all in the Animal Control report."

She closed her eyes, overcome by fear and frustration. When she'd reined in that surge of emotion, Lucia looked over at Hank, venturing softly, "I guess he didn't do himself any favors there."

Rather than answering directly, Hank reached over and took her hand. Interlacing their fingers together, he gave an encouraging squeeze. "I will do everything in my power to ensure he gets a fair shake." Smiling faintly, he said, "I'll even change his name on the paperwork if I have to."

Lucia sat back in mild indignation. "His name? What's wrong with his name?"

"Isn't 'Rocco' a little...you know...on the nose for...." He shrugged and smiled sheepishly, "...a dog in trouble with the law?"

"Would you prefer if he were called, 'Tolldach's Sable Feather'?"

"Nobody in their right mind would prefer that. What the hell is that?"

"That was his show dog name before I named him after *Saint Rocco*—the patron saint of dogs."

Hank tilted his head and stared at her for a second. "Did you just make that up?"

"What the hell kind of Catholic are you?"

"The kind who doesn't have all of the patron saints memorized."

"I don't know all of them. I know mine...and I know that one because when I was in high school my dog Scout got hit by a car, and my grandmother told me to pray to Saint Rocco."

"Did it work?"

"No, Scout died. Considering she was the same age as me, not surprising." Lucia managed a small chuckle at the distant memory. "My grandmother told me God must have needed a good fox terrier up in heaven."

"For the record," Hank said, "I do know my patron saint. I even know yours—Santa Lucia is the patron saint of the blind." Before she could ask, he explained, "My *bisabuela*, great-grandmother that is, was blind and she wore that medal, always."

"Yeah..." Lucia paused to roll her eyes. "My patron saint is not something I advertise much. Kind of ironic for a private investigator, you know?" Hank laughed appreciatively and then stood up and kissed her good-bye, saying he should let her get some rest. Before he could leave, she exclaimed, "Wait, you didn't tell me about Saint Enrique."

He hesitated, studying her for a moment before answering, "He's the patron saint of the handicapped and...the childless."

"Oh." Lucia wasn't often at a loss for words but all she could add to that monosyllable was the less helpful, "Ouch."

Door in hand, Hank ventured, "You know...I've been meaning to ask your opinion on the subject of...adoption. You know—as a general concept."

"As a matter of fact, I am a huge fan of the concept of adoption."

"Good to hear." He shook a finger at her in mock sternness. "Now, get some rest, heal, and do not worry about Rocco. He's in good hands—mine."

Once Hank was gone, Lucia took a moment to weigh the highs and lows of that conversation. She rolled over and picked up the telephone, her hand hesitating over the keypad for a long time. Finally, she keyed in Patsy's number. When he answered, she first assured him she was doing well, then said, "Yeah, it looks like I'm gonna need your dad to pull the trigger on...what we discussed."

Lucia picked at the unappetizing lunch on her tray, glancing occasionally at the clock on the wall. She chided herself for being so nervous—everything was unquestionably going well at Rocco's hearing. She'd made sure of that. Her conscience nagged at her: it wasn't the outcome for Rocco she was worried about *now*, was it?

The aide came and removed the tray, scolding her for leaving her green beans untouched.

"Is *that* what those slimy gray things were?" Lucia protested. "I can get your kitchen staff my great-aunt's recipe for green beans in tomato sauce. She's the head chef at Le Sorelle."

"Ma'am, this is the University of Pennsylvania hospital, not a restaurant."

"Don't worry, no one will ever confuse the two."

Whatever response the aide was about to make was cut short by Max bursting into the room, crowing, "Hail, the conquering heroes!" He was followed by Hank, who didn't look anywhere near as happy.

When the aide had cleared the room, Lucia asked, "The hearing went well? It's over already?"

"It was over before it began," Max answered. "My genius partner, here...." He gestured towards Hank. "...arranged to have Rocco groomed before the hearing." Hank smiled at that pronouncement but Lucia noticed the smile didn't reach his eyes. "You should have seen the judge's face when that shiny, fancy little dog pranced into the room with Juli—after the Animal Control rep had spent twenty minutes indicting him as a vicious and highly dangerous animal. It was priceless."

"Did they let him go? Where is he?"

Hank spoke at last. "Juli took him home with her. You can pick him up when you're released—which will be soon I hope?"

"Day after tomorrow, thank God. Not quite three days in this place and I'm ready to climb out the window." She sat up a bit straighter. "The doctor was in this morning and said I'm doing great. One of the benefits of coming from hearty peasant stock."

Nodding thoughtfully, Hank said, "Great, that's great." He looked back at Max. "Can you give us a minute?"

"Of course." Smiling broadly, he left, calling back with a wink, "Don't celebrate too much—she's still recovering."

"I can't thank you two enough," Lucia said, reaching out a hand to Hank, which he didn't take. She dropped it onto the blanket and waited.

"You know, I was really surprised to see Judge Lauren Bowers presiding at an Animal Control hearing." He paused, studying her reaction before continuing, "She's a traffic court judge."

"Is that right?"

"Yeah, see I ran into her while I was clerking in law school. The lawyer I was working for, Maria Hernandez, told me all about Bowers." His voice honed to a razor-sharp edge as he elaborated, "Maria said she's so corrupt she practically has a price list tacked up outside her chambers." Hank stared down at Lucia, his brown eyes cold and hard as stone. "But I suppose you knew that."

Lucia looked down at the blanket twisted in her fist as she whispered, "Yeah, I knew that."

"What the fuck, Lucia? How could you get me mixed up in this shit? Me! Didn't you think how it would make me feel to be part of that farce?"

"I did! I didn't want you involved once...once I got Bowers. I tried calling you guys this morning but you'd already left for the hearing. Check your messages—you'll see. I wasn't sure until then that...um...the arrangements were in place."

"Meaning you never trusted me at all. You were playing both sides until you were sure your family got a so-called *friendly* judge for the hearing. Can't you see how that's worse?" He didn't wait for an answer but paced away from the bed. "I'm surprised it took them that long to set it up. I guess your *piesanos* are more efficient when it comes to fraud and murder."

"Hank, please—can't you understand? I couldn't take a chance with Rocco's life. I wasn't sure a dog like him would get justice."

"Justice! Is that what you think happened today? Bowers is the judge you get when you're looking to pervert justice. Maria said she took a bribe to let a street racer off with *a warning*—after he had plowed into a playground and hurt a bunch of kids. What justice is there for those kids? Or for anyone who doesn't have a vowel at the end of their name?"

"I'm sorry. I wish I could have done this without you. I tried to—"

"No! You don't get it. You shouldn't have done it *at all*. You should have had a little faith in me—and our system. I guess you can take the girl out of the Mafia but you can't take the Mafia out of the girl, huh?"

Torn between thinking Hank was being overly harsh, and feeling she deserved every last barb, Lucia swallowed down her tears. She looked up at him, stating evenly, "What I did was wrong—I have no illusions on that score. The way I see it, I had no choice. I couldn't live with myself if I let anything happen to Rocco, if I didn't do *everything* in my power to save him."

"It's good you can live with it—because I can't." Hank walked over and clasped her hand briefly. "I'm glad you're doing well and I really hope you'll take this shooting as a warning to...to step away from this whole Colona thing. But as for us...."

Wanting to get it over with, Lucia volunteered, "We're through, right?"

"Yeah, we sure as hell are." He walked to the door not even looking back when he said, "Good-bye, Lucia."

CHAPTER 16
Of Blood and Sorrow

"The past has been a mint of blood and sorrow. That must not be True of tomorrow."—Langston Hughes, *The Collected Poems*

The next day Juli visited, armed with Polaroid's to prove Rocco was in good health, if not the best of spirits. "He is looking *everywhere* for you. I made the mistake of saying your name out loud when I told Dan where I was going, and the poor boy flipped out. I thought about putting him in a duffel bag and bringing him for a visit today but Dan talked me out of it." She laughed, "He was probably worried that tonight's Action News would feature film of his wife getting thrown out of HUP on her ass."

"Probably," Lucia chortled in agreement. "Thanks for taking care of Rocco for me. He'll be out of your hair soon."

"You got somewhere to go other than your office? If not, you should stay with me and Dan."

"Thanks, but my mom and Patsy can barely wait to get their hands on me. My mom swears I've lost weight, which for the first time in my life is apparently a bad thing."

"What about Hank?" When Lucia stared unseeingly out the window rather than answering, Juli said, "I thought something was wrong. You're not gonna tell me what happened?"

"We broke up because...because I arranged for a...let's just say I stacked the deck on that Animal Control hearing."

"Oh, Lucia," she breathed.

"Please don't lecture me. Hank already tore me a new asshole. Not that I didn't deserve it but—"

"I'm not gonna lecture you. Looking at the role models you've had in life, I'm not surprised you thought that was...a reasonable thing to do." Shaking her head, Juli mused, "I don't know what that little dog means to you, but—"

"He's not a substitute child."

"Wow, you almost said that a little too fast but I never thought that. I was going to say, I know he means a lot. And if anything, Rocco's more like a substitute Baccaro than a child."

"How do you figure that?"

"He's almost too good-looking, definitely too much trouble, and has you wrapped around his little finger. Or in Rocco's case, little paw." Her tone softened considerably as she added, "And he loves you more than he loves himself."

"You left out, 'I see the good in him most people miss'."

"If you say so." She gathered up the photographs of Rocco and stacked them neatly on the bedside table, saying, "Speaking of ex-boyfriends, do you know your last one is waiting outside to see you? He requires a private audience and gallantly let me go first but also let me know he's a busy man and I shouldn't take too long."

Lucia looked up, exclaiming in excitement, "Hank is here?"

"Uh, no—your former ex. You know...the WASPy-Green-Giant?"

"Rockingham is waiting to see me? Why?"

"I don't know. Ready to find out?"

"Might as well send him in. I've been shot and dumped already this week. Let's go for the trifecta."

Juli laughed, giving her a sympathetic pat on the arm. "I'll see you tomorrow, hun."

A minute later Rockingham walked in with a large vase of flowers. Lucia thanked him, studying the gorgeous arrangement, thinking the man might have his faults but penny-pinching wasn't one of them. Of course, his trust fund could bankroll a casino on fight night so why should he worry about money? She waited briefly for an explanation for the unexpected visit, finally prodding, "So...business or pleasure?"

"What?"

"Why are you here, Davis?"

"Oh. Well, I wanted to see how you were doing and...and I wanted to talk to you about...." He hesitated, glancing around before continuing, "...the attempt on your life."

"You mean, talk in an official, ADA-type capacity?"

"Yes." He slouched against the wall near her bed, explaining, "When I heard what happened, I focused some of the task force's resources on the shooting. It looks like you were right about Colona. Your assailant was one Jeff Armitage, a known informant of Colona's. And the gun he used to shoot you was the same one used to kill Manny Griffin."

"Holy shit."

"Indeed. All in all, some fairly damning circumstantial evidence against Colona."

"I knew it!" Rubbing her hands together, Lucia asked, "You're gonna arrest him?"

"It's enough evidence for me—but not quite enough for an arrest. Colona could make a reasonable case for Armitage having decided to go after the goods on his own—very much like Griffin did. Which is where you come in."

"I'm listening."

"As soon as you feel well enough, I want you to set up a meeting with Colona, for which you will be wearing a wire."

"Oh, no." Lucia was shaking her head emphatically as she added, "No, no, no."

"There are protocols to ensure your safety—"

"It's not my safety I'm worried about. It's my family. With them...there are lines you don't cross. I wear a wire for you guys, even to get Colona, and that's it, I'm a rat. That's not the sort of thing they'll forget—or forgive. Not ever."

"I see." Davis straightened up and walked towards the window. Turning back, he said, "You've been balancing on that moral fence for some time, Lucia. It looks like you're finally going to have to choose a side."

"Maybe not. I'm really close to blowing this whole case open. If I keep digging, I could find solid evidence of—"

"Absolutely not. Unless it's under the task force's aegis, you need to avoid interacting with Colona from here on out. He's obviously getting desperate. Probably triggered by the fact that the Organized Crime Unit which searched your office appears to be entirely legitimate."

"That would explain Baby-Faced Quint," Lucia interjected.

"I would guess he's petrified that some honest cop will beat him to those elusive goods—the ones he's still convinced you're hiding from him. In short, he's more dangerous now than ever."

"Don't worry, I'll be careful. I really underestimated Colona. I was...okay, I'll say it, a little cocky. My ego almost got me, and what's worse, Rocco, killed."

He strolled back towards the bed, and shook his head at her. "There are two things wrong with that statement. Number one, your priorities appear to be badly askew, and two, the lion's share of the blame does not lie with you. It's true that you have...unique instincts, so I should have believed you about Colona when you first told me. Especially after Griffin was killed. Don't be so hard on yourself."

"Yeah, I guess I can leave that to the pros." She grinned, throwing him a sassy wink. "How is your mother these days?" When Davis frowned deeply in response, Lucia chided, "Aww, don't be like that. It was a joke."

"Sorry, I can't quite find it in me to laugh. Nothing about how I handled that matter is amusing. But how and why I did it is not...my chief regret." As he perched on the edge of the bed, Lucia was silent, wondering if her meds were stronger than she knew. "Would you ever consider giving us another shot?" She didn't trust herself to speak but was reflexively shaking her head. "Ah, because of Narváez, I suppose."

Lucia sighed, realizing she was going to have to talk about this after all. "No, not because of him. I royally screwed that up, anyway. We shouldn't give it another shot because of *us*. You might've spewed some major bullshit when you dumped me, but you were right when you said we don't make any sense as a couple." She held up a hand to halt his attempted interruption. "We'd only end up breaking up again. And that's not something...I want to go through twice." With a shrug, she declared, "Sad truth is, love doesn't conquer all. Love doesn't conquer shit."

"I assume that's the inscription on the flyleaf of the hard-boiled detective's manual?"

"It should be. It's one of the things that keeps us in business."

"It could be you're wrong, you know. If you ask me, it was love that saved your life the other night."

"Get back to me when humans can love as well as dogs."

Davis stood up and stretched. "You get back to me about wearing that wire." He headed out, pausing at the door to say, "The sooner the better. Colona is convinced you have that diamond and those coins—and he's not going to stop trying to get them."

Angie walked into the room almost directly after Rockingham. Lucia searched her face, concerned that her mother might have overheard some or all of their discussion. Angie laid most of those fears to rest by plopping in the chair next to her bed and asking, "Who the hell was that?"

"Davis Rockingham."

"That *stunad* who broke up with you last year?"

"The very same."

"Huh, I wish I'd known—I'd've kicked him in the *cazzo*. What did he want?"

Nodding at the vase of flowers, Lucia gave a ready half-truth. "He wanted another chance."

"You're shitting me?" Lucia shook her head so her mom asked, "What did you say?"

"Well, since I don't have the word 'idiot' stamped across my forehead in big red letters, I said, 'no, hell no.'"

Angie patted her firmly on the arm. "Good for you. Now, maybe you see, after how him and that

245

other lawyer fella done you so dirty, you need to find some nice Italian boy and settle down."

"Stop stalling, Ma, and give me the bad news you came to give." Angie swiveled towards the bed, her weary frown proving Lucia's theory correct. Lucia prodded, "It's *Nonno*—isn't it?"

"Yes. How did you know?"

"Because you have the same look on your face as when Scout died. I figured it had to be someone who you knew I cared about, but you didn't."

"That's not fair. I loved that dog, honey, but...it was her time."

"Yeah?" Lucia said, swiping the hair off of her damp forehead, "I think that Cadillac backing over her might have had something to do with it." Without waiting for a response, she asked, "When did *Nonno* die?"

"A few hours ago. It was peaceful, they tell us." When Lucia said she could start work on the arrangements from the hospital, Angie shook her head. "There's nothing to do. When we was burying your dad, I told Mosti we'd just do all the same for Tony, right down to the casket and flowers. Vince called Father Bruni and also picked out the burial suit. Carmela is arranging the luncheon, of course. It's all done."

"Who's paying this time?"

"Mosti told us Tony's life insurance will cover most of it. Vince will cover the rest, he said, seeing as they were such good friends all their lives." Angie reached over and squeezed her hand. "No one wants you spending your house money."

"When will it be?"

"Day after tomorrow. You gonna be up to it?"

"Yeah, I should be. They're springing me from this place tomorrow. One way or another, I'll be there."

Good to her word, Lucia made it through the requiem mass and the burial but let everyone know she was taking a pass on the luncheon. Patsy offered to stay with her but Angie insisted he go to Le Sorelle with the rest of the family while she drove Lucia back to his house.

While waiting at the gravesite for her mom to free herself from the clutches of the ever-chatty Mrs. Fanelli, Lucia sadly studied her father's headstone. It had been erected since his burial and the finality of it was another icepick to her already sore heart. Out of the corner of her eye she saw a group approach and looked up to accept the condolences of Micky's wife, Lizzie. She was flanked by Gabby and the younger children with Micky bringing up the rear. Lucia nodded at him, hoping he'd respect her pain and move on with the rest of the group.

Consistent with her recent run of luck, Micky stopped next to her, telling Lizzie to take the children to the car without him. He stared at her father's gravestone a moment, before reading part of the inscription aloud. "Beloved father." Eye to eye, as they had been since she was sixteen, he looked at Lucia for a long silent moment before asking, "Was he? Did you still love him?"

"If you must know, yes."

"You had a funny way of showing it. Never seeing him those last seven years he was in Graterford."

Glaring coldly at her cousin, Lucia asked, "And how many times did you visit in all the eighteen years, huh? What was that number again?" She stared up at the cloudless sky, pretending to do the calculations. "Hmm...carry the one and you get...zero, wasn't it?"

"Knock off the comedy. You know why I couldn't see him."

"Oh right, because he violated some stupid fucking code. Not because he killed, but because he killed for himself, that once."

"That's right," Micky snapped. "You think it was easy for me?" His voice cracked a bit as he explained, "We was best friends growing up. Did he ever tell you I wrote to him? Every month your father was there, at least one letter I sent...sometimes more."

Lucia had forgotten that. Moved to pity by such obvious pain, even that of a monster like Dominic Vetere, she admitted, "Yeah, he did tell me that. He appreciated it. A lot."

Not looking up, he nodded, seeming transfixed by Carlo's grave. "I didn't even get to see him. They got to him before—" He stopped short, unable or unwilling to continue. Lucia was, for a moment, tempted to ask Micky what he knew, but quickly realized the futility of it. She watched as he ran a hand over the headstone, murmuring, "He had a lot of secrets, your old man. Things he wouldn't even tell me."

"Like what?"

"Where he picked up the trade, for one thing. That came outta nowhere as far as I could see. Before that, I was always...well, better with a gun than him."

"When was that? When exactly did he start?"

Micky looked over at Angie, tossing his head in her direction. "After they had you. Your dad volunteered for a tricky job, said he needed the boost in pay, said he could do it. I thought he was kidding himself but...damn if he didn't pull it off. All by himself."

"Great," she drawled out. "He did it for me. I needed that extra dose of guilt."

"What guilt? It was your father's decision." His eyes bored into her own, what he was looking for, Lucia wasn't sure. "Is it guilt weighing you down—or is it something else?" He waited for a response, but she had none to give. He muttered, "You got more secrets than your father. *Gabbadost'*." She started to say that hard heads sure ran in the family but Micky had already started on the family's favorite harangue. "If you'd embrace us, embrace your family, like you should, you wouldn't be so alone. Stop playing the *facciadu*, stop trying to have it both ways. That's gonna get you killed. If you was with us, really with us, you wouldn't've needed some mutt to save your ass."

Lucia couldn't help but emit a small chuckle. "Show some respect, Mick. That mutt is a made man, now."

Shaking his head, he put a hand on her shoulder. "I don't know what's gonna get you killed sooner, kid. All those secrets you keep, or that smart mouth of yours."

"I know."

"Yeah? Which?"

She heard her mother call, "*'diamo*" and looked over to find her waving Lucia over, jingling the car keys to show it was time to leave. She started towards Angie, looking back to tell Micky, "Sorry—can't tell you. That's another one of my secrets."

Lucia was sitting at the table in Patsy's sunny kitchen when Angie stuck her head in the door and nodded at her. "You finish your lunch?"

Looking down at the soup bowl she'd all but licked clean, Lucia laughed, "See for yourself," holding it up for inspection. "Who made it?"

"Rosie. She makes better Wedding Soup than Carmela, even."

"You gonna tell her that?"

"Tell Carmela I said that?" Angie sat across from her daughter, taking care not to disturb Rocco, who'd been welded to Lucia's side since their reunion. "No, thanks. She'd run me through with that big carving knife of hers. If you mean Rosie—she already knows. Behind Carmela's back, she says it herself."

Lucia stretched and looked out at the afternoon sun. "Well, you can tell Rosie the soup certainly did its therapeutic job. I feel great and I'm getting out of this house today. I'm gonna take a walk around the block with Rocco now."

When Angie found she couldn't dissuade Lucia, she insisted, "I'm coming with you."

"Fine. If you're coming, you can do the poop scooping."

"Oh yeah...." Angie paused to theatrically roll her eyes. "After all the diapers I've changed in my life, like that's gonna scare me off."

They had strolled along in amiable silence for a few minutes before Lucia ventured, "This walk hasn't been a strain at all. Since I'm feeling so strong, I think it's time I went home."

"Too bad you don't have one." Knowing how much her near-death episode had rattled her mother, Lucia bit back on her instinctively defensive reply. She remained quiet as her mother went on, "Where are you gonna shower, huh? You gonna drag yourself down to the Y? You're not even allowed to swim, yet."

"I can go to the Y and not swim, you know. And if I'm not up to that, I have a basin in the bathroom. I can take a few sponge baths if I need to. I've done it before."

Angie's head was bent, with a hand cupped around the cigarette she was lighting. Without looking up, she replied, "I'll bet you have. Why you wanta live like that...." Rather than finishing the thought, she took a long drag on her cigarette, shaking her head.

"It won't be for much longer. I should have enough for a down-payment sometime next year."

Considering how much income she'd lost lately to personal distractions and now her injury, that was an incredibly optimistic estimate, but Lucia was still intending to make it happen, somehow.

"Is that right?"

"Yes. And I was thinking...maybe you'd like to move in with me when I buy my house."

There were a lot of replies Lucia was expecting but a whoop of laughter wasn't one of them. She bent down to untangle Rocco's back paw from the leash while staring up at her mom. "What's so funny?"

"We'd kill each other inside of a week—and you know it." As Lucia straightened up, Angie patted her arm. "I appreciate the offer, honey, but, no way."

"Okay then, what are you gonna do? Where are you gonna live?"

"I'm not sure, but...." She puffed away in silence for a moment before continuing, "I think I'm really close to having an answer. I'm not staying in Philly, that's for sure. You can bet on me visiting you in that house of yours, so make sure you have a real nice guest room."

Smiling faintly, Lucia promised, "I'll do that."

"You wanta do something else for me?"

"Sure. Whata' you need?"

Angie stopped walking and put a firm hand on Lucia's arm. "I need you to be safe. I lost my husband—if I lose my daughter, too, well, that'll finish me."

"I'll be careful, I prom—"

"No. That ain't enough." Her voice dropped to an urgent whisper. "Whatever Colona or whoever the hell these men are, whatever it is they want from you, it ain't worth dying for. Give it to 'em. Put an end to this."

"I don't—"

"Look, I'm not gonna dig into your business. I'll do for you what I did for your father and stay outta the details but something tells me you know how to end this."

"Ma," Lucia said, gently grasping Angie's hand which still encircled Lucia's arm and releasing it, "even if I had the diamond and coins and handed them over, there's no guarantee that would end things peacefully. That's not how these men operate."

"It is. Trust me on this. I know men like Colona. I know *him*. I've seen a lot more than you, and I know a lot more than you. Whether you believe it or not."

As they restarted their forward progress, Lucia couldn't resist asking, "When you say you know...Colona, um...." Angie was staring at her intently, her cigarette frozen on the way to her mouth. "Were you and him ever...like, did you two ever—"

"What? Are you asking me if I ever slept with that clown?!" Lucia nodded sheepishly. "Did he give you that idea?"

"Yeah, kinda."

"That *schifosa*." She took a puff then scoffed, "He wishes. I never went *near* no cops when I was single. And him? Him, I wouldn't've fucked with a rented vagina."

"Well, there's family consensus on that point," Lucia laughed.

"All the more reason to get that trash outta your life. Give him what he wants and he'll go away." Tapping her on the arm in rhythm with her speech, Angie concluded, "I'm right about this, I promise."

Shaking her head, Lucia remonstrated, "You're always doing that."

"What? What am I always doing? Trying to save your life?"

"No. Making promises you don't have the power to keep."

"Name one time I did that."

"One time?" Lucia stopped walking and faced her mother. "All right. How about when you promised me Dad wouldn't be convicted? And when I was twelve and you swore I was done growing and wasn't gonna get any taller? And when you guaranteed if I ate enough of Grandma's tripe and peas, I'd grow to like it." While Angie laughed, Lucia mumbled, "I still hate that shit."

Angie threw out a cigarette-laden hand, complaining, "Look at this, she has a list ready." She smoked in silence for a moment then asked, "Couldn't you listen to your mother just this once, huh? Just this once?"

Without answering Lucia started moving again since an impatient Rocco had been tugging at the leash the whole time they were stopped. "How much did you listen to your mother?"

"That *buchiach*. All I listened to from her was the sound of her smacking me across the face or screaming that I wasn't doing enough for her and her brats."

"Your real mother, I meant."

"Oh, that one. I barely remember her. I wouldn't recognize her if she walked right past us this minute." Angie dropped her cigarette butt on the ground and crushed it out under the toe of her sandal, muttering, "If she's even still alive."

"You know, I could probably find out for you. It's what I do for a living."

"Lucia, that woman took off on me when I was nine-years-old and I don't give a shit about her." Pointing a finger at her daughter, Angie declared, "You. You, I care about. That's why I want you to promise me, you'll think about what I'm saying. Give that shit up, whatever it is, and get those men off your back. Promise me."

"Okay, I promise, Mama. I promise I'll put an end to this." Lucia was silent on the fact that she planned to do that by nailing Colona's ass to the wall but the words she'd spoken out loud were honest, at least.

CHAPTER 17
The Only Way to the Truth

"...a clearly defined error...is sometimes the only way to the truth."—Benjamin D. Wiker, *The Mystery of the Periodic Table*

It had taken Lucia twenty minutes to assure Patsy she would be fine and would call immediately if she needed him before he could be persuaded to leave her alone in the office. She watched Rocco sniffing around the space which, other than some missing items, showed little sign of the chaos that had reigned there less than two weeks ago. She was relieved to see that the rug which must have been soaked through with both her blood and that of Jeffrey Armitage, was gone. Lucia made a sweeping inspection of the room, stopping to examine the wall behind her desk and easily finding the patched bullet holes. She patted the spots, thinking they'd be a permanent reminder of the danger of overconfidence in her business.

While unpacking she made the discovery that at some point the lock on her bathroom—well, okay not *her* bathroom but the one she made use of, had been removed. The day before her release, Juli had brought a varied assortment of clothing to Lucia at the hospital and hadn't mentioned anything about the lock. Maybe she had considered it a low priority concern at that time. A quick inventory told Lucia that whatever had been the reason for the intrusion, all of her things seemed intact, if somewhat jumbled.

When she made it back to the office, Rocco was still inspecting, snuffling along the baseboards now. She wondered what he remembered of that night. Could a dog understand that he'd killed someone? Would he be in any way haunted by that memory, as she was by the life she'd taken? Lucia wasn't sure and didn't even know anyone she could ask. She looked down at the dog who had finally settled into his bed, looking very contented indeed, glad to see that he didn't seem to be suffering any emotional turmoil. "Looks like somebody's happy to be home."

Before getting down to work, Lucia re-checked her safe. She'd already noted that though it was unlocked, her camera and money were present and accounted for. The police had returned her Glock while she was still at Patsy's house so oddly enough, the only thing inexplicably missing from the office was her stack of active case notes. She needed those notes for her first order of business—finding out if Colona had been out of Philadelphia during any or all of the Specialist's kills. She planned to see if Patty Kourosh had a contact in PPD Records who could check Colona's vacation data on the sly for her. But first she needed that list she'd copied from the alt.true-crime Usenet group.

Ten minutes later she'd come up empty even though she had checked everywhere she could imagine some "helpful" busybody might have stashed her pile of yellow legal pads. She'd combed her filing cabinet without luck. The only notes in there were the ones filed away for all of the completed cases. Hearing a knock at the door, for the first time in her memory, Lucia hoped it wasn't a new client. She opened the door to find Milo Belsky standing on the threshold, holding a clipboard. "Mr. Belsky, hello. Good to see you. Thanks for calling the police and literally saving my life that night."

"Sure thing, Lucia. I'm real glad I was still around. You doing okay? Seems like you are. Looks like you're back on your feet. Good for you. Wasn't that a terrible night, though? Yep, it was, it definitely was. When I saw them paramedics carrying you outta here and all that blood...well, I don't need to tell you how bad it was—do I?"

"No, you sure don't."

"Isn't it funny in all those years Baccaro was running Fidelia, nothing like that ever happened to him? But back then, you didn't have so many clients coming and going, did you? Nope, not even close. Or was that whole thing...er, some kind of...family matter with you?"

"It's hard to say, the police are still investigating. Would you like to come in?"

He looked behind her to where Rocco had appeared and was already commencing with a few low woofs. "No, no, that's okay. About the office, there's just a few things...maybe you can step out into the hall with me?"

Lucia agreed, smiling to herself at the thought that everyone in the building would probably be giving Rocco a very wide berth from now on. Belsky was distracted by the sight of Goldstein's empty shop and started a rambling soliloquy on his son's attempts to find a tenant. When he finally stopped to draw a breath, she redirected him by asking, "You were saying about my office?"

"Oh, right. The police, like you said, they've been through here a few times but day before yesterday they finally let me know it was okay to get things cleaned up. Didn't the janitor's crew do a bang-up job in such a short time? Yep, they got your office pretty ship-shape. They're good guys, and they were real upset 'bout what happened to you, so they cleaned up real good in there. But the rug...it's a goner. And you gotta have a rug in there, don't you? You sure do, so that's gonna have to be replaced." He consulted his clipboard. "That's a good size rug, too, so that's gonna be at least a few hundred dollars, unless I can find something at the thrift store that'll work."

Knowing Belsky was a good-hearted but voluble man who communicated mainly through a series of questions, half of which he went on to answer for himself, Lucia listened in tolerant silence while he rambled on. Waiting patiently for a break in his monologue so she could ask about her legal pads, Lucia had time to wonder if her liability insurance could cover any of the damage. Would she have to sue herself to collect? She immediately discarded the idea of asking Hank or Max, deciding she'd have to bite the bullet and pay her own lawyer for a consultation. Coming out of her reverie, she heard Belsky mentioning the need to replace the padlock on the bathroom door.

"Yeah, I wondered about that—what happened? Was someone in there the night I was shot?"

"No, no, it was one of the police crews who came through. Wasn't it?" Belsky stared up at the ceiling, musing, "Was that the police or was it those task force folks who went at your lock with the bolt cutters? Yep, yep, it was the task force." He faced Lucia, smiling as it came back to him. "That real tall fella you was keeping company with last year, he was with 'em. What was his name? Elvis Rockland."

"Davis Rockingham?"

"I guess that's right. You'd know better than me, wouldn't you? Yep. Anyhow, Rockland's the one that took all of those legal pads of yours."

"He took my case notes? Rockingham took my notes," Lucia repeated through gritted teeth.

"Yep, he took a great big stack of 'em. You'll probably want to get yourself down to the Penn bookstore first thing tomorrow, get yourself a new set, won't you? Sure will, seeing how fond you've always been of those yellow pads, whereas I like—"

"No, Mr. Belsky, I'll be getting those ones back from Rockingham. Or, I'll have a very fancy Main Line pelt you can use as the rug in my office."

"You're gonna get a pelt? No, no, you don't want something that's gonna shed—"

"I know." Reaching out and patting his arm, she assured him, "I was kidding." She took the list of expenses from Belsky, promising to make good on all of them. As soon as the door closed behind her, Lucia made a beeline for her phone. Searching for the number for Rockingham's office, she spun the Rolodex on her desk so fast it almost became airborne.

A few hours later, Lucia walked into Rockingham's office to find him sitting at his desk with his feet up. "Thanks for seeing me on such short notice. I can see how busy you are."

He swung his impressively long legs to the floor. "What's going on? Is this about Colona? You told my admin it was a matter of life and death."

"It is. It's about you butting into *my life* which could be the cause of *your death*."

"I'm not following. Please have a seat and explain why you're here."

"You took all of my case notes, Davis! What was your task force even doing crawling all over my office?"

"Oh." He pointed at one of his guest chairs, so Lucia reluctantly sat down. He steepled his hands in front of him. "You're back to work already? Is that wise?"

"Wiser than you taking off with my notes. What the hell?"

"Please calm down and listen. My task force has jurisdiction over the crime scene at Overbrook." When she went to interrupt him, he wagged his pointer finger at her. "Uh-uh-ah, let me finish. That jurisdiction stems from the fact that we've established Colona as a suspect both in our corruption probe and the attack on you. Therefore, the team thought it prudent to conduct a thorough search of the crime scene and...related areas." He paused, quirking an eyebrow at her. "I suppose it's safe to assume you were aware of the secret compartment hidden behind the back seat of your car."

"Yes, I knew. The original owner, the one before Bac, had it installed."

"Drug dealer?"

"You'd think so, but no. Apparently he was just some gun nut who liked to carry an armory around with him."

"What happened to him?"

"He blew his brains out and his daughter sold the car to Bac."

"I see. How unfortunate. As to your—wait, he didn't kill himself *in* the Chevelle, did he?"

"As a matter of fact, he did. Why?"

"I've been in that car!"

"Oh, grow up. It was professionally cleaned before the sale." Lucia rubbed her forehead. "Could we get back to the reason I'm here? You know, the fact that you stole all of my case notes. Notes you can't even read—can you?"

"No, I cannot. They did not teach shorthand at the Haverford School. As for your hyperbole, I didn't steal them, I confiscated them as possible items of interest in our probe."

"Are you trying to say I'm a suspect?"

"Yes. I *suspect* you're going to go off and try to...to bring down Colona on your own. Which would be not only imprudent but could be considered as interfering in our active investigation."

"And that means...what? You're planning to hold my notes hostage until I either agree to play by your rules or stay out of it?"

Leaning backwards, he swiveled his chair back and forth, the ghost of a tight-lipped smile on his face. "Pretty much, yes."

"My father might be dead but I'm not looking for a new one."

"Considering what I know of your dating history, I'm not sure I agree."

"Wow...." Lucia leaned forward, thumping her hands on the mahogany desktop. "You're not only shopping for a smackdown, you brought a coupon."

Davis held up a hand, acknowledging his blunder. "All right, I'm sorry. That was a low blow."

"It sure was—coming from someone who takes dating advice from his mommy."

"I said I was *sorry*."

Lucia nodded in silent acceptance of his apology before briefly closing her eyes. "Look, I need my case notes. I have to get back to work."

"Would it kill you to take it easy for a few weeks?"

"Yes, it would. It would kill my balance sheet. We don't all have trust funds to fall back on, you know. I've already lost well over a week of revenue and now I've got all that damage in my office to pay for."

"Your liability insurance should cover that."

Her head jerked up in excitement. "Will it? Even though it wasn't strictly related to a case?"

"That's a good point. You should consult an attorney—the right kind of attorney. Not me, that is."

"Yeah, so that's another bill to pay."

"You have savings, don't you?"

"I'm not touching my house fund! Besides, it's not only the money—I have clients who are expecting updates, who need the information they hired me to get."

"Point taken." He got up and walked around to the front of his desk and perched on it, facing her. "I will give you back your case notes. *Providing*, that is, I have your word that you will not interfere in the Colona investigation in any way."

"Define...." She paused to make finger quotes. "...interfere."

"What is it you intend on doing?"

"I need to cross-check some dates. That's all."

"What dates and with whom are you going to check them?" Something about the idea of being wholly transparent with Rockingham didn't sit well with Lucia. She was especially hesitant to mention Patty Kourosh who hadn't even yet agreed to any further involvement. Moreover, Bac was whispering in her ear that the only person's motivation she could ever be sure of was her own. "What's the problem? Why the hesitation?"

"I'm not quite ready to hand everything over to the Feds. Not yet."

"Since when am I 'the Feds'?"

"The 'F' in FBI doesn't stand for friendly. They gotta be the ones helping you on this task force. You don't use cops to investigate cops."

"Touché." He tossed his head in acknowledgement of her perceptivity. "How about this? You tell me, as narrowly as possible, what it is you're intent on checking, and if I can do it myself, I will do so."

"Okay. I need to check Colona's attendance record."

"What?"

"I need to see if he was on vacation on these...on certain dates. Over the past decade."

"That's it? I should be able to get that done discreetly. What will it tell you?" When she was silent, he pressed her, "Lucia, I'm not doing this blindly."

Rubbing a finger across her lips, she weighed her options carefully. At last, she looked up at him with a smile. "If the records show Colona was out of town at the times I give you, then my theory is probably correct, and I'll give you everything I've got on him. If there's no match, then my theory's a bust, and...." She exhaled slowly, aware of the risky gamble she was about to make. "...and I'll wear the wire for you guys."

Davis bit his lip for a moment, staring down at her. "You will? You swear on your grandmother's grave?"

Lucia rolled her eyes, regretting she'd ever shared that bit of Italian-American lore with him. "Yes, I swear it. On my grandmother's grave."

Rockingham produced her legal pads from a locked drawer in his desk and Lucia swiftly found the one she needed, and wrote out the dates of the Specialist's deadly activity as provided by Hugo. Davis promised to have the dates checked within a few days' time. As she was gathering up her notes, he asked, "What is it about your grandmother's grave that is so...weighty? Is it...how she died that provokes so much superstition?"

"What? No, she died of pneumonia. It's because she's my grandmother and...." She shook her head, at a loss for words. "I don't know how to explain this to a '*Madigan*. You don't tell a lie after swearing on your grandmother's grave. It's an *infamnia*."

"If you say so."

"What is it your people swear on? Your polo ponies or yachts or something?"

He smirked at her, explaining, "We don't have to swear on anything; we don't lie."

Stroking her chin, Lucia retorted, "Really? I seem to recall a time when you tried to convince me you'd shouted, 'darling' when it was *clearly*, 'Daria'."

He crossed his arms and glared down at her. "Don't you have to be going? You have all that work to do." As she was heading for the door she heard him mutter, "You have a memory like an elephant."

Hand on the doorknob, she laughed, "Nope, like a Sicilian."

With nothing better to do while Rockingham checked the dates for her, Lucia put her head down and went to work. She cleared up a dozen cases in three days, including the slip-and-fall for the insurance company and the skip-tracing one for Maddie Forrester. Lucia had found the missing witness to the hit-and-run hiding out at her sister's house in Kensington. The woman was reluctant to come forward since she had almost $500 in unpaid parking tickets which she feared would come to light if she testified.

After laying out a sob story about the hit-and-run victim which admittedly wasn't entirely factual, Lucia saw the woman wavering so she made a quick call to Fritz, Fritz, and Bailey. The law firm, as she'd suspected, was willing to pay off the witness's fines in exchange for her testimony. Using those combined strategies, Lucia persuaded the witness to accompany her to the police station and give a statement.

Despite noting the re-emergence of her police tail, Lucia was in an ebullient mood when she made it back to her office building. Her relief was so great that she hadn't blown it with the high-powered law firm that she breezed into the lobby oblivious to the fact that Hank and Max were waiting at the elevator. That is, until she almost bumped into them. She momentarily froze, thinking the only missing element in her day up until then had been this free ride on the awkward train.

Feeling an almost manic need to escape, she blurted out, "Hi, guys. Good to see you. Maddie says, hi, by the way." Without giving them the smallest chance to respond, she hurtled towards the stairs calling behind her, "I gotta run. Have a great day...um, have a great rest of the day."

When she made it to the safety of her office, she slammed the door behind her and leaned against it, breathing heavily. Looking down at Rocco, who was jumping up at her in his usual frantic manner, Lucia laughed, "Well, I didn't sound the least bit rational up there, did I? Nope, no chance they'll think I'm not a crazy woman, now." The more she thought it over, the harder she cringed. "Rocco, I think you're gonna have to help me dig a tunnel out to the street so I never have to show my face in the lobby again." She shook her head, looking up at her crystals glinting in the few beams of sunlight which had managed to steal into the basement. "If only those windows opened."

The ringing phone presented a welcome distraction from her replaying that humiliating scene over and over in her head. She answered to find it was Davis Rockingham calling with an update. She closed her eyes, briefly praying for some good news, as he droned on about the hoops he had to jump through to check Colona's vacation records. "Cut to the chase. What did you find?"

"Nothing. His vacation records show no correlation with those mysterious dates you gave me."

After a moment of shocked silence, Lucia whispered, "*Fanabola. I malano miau.*"

"Translation, please."

Listening more to the ghost of Baccaro in her head than to Rockingham on the other end of the line, Lucia struggled to integrate this information. "Yeah, I really dogged this one."

"Dogged? Does that mean solved? Because I thought you were hoping for the opposite result?"

It suddenly came to her that there was another person in the metaphorical room. "Uh, yeah, I was. I was expecting the opposite. 'Dogged' means, you know, I missed my shot, screwed up. It's pool talk."

"Pool as in swimming or—"

"Billiards, okay?" While she ran a hand through her curls, Lucia muttered, "For those of you born with a silver cue in your hands." She sighed heavily before admitting, "Okay, looks like I lost, big time. I know I gotta pay up. How does this wire thing work?"

"You're not walking the plank, Lucia. You're going to help us apprehend a highly corrupt and dangerous LEO. An admirable endeavor."

"Easy for you to say."

There was a long pause, that had Lucia wondering what Rockingham was doing. "I suppose it is easy for me to say." He cleared his throat. "There is a chance, you know, that your family can remain entirely ignorant of your role in this matter."

"Yeah...." She gave a particularly mirthless chuckle. "A really bad chance. You're talking to the granddaughter of one of the best bookies Philadelphia ever knew. I can lay out the odds right now. Most likely outcome is everyone finds out because Colona kills me." Rockingham started protesting but Lucia went on undeterred, "Next likely is we walk away with nothing but my involvement is still broadcast, then comes this being a grand success with everyone, of course, finding out my role in it. Most unlikely of all is *anyway* in which I come out clean."

"We will do our utmost to maintain your anonymity. It's best to discuss any further particulars in person. We can go over the details of the operation with you tomorrow. Here at my office. Say...ten-thirty?"

"Who is this 'we' you keep referring to?"

"Ah, yes. There will be a couple of...FBI agents participating in these discussions."

"Ha, I knew it. Okay, tomorrow at ten-thirty. If I'm a little late, be patient. It means I'm being followed and have to lose the tail."

"Are you...are you being serious? Do you think your family is having you followed?"

"No! Not my family. Some cop's been tailing me, on and off for weeks now."

"A cop? Is he with Colona? Or perhaps someone with the Organized Crime Unit?"

"I don't know, Davis. They don't come with 'dirty' and 'clean' stickers like a dishwasher." Before he could make any long-winded response, Lucia said, "Bye. See you tomorrow."

CHAPTER 18

Sand Turns Traitor

"Nothing in this world is hidden forever. The gold which has lain for centuries unsuspected in the ground, reveals itself one day on the surface. Sand turns traitor, and betrays the footstep that has passed over it...."—Wilkie Collins, *No Name*

The next day Lucia was ushered into Rockingham's office where he was standing with his FBI associates, Special Agents Jane Chen and Nicholas Franklin. Chen looked to be about forty-five, and as they were introduced, Lucia reflected that it was true, someone as short as Dana Scully could be an FBI agent. Franklin, on the other hand, seemed to be in his mid-thirties at most, and was as tall as Lucia. He bore such a striking resemblance to Lenny Kravitz that she found it impossible not to say so as she shook his hand.

Franklin flashed a brilliant smile. "I hear that all the time."

"But tall. I mean, you're tall, he's short."

"I wouldn't say Lenny Kravitz is particularly short," Chen objected.

Considering Chen was the only one in the room under six-feet tall, Lucia felt it best to hastily retract her assessment of the singer's height and was about to do so when Rockingham impatiently interjected, "Shall we get down to business?"

Nodding in agreement, Chen swung into action, expertly explaining the technical aspects of wearing the wire, or as she called it, the covert listening device. It consisted of a transmitter, microphone, and battery pack, all of which Lucia would have to conceal on her person. Chen gave several options for placement but Lucia figured the bra was the best and most comfortable of them. Chen handed the device over, advising Lucia to do some practice runs with it before showtime with Colona.

Franklin then launched into some best-case scenarios for the meeting place; he advised it preferably be a public space but most importantly, a quiet one. He gave examples such as a parked car, empty bar, public park, even her office after hours. "Anywhere there won't be too much background noise, where nothing will interfere with signal transmission, and where we can park our van close by yet remain inconspicuous."

Lucia nodded, thinking it all seemed pretty much common sense. "Got it."

"Any ideas," Rockingham asked, "how to entice Colona into a one-on-one meeting?"

"Yeah. I was thinking of letting him know, once and for all, that I don't have the diamond and coins but if he'll promise to leave me alone, I'll give him back the twenty-five-thousand dollars he paid my father to kill Guenther."

The agents swiveled around in unison, staring at Rockingham who, in turn, stared at Lucia. "What? He did? You wasted my time looking up his vacation records while you sat on something like that? When were you planning on telling me?" He pointed an angry finger at her. "And don't you dare say, 'I just did'."

"You've really limited my options here." Since no one else in the room cracked a smile, Lucia rolled her eyes and explained, "I haven't mentioned it because I don't have any hard evidence, you know, of the kind you folks like. It's an educated guess." She filled them in on the exchange with Colona outside her office.

Franklin tilted his head, spearing her with a penetrating look. "Meaning you don't actually have the money, correct?"

"My parents weren't rich enough to sit on a windfall like that," Lucia evaded. "But Colona doesn't need to know that. I can tell him my grandfather was holding on to it all these years."

"If you don't know for sure, and you don't have the money," Chen said, "then where are you getting the twenty-five-thousand-dollar figure?"

"Also an educated guess based on...well, things I overheard as a child."

While Franklin chewed his lip thoughtfully, Chen was shaking her head in vigorous protest. "If you're wrong about the amount," she objected, "it could tip him off to your bluff. Don't be so specific— just say you have his money, it came from your grandfather—" She stopped abruptly. "Is there a good reason for mentioning your grandfather?"

"Yeah. It would make sense that I got the money from him. He just died a couple of weeks ago, after a protracted illness."

"I didn't know that," Rockingham replied. "I'm sorry. On top of your father's recent passing...uh, that's a lot."

The agents said nothing but the room was so thick with pity that Lucia thought it might choke her. She clapped her hands and rubbed them briskly. "Okay, I will take Agent Chen's advice not to mention a specific amount. Anything else?"

Rockingham nodded. "Yes, there's the matter of how to get the initial message to Colona. Contacting him on his police line is not the best way to launch this. We want something a bit more...organic than that."

"If I don't run into the man himself today, then I could accost the cop who's been following me. Say I've had it with the surveillance and I want to meet with his boss. Make him an offer he can't refuse." Noting Franklin's quiet chuckle, Lucia was pleased to learn these FBI agents weren't total stiffs.

"And if your police tail is not with Colona?" Rockingham asked.

"Then I'll probably get a call from Lieutenant Daniels urging me to seek the services of a mental health professional."

Chen smiled approvingly. "All and all—not a bad plan."

Yep, definitely not a couple of stiffs, after all.

Lucia had just agreed to have lunch with Juli when their conversation was interrupted by the ringing phone on Lucia's desk. One glance and Lucia knew immediately who was calling. She could now easily recognize Davis Rockingham's cell phone number since it was his fifth call to her since the previous day's meeting. Without greeting him, she said, "He hasn't gotten back to me yet."

"It's been nearly twenty-four hours. What's his game?"

"I don't know, he probably has a lot of dirty irons in his corrupt fire. He might be distracted by a teenage hooker or an illegal poker game right now. I will let you know as soon as he contacts me."

"No matter when, right? I have my phone on me—"

"Yes. We've been over this. I will. Good-bye."

Juli, who'd been examining the set up on Lucia's desk, asked, "What was that all about? Colona?"

"Got it in one."

"Do I want to know who was calling and why?"

"Rockingham was calling and why...is kind of complicated. It's connected to him showing up in my hospital room. Nothing to worry about though."

Studying her with narrowed eyes, Juli said, "Uh-huh, I'll bet." She gestured to the desktop where Lucia had used her snow globes to build a little three-dimensional schematic of the cities the Specialist had worked in. "Planning a vacation?"

The truth was that Lucia was still obsessing over the thread that tied together her father, Colona, and the Specialist. She was convinced there was one, there was too much overlap, too many coincidences, too many parallels between those three individuals. Though she felt guilty about feeding Juli half-truths, she also didn't want to burden her friend with the whole story. "Just playing around. I think I have too many of those things. I might weed some of the uglier ones out."

"I'm relieved to see you aren't thinking of chucking any of the ones Dan and I got you."

"No worries—your taste in snow globes is impeccable." Lucia told Rocco to be a good boy and they headed out the door together. Juli had suggested a visit to Salad Alley since she held that Lucia was still recovering and needed a nutritious lunch. "You're gonna drag me ten blocks to eat rabbit food?"

Laughing, Juli said, "Since you can't swim yet, you might as well walk."

"Good point—it's not like I have to walk my dog four times a day or anything. And my stitches are coming out this afternoon. I'll be back in the pool first thing tomorrow morning."

Juli congratulated her before looking up at Lucia with a tilted head and raised eyebrow. "Speaking of getting back in the swim of things...I was talking with Hank the other day and he seems to think you're avoiding him."

"Oh, he probably just feels that way because I'm avoiding him." Without even listening to them, she interrupted Juli's gentle remonstrations. "One trauma at a time, please. Let me close the book on this Colona mess, then I'll think about facing Hank."

"And how are you going to do that? Close the book on Colona, I mean."

With a shrug, Lucia evaded, "The ball's mainly in Rockingham's court, there. He claimed it as his purview."

"Good. That's a relief." Before Juli could inquire into the matter further, Lucia changed the subject to her upcoming babysitting duties at the Bennett-Channing house.

Her ploy worked and they discussed plans for that evening and other matters of little consequence throughout lunch. Still, the Colona mess, as Lucia had termed it, was never far from her mind. She was still musing on the matter when she came back from taking Rocco on his last walk of the day. When the phone rang, she was prepared to pick it up and tell Davis Rockingham to get a life—except on inspection it wasn't his number. It was Colona.

Without preamble he stated, "I understand you want a meet with me."

"That's right. I have some...cash you might be interested in. Does twenty-five thousand dollars ring any bells?"

"That much money rings a lot of bells with lots of people. What're you getting at?"

"My grandfather left it to me but I'm pretty sure I'm not the rightful owner and I think you know who is. Let's meet in person and see if you can come up with a name. I want that person to have the money and...and thereby end our dealings with each other."

"Fine. My terms, my turf. Come alone, no weapons. I'll do the same. The concrete tower in Gray's Ferry tomorrow night at six-thirty PM."

"The Concrete Tower? Is that a bar or something?"

"What are you, stupid? You can see it from the Schuylkill."

"Are you talking about that abandoned silo thing? Are you *nuts*?"

"Nah, I ain't nuts—what I am, is smart. Lot smarter than you." He gave a particularly self-satisfied chuckle. "It's a' interesting place and I happen to like the ambience. It's very...secure."

"I'm pretty sure that thing is not open for tours."

"I got my ways. You'll find it open—if you got the nerve to show up."

"Yeah, I don't think so."

"Suit yourself, Scafetti. You're the one who wanted the meeting." He hung up as abruptly as he'd begun.

Lucia looked down at Rocco saying, "That man is not right," as she dialed the number of the cell phone Davis said he carried everywhere these days. Apparently, Lucia was among the last ones to jump on this new cell phone trend. Davis's line rang several times, while she chanted, "Come on, come on, come on. It's not like you're not there."

At last, he picked up. "Lucia? What's up?"

"Let's just say, contact has been made but it's complicated. Can you talk?"

"Uh, no, not really. Just tell me clearly—is this in reference to the meeting you've been trying to set up?"

Rolling her eyes, she snarked, "No, this is a booty call. Get those pants off and get over here and do me, big boy." The line went silent except for the sound of a woman loudly clearing her throat. "Um...where are you? Is someone with you?"

"I'm in the vestibule of Le Bec Fin and yes, *my date*, who overheard that, is here with me."

"Shit. Sorry 'bout that." More loudly Lucia called out, "Sorry, Muffy. It was a joke."

"Oh, yes, I'm dying with laughter here," a sharp voice returned. "And the name is Philippa."

Lucia muttered, "Yeah, like that's so much better," before saying to Rockingham, "Our man wants a meeting tomorrow night, in a very sketchy place. Can we talk about this in person—in your office tomorrow morning?"

"Yes. Be there at seven AM."

"Okay." In a whisper she added, "Good luck, she sounds *lovely*."

The next morning Lucia sat at a table in a small, very secure conference room with Rockingham, Chen, and Franklin who had been joined by their grizzled, barrel-chested superior, Special Agent Ron Germano. Germano seemed rather inattentive to the proceedings, since he had contributed little to the discussion and was more focused on skimming through the stack of file folders in front of him. Working around his disconcerting presence, the team had reached consensus on the fact that Colona's suggested meeting place proved he was suspicious of Lucia's motivations.

Franklin said, "I've had a quick look at the specs on this...abandoned silo and you couldn't pick a better place for avoiding surveillance. There's no way to see in, there's no way a transmission will get out, and the place is like a fortress."

"Tells you a lot about Colona that he even knows about that place, doesn't it?" Lucia asked.

"Yes," Rockingham agreed. "It tells us that Colona is going to be rather more difficult to snare, then we had hoped."

Twirling a strand of her straight black hair around a finger, Chen leaned forward, her eyes unfocused, seeming lost in thought. After a moment, she addressed the group. "We're going to have to wait him out. I find it hard to believe he'll pass up the chance to reclaim such a considerable sum of money. He'll eventually cave on the meeting place." She looked at Lucia. "I think this initial suggestion was to gauge whether you're making a good faith offer."

"Or...." Lucia paused until she had everyone's attention—everyone but Germano, that is. "Or, we increase the prize. Substantially. I wire up, then drive out of the city. He'll assume I'm traveling *with* the goods he's had his tongue out for all these years and—"

"I don't know that that will work," Chen interjected. She shook her head, expounding, "I would guess that Colona knows how thoroughly your office was searched after...the attack by Armitage, and has perhaps deduced that you never had the items in question. I guess that's why his interest in meeting with you has waned a bit."

Germano looked up at last. "Good point, Agent Chen. This seems like a dead end." He closed and tapped his stack of folders. "And it seems like there are much more enticing targets to spend your valuable time on, yes?"

"No," Lucia said. "Not so fast. Colona still has someone following me around. Hope dies hard for some people—and he's one of them. He didn't give up after nearly twenty-years and he's not going to give up—"

"Look, honey," Germano sneered. "I don't know exactly whose disgruntled mob wife or mistress...or whatever, you are, but you don't get a vote here. I said we're through and we're through."

The room went deadly silent as Lucia took a moment to tamp down her spike of temper. In a low voice dripping with honeyed venom she said, "Oh, you don't know who I am? Well, I know who you are. You're the guy who should have read the whole case file before he walked in here." Germano started to talk but Lucia ignored him. "Now, I'm going to tell you who I am. I'm the PI who single-handedly brought down Mad-dog Murphy." She saw the light of recognition in Germano's eyes and closed in for the kill. "That's right. At age twenty-three I nabbed his girlfriend with nothing but some zip-ties and ingenuity." She raised her voice ever so slightly, as Germano once again tried to interrupt her. "*Then*, I dropped Murphy with one bullet while he was blasting at me with a sawed-off shotgun." Since Germano was hurriedly flipping through the Colona file, obviously trying to get up to speed, she had time to slip in one last barb. "I would guess when you were twenty-three, they were still teaching you which end of a gun to hold."

In a stilted tone, Germano said, "However notable it was, Ms. Scafetti, that accomplishment does not render you an FBI agent."

"Wow, I guess brilliant insights like that are what puts the 'special' in special agent."

Lucia looked past Germano to see Franklin stifling a laugh. She winked at him as Rockingham took charge of the meeting once again. "While Ms. Scafetti is not an FBI agent, and never claimed to be one, I think we can all agree she's earned her place at this table."

The meeting proceeded with no further outbursts from anyone, with the team eventually settling on Agent Chen's plan to wait Colona out, at least for a few days, before trying Lucia's idea.

To her surprise, Germano offered Lucia a handshake upon leaving the room. "I'm impressed that despite your somewhat over-inflated ego, you can be persuaded to see reason, Ms. Scafetti."

She shook the proffered hand, answering, "And I'm impressed you stuck around after I schooled your ass that hard. We're both full of surprises, Germano."

Germano's only response was a poisonous glare, and he left the room, saying, "I'd like to see that Task Force summary tomorrow, Rockingham."

Franklin followed him out while Chen hung back to whisper, "He's actually lucky you weren't a mob wife. I've known ones who'd have taken him out, right then and there."

"I do, too. I know one *real* well."

When they were alone, Lucia could tell Davis had something on his mind. She figured she was going to get a lecture on deportment, or being a team player, or some such bullshit. She raised an eyebrow at him, saying, "Yes?"

He tugged at his ear in silence for a moment, then shot a surprisingly pensive look at her. "I always thought the...the Murphy incident was one of the most traumatic experiences of your life."

"It was. It still is." She shrugged. "I'm not above using my trauma to score points on an asshole like Germano."

"Lucia Scafetti," Davis laughed. "You are an enigma."

"Nah, I'm just not a very good person."

Due to the early morning meeting, Lucia had missed her morning swim. Having just regained the privilege of swimming when her stitches were removed, she did indeed miss it. There was nothing like a swim to relax her body and clear her head, so after lunch she grabbed her gym bag and headed for the YMCA. The simple sensation of slipping into the pool, immediately eased the tension from her muscles—tension which had built up immeasurably at that morning's meeting. She started doing laps, ruminating on the Colona case, that Germano asshole, and all that had gone wrong in her life since the day her father showed up outside her office.

She always thought better in water than anywhere else, so in preparation for her eventual meeting with Colona, she was running over the things Chen had said at the meeting. She faltered slightly as a thunderbolt of revelation broke over her. The realization was so shocking that she swam right into the pool wall. Luckily, Lucia was in the shallow end, so she stood up, dazed, murmuring, *"Gesù, Giusep, Marie. I malano miau.* I can't fucking believe it. Holy fucking shit."

The woman in the next lane stopped swimming; hanging on to the lane divider, she asked Lucia, "Is something wrong?"

Still talking to herself, Lucia murmured, "He wasn't saying, 'the loon'—he was saying 'la luna'."

Gaping openly at her, the other swimmer asked, "Do you need some help?"

"Yeah, I sure do." Vaulting out of the pool, Lucia called back, "Thanks, but I'll handle it."

Out of breath from running the four blocks from the Y to her office, Lucia burst into the room. She greeted Rocco distractedly, then sat at her desk, studying the notes she had on the Specialist and staring at the snow globe tableau on the desktop. After a few moments, she said aloud, "It's true. It has to be." She dialed the phone, and when Colona answered, she didn't bother to greet him. "You're on. Cement tower, tonight at six-thirty. If you want your money, don't be late."

"Are you fucking serious?"

"Deadly." She slammed the phone down and looked at Rocco. Still slightly dazed, she went over to the couch and flopped down, calling him up beside her. She stroked his long body, saying, "Let's hope I'm right this time, boy. Otherwise, you're gonna go live with Uncle Patsy." She looked over at the bookcase. "And I'm gonna move in with my Aunt Lidia."

CHAPTER 19
To Cheat the Devil

"'Tis no sin to cheat the devil."—Daniel Defoe, *History of the Devil, Part II*

Only a few rays of sunshine made it through the filthy windows at the top of the structure, so Lucia cautiously picked her way through the dimly lit space, her gun at the ready. There were a few rusted-out pieces of unidentifiable machinery to be seen, tiny mountains of trash here and there, but no evidence of Colona. At the sound of a door opening behind her, she whirled and pointed her weapon, finding Colona already doing the same.

"Interesting satellite office you have here, Lieutenant."

"Yeah, I find it cozy—and safe. Transmissions can't penetrate—but then, I bet you already knew that." There was a moment of silence, Colona apparently expecting a response. Lucia didn't give it to him. "I told you to leave your gun at home."

"Yeah, and you promised to do the same. Looks like we're both liars, Cuckoo."

"Call me that again and you're not gonna walk outta here. Tell me what it is you want, now."

"What I want is for this shit to be over." Lucia held out the green Hallmark envelope she'd found in Lidia's urn. "I have the money you paid my father to get that diamond and those coins for you." She pointed to a barely recognizable rusted-out lathe. "I'm gonna put it on that thing, right there. Take it, and we can end this stupid feud and get back to our lives. Mine of solving crimes and yours of committing them."

"I think you have that backwards."

"What audience do you think you're playing for, Colona? Like you said, transmissions can't penetrate this place. I mean, you pulled off a masterstroke there with my father, playing both ends against the middle. You should take the credit."

Colona shook his head and emitted a rusty chuckle. "You trying to entrap me, kid? I been outsmarting punks like you since you were in diapers. Tell me what this is really about." He moved closer and his voice dropped to an undertone. "I'd hate to think a Scafetti is wearing a wire."

"Nah, I don't do that kind of shit. My family would never forgive me." Her tone sharpened to a knife edge as she continued, "By the way, they do know about me meeting with you. And they'll know exactly what happened if I turn up dead. And they won't sit still for that, no matter who you know or who you work for." Edging over, she placed the envelope on the lathe without lowering her gun or taking her eyes off Colona. "Take your money back. It's only right—you never got what you paid for." She paused, cocking an ear towards a sound, finally identifying it over the noise of the rats scurrying in the dark corners of the structure. "I don't have the diamond—or the coins. I never did. It looks like my old man didn't, either. Enough people have died for a mirage. Right?"

"Mirage, huh? You lying bitch. That was your last chance. I was gonna let you walk away if you gave me my goods. I hope you're not depending on your family—or the fucking wire I know you're wearing, to save your ass. 'Cause neither will. I'm sick of you. I'm sick of your games and I think it's time I made an example out of you. But thanks for the money. That'll come in handy." He started advancing on her. "Real handy."

"Stay right where you are."

Colona kept walking towards her, so Lucia backed up to maintain the distance between them. Suddenly she bumped up against something solid— and human. Lucia froze at the feel of a gun barrel pressed up against her neck. "Well, well, lookee here. Seems like you bumped into my old friend, Dixon."

Dixon growled, "Drop it."

As soon as her Glock clattered to the ground, Colona jeered, "You *are* as dumb as your old man. Thinking I won't take you out 'cause of your family. I ain't afraid of that bunch a' low-life crooks—you'll learn that the hard way. Just like Carlo did. Only you ain't going to Graterford; we'll skip that step and send you directly to hell."

Her voice low and steady, Lucia warned, "I wouldn't do that, if I were you. I am wearing a wire. They'll find it when they find my body, they'll hear this whole conversation." She turned her head ever so slightly towards Dixon. "I'm just gonna show him. That's all. It's right on my shoulder. Under my bra strap."

"That only works if they find your body, which ain't gonna happen." He looked at Dixon, commanding, "You know where to take her. Pike's waiting there—he can help you dig."

"Yeah, I know...but all the same...." Dixon reached in and yanked the battery pack off of Lucia's shoulder. "Better safe than sorry."

He tossed the battery pack to Colona who caught it with one hand. Colona crushed it under his heel taunting, "You really thought I would come alone, Scafetti? You're a bigger sucker than I thought."

"No, I knew you wouldn't come alone." Lucia smiled broadly, taking a moment to enjoy the look of confusion it provoked from Colona. "But it's funny how you idiots think *I* did."

"I don't think you did," he snapped, "I know you did. Dix followed you all the way."

"I know, I saw him. But who followed you, Cuckoo? Who's been following you for weeks, now?" Colona stared at her, his expression wary, and she could feel the uncertainty in the slight waver of

Dixon's gun. Knowing the time was ripe, Lucia yelled, "Come on out, Ma!"

"Are you serious? You brought *your mommy* as back-up?" Colona doubled over in laughter. "This is great! I can take care of her at the same time. A two for one special."

His laughter only increased when Angie called, "I'm here," from the metal walkway above them. Out of the corner of her eye, Lucia saw her mother emerge from the shadows. Colona's laughter died abruptly when he noticed Angie had one Sig Sauer in her right hand pointing at him, and another in her left trained on Dixon.

"Hey, now, put those things down, Angie. You could hurt somebody," Colona wheedled.

"Oh, I ain't gonna hurt you, Colona. I'm gonna kill you." Without changing her focus on Colona, she added, "And you over there, you hurt my daughter, and you're gonna die, too. I'm almost as good with my left as I am with my right. Make no mistake about that."

"What is this shit? The waitress thinks she's a gunman, now?" Colona sneered. "You can't possibly be this stupid."

"I'm stupid? That's rich. All you men with your chests puffed out, throwing change at the poor little cocktail waitress. None of you ever figured it out. You thought Carlo just suddenly picked up the trade one day. He didn't learn it, you *mameluke*! He married it."

"You think I'm buying this bullshit, bitch, you better think again."

"I ain't surprised. You always were dumber than fly-shit. You tipped off D'Amico about Carlo's release thinking he'd kill 'im and split the goods with you. He killed 'im all right. But he never intended to give you nothing." Angie shook her head. "All these years an' you still don't have the *cazzo* to do your own dirty work."

"And you know all a' this, how?"

"Oh, Frankie spilled his guts, bawling like a baby—right before I put a bullet through his eye."

"You?" Colona stuttered. "You were the one....? No way."

"Really? You mean you didn't find him face down in that alley behind the Goodwill where I left him?" Lucia had to admit to herself that she enjoyed watching Colona's face go especially pale at that detail from her mother. "He paid for what he did, and now it's your turn." She spared a glance for Lucia and Dixon. "I'm warning you, let my daughter go right now, and maybe you get to walk away." She paused, her tone growing more chiding than angry. "Then, honey, you go over there and get my money for me. What're you thinking?" She pointed her chin at Colona. "He got what he paid for—Guenther dead. That was the deal. It ain't my fault he didn't have the goods."

More than seeing it, Lucia could *feel* her mother preparing to shoot Colona. With no time to waste, she grabbed the arm Dixon was holding her by and pulled him tighter against her, throwing all of her weight up and back, slamming the man's head into the steel pillar behind them. In the same swift smooth motion, she reached for his gun hand and put her hand over his, her finger over his trigger finger and jerked the gun towards Colona—and fired. John Colona crumpled to the ground, dead, one bullet through his left eye.

Gulping huge lungsful of air, almost giddy with relief, Lucia stepped away, allowing Dixon's unconscious form to slide onto the floor. She checked for a pulse and by the time she found it, thready but present, Angie had clattered down the steps. She walked over, stopped next to Lucia, and pointed one of her guns at Dixon's head.

"Are you fucking nuts?" Lucia grabbed the Sig away, snapping, "Give me that."

"We can't let him walk away. He heard the whole thing."

"He's not walking anywhere." Gesturing at the unconscious figure, Lucia explained, "When he finally comes to, he'll be lucky if he remembers what year it is." She strode over to Colona, adding, "And if Dixon *does* remember, when he tries to tell them that *my mom* was here, and is the real Sure-Shot Scafetti, they'll just give him another CAT scan." Lucia looked at the gun in her hands and the one now slung on her mother's back. "Which gun did you use to kill Frankie and Lugano?"

"That one. It's my go to."

"Not anymore." Lucia had reached Colona's body and nudged him slightly with her foot while using her shirt tail to carefully wipe down the Sig.

"What're you doing?"

"Getting my prints off it; unlike the expert hitman you are, I'm not wearing gloves." When Angie gave her a puzzled look, she explained, "I'm gonna plant it on Colona so they'll pin Frankie and Lugano's deaths on *him*." While working, she glanced up at her mother. "I assume it's clean."

"Cleaner than your smart mouth." When Lucia glared at her, she added, "Yeah, it's clean. Nobody is ever gonna trace that piece."

"Loan me those gloves, would ya'?" Angie tossed the gloves to her daughter and, after a struggle, Lucia managed to get them over her much larger hands. As she carefully and gingerly curled Colona's dead fingers around the gun, Lucia asked, "Where've you been keeping the guns?"

"What's it to you?"

"I'm curious."

Angie gave her a knowing grin. "You wanta learn the tricks of the trade, huh? Why not?" She shrugged before advising, "They've been in a locker at 30th Street Station between uses."

"Good to know," Lucia muttered, shuddering slightly at the euphemism for killings. She picked up Colona's service revolver and handed it to her mother along with her black leather gloves. "Get rid of that somewhere, would you? It wouldn't make sense for him to bring two guns."

"Why not?" Angie smirked. "I always carry a back-up. Comes in real handy—as you saw."

"I don't have time for this discussion, Ma. Could you please just dump that gun for me?" When Angie agreed, Lucia said, "Okay, you better get going."

"Let me grab that money, first."

"Don't bother—that envelope is stuffed with old receipts. I didn't actually bring twenty-five-thousand dollars to a meeting with that slimy *disgraziat'*."

"Where is it? Did you ever find the rest of the goods?"

"Meet me at my office tomorrow and I'll give you what I've got."

"Why can't we do it tonight?"

"Because I've gotta contact Rockingham immediately so this...." She gestured around the space. "...looks at least a little bit legit. Then I'm gonna be cooped up with the Police Corruption Task Force for hours, lying my ass off about what happened here. *Capish?*"

"*Capisco*." Angie pointed at the crushed battery pack lying next to Colona. "And get ready, we're gonna be discussing that."

Lucia waited until her mom was a few feet away to mutter, "That's what you think." Suddenly remembering a recent incident with the Sig she'd just planted on Colona, she called out, "Wait a minute!"

"What?"

"You shot at me on the dock. The day I found dad's body. What the hell, Ma?"

"Oh, I was trying to scare you off. I didn't want you to find your dad. I heard Micky'd paid you a visit so I was keeping an eye on you. I thought you'd run—not dive in the water like an idiot."

"It was a smart move. Bullets can't penetrate very far into water."

"You jumped in the fucking Delaware! You could've drowned."

"I'm a good swimmer."

"With all your clothes on? No one's that good."

"I'm still here."

Angie turned to leave, muttering, "Yeah, because God watches out for children, fools, and foolish children."

Lucia watched her go thinking that when two people who know you well hurl that same sentiment at you, it was probably time to reassess your life.

Lucia looked up at the clock in the conference room near Rockingham's office, thinking she couldn't believe it was only ten PM. She would have guessed at least a half a day had passed since she walked into that abandoned silo.

For no less than the third time, the FBI agents, who had all long since shed their jackets and rolled up their respective sleeves, were listening to the recording from the wire Lucia had worn to the meeting with Colona. Lucia was seated at the small table across from Franklin and Chen, while the other two stood, Davis lounging against the wall while Germano alternated between pacing and looming over the table, hands on hips.

When the recording finished, Chen asked, "Why, exactly, did you tell them at that point about the wire? You must have known they'd disconnect it."

Lucia answered, "Because shit was going south fast right then and I needed to stall for time. I used it as a distraction to get Dixon in position."

"Colona had his gun pointed at you right then, correct?" Franklin confirmed.

"Correct." She stretched and yawned, adding, "He had it pointed at me the whole time."

"We haven't yet located his service revolver," Chen announced. "We had an agent check his desk and locker. And I heard from the team at his house ten minutes ago. Nothing."

"My guess is...." Lucia paused to rub her chin in feigned concentration. "...that maybe he'd swap it out for the Sig, whenever he grabbed that weapon. It's probably wherever he's been hiding that."

Nodding along, Franklin said, "Yes, that makes sense. Hopefully, we can figure out where that hiding place is." Looking up at Germano, he explained, "Dixon is still unresponsive but Pike is currently being sought. Maybe when we speak to—"

"What the hell do we need that for? We literally have Colona's taped confession that he was planning to kill Scafetti, here," Germano snapped, gesturing angrily at Lucia, "and him in possession of the weapon that killed Tumino and Lugano. Murders he apparently planned to frame her for unless she gave him what he wanted. I don't give a shit where he's been hiding the gun between kills."

Rockingham interjected, "Speaking of things that are not necessary...I'm still wondering how any of tonight's revelations tie in with those dates you had me check. What was that exercise intended to prove?"

"Oh yeah." Lucia shrugged. "I had this wild idea that Colona was that hitman I asked you to check on way back when. You remember...the Loon?"

"Right. The Loon." Eyes unfocused, Davis nodded. He glanced at Lucia to ask, "Are you still thinking there's some connection between Colona and...that individual?"

"No, looks like he never even existed." She ran her hands through her hair, murmuring, "I might as well have been chasing after the moon."

Chuckling ever so slightly, he replied, "The moon. Ah, very clever." At Franklin's puzzled look, Rockingham expounded, "In Italian, the moon is *la luna*.'"

"Uh-huh," Franklin replied, looking supremely bored with that aside. He tapped the playback device. "Was anything said after the wire was disconnected that we should be aware of?"

Her focus momentarily switched to the table surface as Lucia took a deep breath. She looked back up at Franklin. "Nope. There wasn't really time. When Dixon grabbed for the battery pack is when I made my move on him."

In a low voice Germano said, "Yeah, I guess we have the whole picture here. Oh, except for one thing...." He paused, leaning down to bellow at Lucia, "...what the fuck you were thinking, meeting him alone like that!"

"Is that your Columbo impression?" she asked. "Because I've heard better."

"Lucia, please," Rockingham said. "We need, nay, we deserve an explanation."

"All right." She sighed heavily and rolled her shoulders, while looking off to the side. Frowning wearily, she addressed the group. "I told Colona the truth—I wanted this to be over. I want my life back. I'm tired of being threatened, followed, monitored. It came to me this afternoon that I just couldn't take it anymore—I *had* to bring this ordeal to a close. Meeting with him there in Gray's Ferry seemed to be the fastest route to that end."

Her lips in a hard line, Chen shook her head, causing her bobbed haircut to sway gently. "You promised to wait."

"No, I agreed that waiting was a good idea. I just...didn't. I'm sorry—patience is not one of my virtues."

Germano, who had turned away in apparent disgust, spun around to face her again. "Do you have *any* of those, Scafetti?"

"Yes. The ones I can talk about in polite company, though are limited. I'm a determined detective, a crack shot, and...." Lucia stared up into Germano's eyes as she finished, "...I'm fairly decent at suffering fools, if not so gladly."

"You know," Germano said, looking at Rockingham, "this morning I was actually starting to think maybe she could be a reasonably competent ally to this task force."

Despite not being addressed, Lucia answered, "And I thought you might improve on acquaintance. Guess we were both wrong."

Ignoring Lucia's interruption, Germano continued, volume increasing with each word, "Now, I see she's a crazy, reckless ego-maniac who almost got herself killed...." He paused and glared at Lucia. "...and risked blowing this whole operation to Kingdom come!"

"That would be the operation you called, and I quote, 'a dead end.' Right?"

For a moment Germano looked like he was going to respond but instead suddenly announced, "I need a break," as he stormed out of the room.

As soon as he was gone, Davis leaned down and put his head mere inches from Lucia. "Would you *please* stop antagonizing him?" He straightened up, sighing, "I would like to get home before dawn."

"Whereas I," retorted Lucia, while throwing out a hand, "haven't had this much fun since I woke up with a gash in my side and my spleen missing."

"Maybe we should take a break, too," Chen said. She rose from the table and with a jerk of her head, indicated that Franklin should join her.

As soon as they were gone, Davis said, "Now that we're alone, I have to tell you, I'm very disappointed in you. I believed you when you said you were through taking foolish risks."

She bristled at the fatherly tone but also realized she'd put him in a difficult position. He'd vouched for her pretty strongly. "You're right...and I'm sorry. I'll make it up to you."

His Adam's apple bobbed nervously before he finally responded, "Um, I don't think that's a good idea. You see, Phillipa and I are still—"

"Oh my God, get your mind out of the gutter. I was talking about letting you take credit for bringing the Kimberly Star and Double-Nine Ponds in as evidence. As long as you promise to make sure they eventually make their way to the South African Embassy." While Davis was staring at her, she asked, "They have one now, right? They became a true democracy last April. I looked it up and—"

"Lucia, are you having some kind of cognitive break right now? I mean, with the stress you've been under and everything, it wouldn't be surprising. Perhaps you should have been taken to the ER before we came here."

"If that's rich people speak for 'Lucia, are you batshit insane?' the answer is no." She laughed gently. "What I am, is in possession of the diamond and those coins."

"Where? Where do you have them?"

"In my office. Well, the diamond is in my office and the coins are in the bathroom."

"Since when?"

"Since...." Lucia paused to think back. "...shortly after Griffin was murdered."

"Be serious. Those premises have been searched several times since then."

"Yeah, I know. I also know where to hide things." Seeing his doubtful expression remained unchanged, she said, "It's clear you don't believe me.

Fair enough. We should visit Overbrook together, I guess."

CHAPTER 20
Fallen Angels

"I know—from experience—how much beauty Satan carried down with him when he fell. Nobody ever said the fallen angels were the ugly ones."—Graham Greene, *The Power and the Glory*

Not only Davis but all three FBI agents accompanied Lucia to Overbrook. She left them waiting in the office, with Rocco growling at them all from his crate, while she retrieved her cashmere car coat from the bathroom. Immediately after crossing the threshold, she tossed it to Rockingham.

"What's that?" Germano asked. "It's a goddamned coat. You said you were going to get the coins."

"They're sewed into the coat. I used them as hem weights. I needed twelve and there were only eleven coins but I made do."

"Hem weights? What is that? Some kind of joke? Like 'what's a hen weigh?'"

Rockingham stared at Germano as if he'd just asked what a zipper was. "A hem weight is just what it sounds like—a weight used to weigh a hem down so it hangs properly."

"Give me that." Germano grabbed the coat from Rockingham and inspected the hem. "There is something in here." He looked up accusingly at Chen. "Why didn't your team find this damn coat?"

"I'm sure they did, sir. They just thought it was...well, a coat." She walked over and inspected the garment Germano was holding up to her. "That hem looks finished. I mean, there's no sign of amateur work on it."

Brightly, Lucia said, "Thanks. I've been working on that stitch for a while."

Rolling his eyes, Germano demanded, "Anybody got a knife or scissors?"

Lucia said, "Don't you dare. I'll get a seam ripper." As she moved towards the desk she called out, "That's vintage cashmere."

Rockingham pulled her back by the sleeve. "It is truly a lovely piece and you can take your time extracting the coins for us later. But I, for one, would like to see the diamond."

"Okay." All eyes upon her, Lucia walked behind the desk, pushed the chair against the wall and climbed up on it. She reached up and removed the diamond from where it had been hanging from a fishing line in the left-hand window, hidden amongst her crystals.

"No fucking way," Franklin breathed.

When Lucia jumped down, Chen reached her hand out so Lucia put the diamond in it. With wonder in her voice, Chen exclaimed, "It is...I think it *is* the Kimberly Star."

"Are you nuts?" Germano demanded. "You had a thirty-three-carat diamond hanging in the fucking window? You are crazy. You are certifiable."

"Crazy like a fox," Davis laughed. "The best place to hide a book is in a library." He looked at Lucia. "Right?"

Smiling briefly, Lucia shook her head. "Actually, there are only two places to hide *anything*: where no one will look, or where no one will see." She nodded at the coat, repeating, "That's where no one would ever look," before pausing to point at the window. "And that's where no one would ever see."

"That's pretty good," Franklin murmured, before looking at Chen. "Is that from Confucius?"

Lucia replied, "No, it was from Baccaro."

"Okay," Germano announced, "I've had enough. I need a drink, some sleep, and to return to a world where things make some goddamned sense. In that order." He looked back, barking at Chen, "Get those damn things logged into evidence *tonight*."

"No," Lucia objected. "I said Davis could have the honors. He gets the credit."

Germano side-eyed both of them. "Oh, I see." He then turned a full-bore glare on Rockingham. "I thought you said you two were done playing footsie." He stalked from the room without a backward glance.

Chen went to follow him out, handing the diamond to Rockingham. "Congratulations."

Franklin lingered behind, looking back and forth between Lucia and Davis. "So, you two are...?" When they both loudly proclaimed how over that liaison was, Franklin asked Lucia, "Does that mean you're single?"

"Yeah, as a matter of fact I am. But I recently got out of a relationship and...I'm not really ready to dive back in."

He handed her a business card. "Well, when you are ready, give me a call. I'll buy you a well-deserved drink." She looked down at the card, asking if he was likely to still be available in a month or more. Franklin answered, "Absolutely. I'm always available. I believe in keeping things light and loose. If that's the sort of thing you're looking for this time...." He pointed to the card. "You know what to do."

"Thanks. I'll keep that in mind and...I'll hang onto this."

Once he left, Davis walked over and tried to confiscate Franklin's card, saying he intended to save her from herself, provoking Lucia to tersely demand an explanation. "I happen to think you deserve better."

"Better than a tall Lenny Kravitz?" Lucia put Franklin's card under her desk blotter while retrieving a seam ripper from the drawer. "Are you kidding?"

"Better than a tawdry, meaningless affair, yes."

She started removing the coins one by one from the coat, observing, "You know what? You're a prosecutor, not a judge, so stop judging me and worry about you and Petunia."

"Phillipa."

"Whatever." She glanced up from her work to see him looking rather glum. "What? Is something wrong between you two?"

"You might say that. Phillipa is...upset with me right now. I made a bit of a...faux-pas the other night."

"Okay, I know you didn't use the wrong fork or shake hands with her butler so I'm gonna guess that you...called her by the wrong name in bed?" He admitted both that she was right and that it had been her name. "Dude, you have got a problem." She put a coin on the stack on the desk and moved onto the next one. "Go ahead and tell her you did it to me."

"I did—she said that made it worse."

"I...I don't see how. Send her some flowers, then."

"Phillipa Annenberg is not likely to be impressed by a dozen roses."

"Oh, wow. An Annenberg. Yeah, don't blow this one." Lucia stood up and dropped all of the coins in Davis's jacket pocket. While walking him to the door she suggested, "Okay, roses are out, so send her something rich people like. You know...orchids, or a tax shelter...or one of those ugly pocketbooks that looks like a basket."

He paused at the door to ask, "Where is that handbag I gave you?"

"Check the consignment shop off Rittenhouse."

"Nice."

"Hey, that exchange paid my utilities for three months. Now, happy birthday—that's a gift." As she was closing the door on him, Rockingham held out his palm to stop it. "What?"

He pulled the diamond out of his pocket and held it up. "Why did you hold on to these things for so long? You could have turned them over to the authorities as soon as you found them. You could have even handed them over to that state trooper you told us about. Wouldn't that have redirected Colona's attention away from you?"

"I wasn't sure who to trust." Lucia looked away, up at the window where, until recently, the diamond had sparkled. She looked back at Davis. "I had to be sure they wouldn't fall into Colona's hands."

Davis stared down at her, his lips pursed, searching her face, for what she was not sure. "Is that the truth?"

She took a moment to tamp down her surge of annoyance in the face of his suspicion. "You don't think I was going to fence them, do you?"

"No. I know you better than that. That's what has me so puzzled."

"Colona tipped off D'Amico about my father's release. He had my dad killed for those lousy bits of metal and carbon and I was gonna make damn sure he never got his hands on them. The only way I could be absolutely sure was to—"

"—hold onto them until Colona was dead," he finished for her, his voice imbued with rising comprehension. He continued to stare at her in silence for an unnerving moment. "When you went to meet him tonight, you knew that...he would never settle for the money. You knew that one of you wasn't going to walk away. Didn't you?"

"I really need to let Rocco out—"

"He seems to be sleeping."

The only sound for a moment was Rocco's snoring, corroborating Rockingham's statement. "Yeah," she sighed. "You're right. I knew. I also knew it would be him." Lucia waited for a response—condemnation, accusation, disgust. All she got was Davis continuing to look at her with the same pensive frown. "I told you—I'm not a good person. But you have to admit...I come by it honestly." With that pronouncement, she finally closed the door.

Lucia got no sleep at all and in the morning was more walked by Rocco than walking him. Afterwards, she sat down blearily at her desk and dialed Patsy's number. She was hardly surprised to hear that her mom was already on her way over. She sipped her coffee, thinking of what she needed to say and gathering her strength for the looming confrontation. The phone rang. It was Agent Chen, with the grim news that Pike had committed suicide.

"He ate his gun?"

"Yes."

"When?"

"This morning. When some of our agents caught up with him at his daughter's house in Fort Washington."

Sighing, Lucia murmured, "What a thing to do to your kid." She shook her head. "Looks like he died like he lived, like all three of them lived—selfish, cowardly assholes." While thanking Chen for letting her know, she heard her mother's quick knock at the door.

Hanging up the phone, she called, "Come on in, Ma," and rose to meet her.

Angie practically bounced into the room. She gave Lucia a hug and then dropped down on the couch. "Come, sit," she said, patting the space next to her. "I get a crook in my neck looking up at you." She pulled out a pack of cigarettes, asking, "Did you have a bad time with those Task Force goons? Did they buy your story?"

Lucia declined to sit, answering, "No, it was okay. They bought enough of it. The stuff they got off the...the device, matched up well with...what I told them."

"The device," Angie sneered, using the lighter from the coffee table to light up her cigarette. "The wire, you mean. *Che disgrazia*. I'm ashamed for you, Lucia."

"*You're* ashamed? You're ashamed of *me*? I don't fucking belie—" Incoherent fury left Lucia struggling for words for a moment. Finally, she ground out, "There was a shattering revelation of moral corruption about one of us in that silo...but newsflash, Ma, it wasn't me!"

312

"Moral corruption...." Angie waved a languid hand at her daughter, the smoke from her cigarette leaving trails in the air. "*Gesù, Giusep, Marie.* You can be so melodramatic."

Lucia threw up her hands, admitting, "Yeah, maybe I am being melodramatic. But, I'm sorry, I don't know how it is you're supposed to act when you find out your mother is...the Specialist, *La Luna*, Sure-Shot—what the hell is your handle, anyway?"

"They called me *La Luna* at first, but I shed that moniker fast as I could. I never wanted a handle. Men love that kind of shit, me, I just do my job. A job I'm not gonna defend to you. I don't have to defend myself to you—I'm *your mother.*"

Frustrated and stunned as she was by her mother's stonewalling, Lucia pushed those feelings aside. The detective in her still needed some answers. "I'd like to know what your plan was. With the Guenther killing, I mean."

"Whata you mean, what was the plan? Ain't it obvious? Me and your dad were gonna fence the goods outta town...use the money to start a new life."

"With me?"

Her mouth hanging open, Angie finally seemed stung by something Lucia had said. "Of course, with you. The three of us were gonna start a new life together." She took a long drag on her cigarette saying, "We were thinking the Caribbean. You would've loved that, how you always loved the shore."

The aching note in her mother's voice had Lucia wiping away a stray tear. She needed to get this conversation back on a less personal track. Taking a huge gulp of air, she said, "I still don't understand how you and dad ever thought Colona was gonna let you get away with it. You should've known he'd rat you out if you kept the goods."

Leaning back, Angie explained, "Your father was drinking with Colona a few nights before Guenther was due in from Amsterdam. Colona laughed about it being the biggest gamble of his life, putting fifty-grand on a rumor. Then we knew he wasn't really sure that the mark had the goods. We thought he'd believe it when your dad told him there was nothing of interest on Guenther except ten phony passports."

"Okay, that's not the smartest thing anyone's ever done but okay. I still can't believe you decided to keep them *after* dad was arrested! Why not use 'em to get a deal?"

"Don't you take that tone with me. That was your father's choice. All of it. He wanted to take the fall rather than let people know he wasn't the real Sure-Shot and he wanted to sit on the goods until he got out. That's why he had his mother hold on to everything."

"You mean, 'cause he didn't trust you."

Angie swallowed hard, nodding silently for a moment. "Yeah. Maybe not...but that was Tony's doing. The old man kept whispering in your father's ear. Saying 'Money sticks even in the hands of saints, and she ain't no saint.' I didn't care—I was willing to wait. Thought we'd enjoy it together." She dashed an arm across her damp eyes. "That was our gamble."

314

Pulling herself together, Angie sat up straight. "Why are you asking this? You found the diamond and the coins, didn't you?"

"Yeah, I did."

"I knew you would—you're so smart. You get that from me." She smiled proudly. "Among other things." Oblivious to Lucia's shudder of revulsion, Angie chattered on. "You should come away with me—we'll live like queens. I'm heading for Monaco, first, I think."

"No, you're not. Not unless twenty-five thousand is enough to get you there. I turned the diamond and the ninety-nines into the authorities."

"You didn't!"

"I did. They're finally going back to their home country. South Africa is a democracy now, so—"

"You *stunod*! How can a daughter of mine be such a fool? You said you'd give them to me."

"No, I said I'd give you what I have. Which at this point is just the money. I thought long and hard about it—but in the end, I decided you should keep it. After all, you earned it. Didn't you?"

"I sure as hell did." Angie didn't meet her eye, tapping the ash off of her cigarette into the ash tray, while coolly asking, "How long have you known about me?"

"Not long." Lucia gave a mirthless laugh, realizing that though it seemed like an eternity since the realization had burst upon her, it was in reality less than a day. "I finally put it together yesterday—right before I said I'd meet Colona."

"What tipped you off?"

315

"A lot of little things hit me at once. No matter how I kept adding them up, the sum was always...you. Dad suddenly started taking contracts after he married you; Paulie knew his assailant, Paulie knew you; you searched my office, pretending you were rearranging the furniture. You were in all the right places, at the right times. Motive, opportunity, means. Bam." She pointed at the filing cabinet where her snow globe collection sat. Her tone incredulous, she said, "For God's sake, Ma, you sent me a snow globe from every city where you...you had a contract." More calmly she concluded, "Once I figured it out, it made sense why you'd been pushing me so hard to turn the goods over to Colona. You were planning to kill him and take them back. I knew then you were keeping a close eye on him. And would definitely show up at our little meeting."

"The meeting you came to wearing a wire."

"Yeah, we've been over that. I can't believe we're talking about that, and not, you know, the *twenty people* you've killed in your life. Is it only twenty—or are there more I didn't dig up?"

After smoking in silence for a moment, Angie dodged the query by stating defiantly, "Everyone I killed...they had it coming. One way or another."

Her head in her hands, Lucia groaned, "Holy shit, he really did learn that from you." She looked up. "You're not God! It's not your place to make that call. Maybe those people were gonna change, reform, I don't know, something—you cut them off from that."

Grinding out her cigarette butt in the ash tray, Angie rolled her eyes. "You think people like Colona, Joe Morello, Bernie Terranova—were gonna reform? Come on...you're not that naive, Lucia, you've seen what guys like that can do."

"Yeah, I know, but...but they still deserved the chance. We all do." Lucia stared at her, trying to reconcile this remote stranger with the mother she'd known and loved all her life. "It doesn't bother you? You don't worry about getting caught, going to prison, going to *hell*, even?" Angie had no response other than a slight shrug. "I know you believe in God, Ma, you don't think He's gonna punish you for this?"

"He punishes, but He don't wait for death." Angie exhaled a melancholy breath before elaborating, "I'm not so sure hell is another place; I think it's always been right here," she said, throwing her arms open. "I think God sends His punishments to us on Earth. Like your father never getting to enjoy the wealth he sat in prison for all them years, or me having my daughter acting all high an' mighty, judging me, despising me for something she refuses to understand. And how 'bout *you*?" Her arms crossed, Angie leaned forward, shaking her head in admonishment. "God fixed it so you can't bear a child after having that abortion." Lucia stiffened, staring her mother down, but remaining silent. "You're not gonna bother denying it this time?"

"No. You say you don't have to defend yourself to me? Well, I don't have to defend myself to you. Not anymore. Never again." She walked over to the desk, picked up a fat white envelope and handed it to her mom. "Here's your money."

"This wasn't in the office when I searched it, was it?"

"Yes, it was. I had it sewed into the lining of Rocco's bed." After a pause she whispered, "Where no one would look...."

"What was that?" Lucia waved her hand in a 'never mind' gesture as Angie opened the envelope and rifled through it. "There's four-thousand missing."

"Oh yeah, that's right. I have to pay off my medical bills at HUP—*and* the judge who sprung Rocco. I figure, in the end, that's all on you, so you can pay for it."

"I don't mind. I would've given it to you if you had asked." Angie stood up. "Well, I've imposed on Patsy long enough. It's time for me to get back on the road. I'll be leaving as soon as I can get a flight."

As she pulled Lucia in for a hug, Lucia asked, "Where will you go?"

"First, I'm headed for Rancho Valencia."

"What is that?"

Angie stepped back and looked up at her daughter. "It's a spa in Santa Fe I've been to a few times. Very plush. Wanta come with me?"

"Something tells me I can't afford it."

Waving the envelope, Angie laughed, "This would cover us both." When Lucia shook her head, Angie shrugged. "Suit yourself. I think I'm overdue for some pampering. Then I'm gonna travel around for a bit. Clear my head." She studied Lucia's face for a moment before asking, "When I come back—am I still welcome to stay in that guest room of yours?"

"As long as you're not...." Lucia paused, afraid of the answer but finally, needing to know, she forced herself to go on. "You're not going back to the trade. Right?" As if she could speak her hope into reality, she reiterated, "You're through with contract killing—aren't you?"

"How long do you think twenty-one-grand will last me?"

"You could do something else. *Anything* else."

"What?" Angie scoffed. "Waitress?" Her lips held in a hard line, eyes half hooded, she shook her head. "I did that for real those eight years after your father was sent up. Never again."

"Then you don't have to work—you can live with me, like I said."

"I've been on my own since I was sixteen. I never depended on anyone since then and I ain't gonna start now." Arms akimbo, she announced, "You told me you do this detective shit because it's what you were born to do. Same's true for me."

"Ma—you were not born to be a paid killer."

Flashing a brief weary smile, Angie made no direct response. "You didn't answer my question. About the guest room."

Lucia cleared her throat several times, desperate to halt the tears she could feel coming on. "When you stop...when you're done with that life...forever, that room will be waiting for you. I'll be waiting for you."

Her mom nodded, her own eyes damp. She pulled Lucia into a bruising hug, whispering, "I understand." She stood up on tip-toe to kiss Lucia on the cheek. "But don't hold your breath, honey."

Closing her eyes against the pain and the tears she could no longer hold back, Lucia choked out, "I have to—it's one of my gifts."

Angie finally released Lucia and gathered up her things. She moved to the door, turning back to say, "You'll always be my daughter, and I'll always love you. I love you, Lucia. You know that—don't you?"

"Yeah, I know." Lucia sobbed, "I love you right back, Ma." Angie smiled and left, softly closing the door behind her. Lucia repeated, in a whisper, "I love you, too, crazy lady."

EPILOGUE

A Home and People to Love

"If there's one thing I learned, it is that blood families can sometimes be the pits; it's the one you make for yourself that really gives you a home and people to love."—Joss Stirling, *Stealing Phoenix*

Lucia unpacked the box of kitchen staples, spices, and condiments while Juli and Dan watched. "Wow, you guys thought of everything. Thanks. Though the champagne would have been plenty."

Dan's broad smile gleamed against his dark complexion as he waved his meaty hand at her. "It's nothing. Juli and I remember how hard it is getting set up in your first home. Seems like there's always one more thing you need to buy." He looked around the kitchen, observing, "This is a great place. I was worried when Juli told me you bought the first house you looked at, but—"

"It wasn't the first house! I just found it on the first day I looked."

"Oh, that's very different," Juli laughed, turning towards her husband. "I swear, she would've bought a chicken coop if it'd had a screened-in porch for Rocco." She looked down at the dog who was watching the proceedings. "Though I suppose you deserve it, Mr. Life-Saver."

Nodding her head, Lucia said, "Damn right, he does." She stowed the perishables in the fridge and added, "Now, I'm almost ready for my first dinner party." She swiveled around to face her friends. "What shall it be?"

"Tess has requested your spaghetti and meatballs," Juli replied, "like you made at our house last time."

"That's all I ever fix for you guys." She escorted them into the dining room offering, "How about...'trippa cu' sucu e piseddi' instead?"

Dan scratched his head. "What is that?"

"Tripe and peas in tomato sauce."

"That sounds...." Juli hesitated, her head cocked to the side. "...positively disgusting."

Lucia chuckled before admitting, "Oh, it is. It really is. Okay—spaghetti and meatballs is on the menu instead. Next Saturday, right?"

"Right." Dan looked around the room. "I guess we'll be eating in the kitchen—or will you be getting a dining room set before then?"

"Um...actually...I was thinking about putting a pool table in here."

"No. Lucia, no." Juli put her hands on her hips and drew herself up to her full height. "This is your home—not Otto's Tavern."

"Where would I put it then?"

"How about the basement?"

"Ugh. I lived in a basement for nine years. That's enough."

"Then put it in the spare bedroom," Juli answered as she scrutinized the dining room and the living room it adjoined. "You still need something on these walls but you did a great job on the curtains and blinds. These rooms look so much better with those up."

"Actually, that was Patsy's doing. He was so worried about some 'crazy guy' peeping in on me, as he put it, that he worked all day yesterday to get them up." She shook her head. "Like him buying me all the porch furniture wasn't already too much."

Dan studied her for a moment before asking, "And the rest of your family? Have they come around?"

"No. They'll never come around. I not only wore a wire, I did it for the Feds. They're through with me—forever."

Patting her on the arm, Juli murmured, "I'm sorry."

"It's okay. I knew it would happen as soon as I signed on with the task force." Lucia shrugged, adding sadly, "In a way...it was inevitable." Juli and Dan both nodded in clear agreement.

Dan clapped his hands together. "Well, we should get going. We gotta get the girls soon; they only have a half day today—first day of school, you know."

Lucia walked them to the door and was about to establish a firm time for the dinner on Saturday when the doorbell rang. She opened the door to find Hank Narváez standing on the threshold, holding a potted plant. "Uh, hi," she stuttered, frozen in place, while Rocco barked a noisy welcome.

Juli and Dan quickly greeted Hank, said their final good-byes to Lucia and rushed past Hank. Lucia came out of her stupor realizing Hank was still standing on the porch. "Please come in," she said. At the same time, she ordered Rocco out onto the porch where he happily settled into what was quickly becoming "his chair."

Hank stepped into the living room and handed her the plant, saying, "Congratulations on your new home."

"Thanks." Lucia looked down at the plant then back up at Hank. "How did you know—Oh, Dan or Juli told you, I guess."

"Yeah. Dan told us. He said you got a big reward from the South African government—for giving them back the diamond and those coins. And that's how you got your down payment?"

"Yep." She forced out an unconvincing laugh. "If I'd known there was money in it for me, I would've turned them in right after I found them."

"When was that?"

"Remember that day you saw the blinds drawn in my office? The night before that."

"Oh, wow, yeah. I remember that. Did you really have the diamond hanging in your office window?"

"I did." She pointed out to where the crystals now hung from the porch ceiling. "In fact, I've got a few more up there. See if you can pick them out." Hank's genuine laugh relaxed her enough that she finally remembered her manners. "Hey, would you like a beer?"

By the time they'd settled onto the porch with their beers, Lucia was able to act like a true hostess and calmly ask about Max.

"Max is good, he says hello." Hank tipped his beer at Rocco. "Looks like he's happy with the house you bought for him." After Lucia agreed that no one was happier about the house than Rocco, Hank cleared his throat. "Um, Juli told me about what you did—wearing the wire and everything. That was...brave. Really brave of you."

In an effort to hide both her face and her emotions, Lucia took a long pull on her beer as she asked the next question. "Did she also tell you...about me killing Colona?"

"Yeah, she did. She told me how he'd planned the whole thing as an ambush." He leaned forward, his beer dangling from the right hand. "I'm sure glad it was him—and not you who died that night." As she was searching his face for any lurking judgment, Hank asked, "How are you doing...with that?"

"Okay, I guess. Not as bad as it was with Murphy, for sure." She sat back against the cushion, considering whether she wanted to talk about this or not. Deciding she had to know how Hank would take her full confession, she said, "That's the scary part, you know? Not just reliving it, or the nightmares, but that...that it got easier this time." She took a sip before murmuring, "Guess that's how people like...you know, like my family, end up who they are."

"You don't think it was easier this time because of all that Colona put you through? That maybe this time, it was a lot more personal?"

"Maybe." She chuckled ever so briefly. "I'm gonna tell you a secret though, any time someone points a gun at you—it feels pretty goddamned personal."

"I'll bet." While she was searching for a way to change the subject to something lighter, Hank went heavier. "Speaking of your family, how did they react to...all of this?"

"Oh, I'm dead to them now. I got the word directly from the family matriarch, my Zia Carmela herself." She shrugged slightly. "I was just telling Juli and Dan that part was inevitable. The family has always called me a *facciadu*, a two-face. It's a wonder they didn't cut me out long before this."

"There's no one sticking by you?"

A fond smile lit her face as she said, "Patsy is. He seems more worried I'll cut him out. He warned me if I disappear on him again, he'll hire a PI who's even better than me to hunt me down."

"Disappear?"

"Yeah," she answered with a laugh. "That's what he calls that time I was out of his sight for a few months." Hank still looked puzzled so Lucia elaborated, "When I went up to the Poconos after Bac died."

"Ah, I see." After a brief pause, Hank said, "And your mom, too. I'm sure you still have her on your side."

Exhaling deeply, Lucia scrambled to find the right answer. Finally, she looked at Hank, shaking her head. "Not really. I don't think I'll be seeing much of my mom anymore. Maybe not even...ever again." Eyes unfocused, she gazed out at the street over Hank's shoulder. "We don't see the world in the same way. Truth is...we never did. It was staring me in the face all along but...I was too blind to see it." She took a drink before laughing bitterly, "She named me well, that woman. Santa Lucia—patron saint of the blind."

"Don't be so hard on yourself. No one wants to think...badly of their mother. It's love that's blind—not you."

Lucia couldn't help but grin upon hearing that first sentence from Hank. "That's two ex-boyfriends who've told me not to be so hard on myself. Must be something there—I'll have to think about that."

"I don't like to think of myself as your ex-boyfriend."

"Oh." Gathering her courage, she finally forced out the question that pronouncement had raised. "How do you like to think of yourself?"

"As a friend? I hope we can be friends."

As good as she was at hiding the truth from herself on occasion, Lucia couldn't ignore the pang of disappointment she felt. But she could argue it down, knowing that there was now a wall between her and the future she'd once glimpsed with Hank. An impenetrable wall built of pernicious lies and ugly truths. That reflection allowed her to bestow a genuine smile on Hank as she said, "I'd like that. I'd like that a lot."

"I'm glad—I've missed you."

"I've missed you, too."

Hank chuckled slightly, saying, "I wouldn't have guessed it—not with the way you've been avoiding me."

"Yeah." After pondering how best to field that one, Lucia decided on sheer honesty. "It was hard to face you...after what I did." She cleared her throat, adding for good measure, "I was embarrassed."

"Does that mean...you're sorry?"

Shaking her head, Lucia declared, "No. I can't go that far. I'm sorry I got you involved, and I can offer a belated apology for that, but...I'm not sorry I did it." She studied him for a moment but his expression was inscrutable to her. "Still want to be friends?"

After putting his beer down on the side table, Hank leaned forward, elbows on his knees. "The question of wrong or right there is something I think we'll never agree on but I think we can both agree to put the whole mess behind us." He smiled brightly as he picked his beer up again. "So, yes, absolutely, I still want to be friends."

"That's great. I can use all the friends I can get— I'm building a new family from the ground up." Lucia made a mental note that the door which had just slammed shut on her and Hank, allowed another door to open up. She could now dig out that card and give FBI Agent Nick Franklin a call.

"How about we celebrate our new-found family tonight. What do you say to a round of pool with me and Max at Otto's? Only tonight, I want that...weight, you offered last time."

"Can I get a rain check? Maybe tomorrow night? I have a date tonight."

"Good for you." Hank reached over and clinked his beer against hers in a congratulatory gesture. "Why don't you bring him along?"

"He's nine-years old."

He polished off his beer while staring at her, eyebrows raised. "Um, what?"

"It's for a case."

"Is he cheating on his wife?"

"No." She scratched her forehead, her lips twisted into a half smile. "I'm getting a picture of him for his birth mother. I do it once a year for her. Around his birthday."

When Hank asked if the boy's family knew about this practice, she had to admit they did not. They didn't even know that his birth mother had located them. "Uh, Lucia, I hate to say it but...that almost sounds...a little bit like stalking."

"Oh, it's absolutely stalking." When Hank protested the risks and intrusion, Lucia explained, "She's not a danger to this little boy, not in any way. I'd never do this if I wasn't sure of that. Trust me on this."

Hank stared into her eyes, then nodded. "Okay, I do. I do trust you." He left only after securing her promise to meet him and Max at Otto's the next night at six PM sharp.

By five o'clock that night, Lucia was standing outside a soccer field in North Wilmington watching a group of boys play a fairly disorganized game. No one paid her any attention. Casually attired, with camera in hand and Rocco on a leash she probably looked like someone's older sister or aunt, trying to get a good picture for the family photo album. Due to them all wearing identical uniforms, it took a moment to distinguish the boy she wanted. But finally, he turned around and she spotted those beautiful turquoise eyes, like none she'd ever seen, the eyes he'd inherited from his father.

She snapped several great shots, and watched the boy score a goal before getting in the Chevelle and heading back to Philadelphia. She glanced over at Rocco, who was watching the other cars suspiciously as he always did. "Robbie's getting tall, isn't he?" Rocco didn't answer, of course, but Lucia hummed to herself, secure in the knowledge that her son was happy and safe where she'd hidden him away—where no one would ever see.

Italian-American Glossary

Assassino —Murderer
Buchiach —Bitch (but so much worse)
Capisco —I understand
Capish —Understand
Cazzo —Testicles
Che cozz' —What the fuck are you doing?
Che fai —What are you doing?
Che disgrazia —What a disgrace
Colpa mia —My fault
'Diamo —Let's go
Disgraziat' —Sleazeball
Facciadu —Two-faced
Fanabola —Shit/Damn it
Figliocce —Goddaughter
Gabbadost' —Hardhead
Gavone —Greenhorn/Rube
Gesù, Giusep, Marie —Jesus, Joseph, Mary - references the Holy Family
Hai capid —Do you understand?
I malano miau —I don't believe it
Infamnia —Infamy

La Famiglia —The family
Lasciato —I allowed
Le Sorelle —The Sisters
'*Madigan* —A non-Italian-American
Maliocch —The evil eye
Mameluke —Idiot
Managgia —God damn it
Mio figlio —My son
Nonno —Grandfather
Povaretto —Poor little one
Schieve —To have disgust or loathing
Schifosa —Disgusting person
Stunad —Stupid
Strunz —Turd

ABOUT THE AUTHOR

Felicia Watson started writing stories as soon as they handed her a pencil in first grade. She's especially drawn to character driven tales, where we see people we recognize, people who struggle with their mistakes and shortcomings, acknowledge them, and use that knowledge to grow into wiser human beings.

When not writing, Felicia spends her time chasing after her not-so-brilliant, but darling and beloved dogs, being chased by her truly brilliant, darling, and beloved husband, is known to friends and family as an amateur pastry chef, and still finds time for swimming and her day job as a scientist.

Her debut novel, *Where the Allegheny Meets the Monongahelia*, an LGBT romance that breaks the "romance mold," was very well received. Her *Lovelace Trilogy* of science-fiction novels brought that same outside-of-the-box style to the science fiction genre. So it was not surprise when she did the same for the detective novel with *Where No One Will See*.

Chad Bordes.......THE RUINATION OF DYLAN FORBES
S. W. Capps..RUNAWAY TRAIN
Karuna Das...KAT'S CRADLE
SEX, DRUGS & SPIRITUAL ENLIGHTENMENT
Courtney Davis.................................A WEREWOLF IN
WOMEN'S CLOTHES
A LIFE WITH BEASTS
SUPERNATURAL P.I.
SECRETS AND STALKERS
Eileen Joyce Donovan.......THE CAMPBELL SISTERS
Therese Doucet.........THE PRISONER OF THE CASTLE
OF ENLIGHTENMENT
Samuel Ebeid ....THE HEIRESS OF EGYPT
THE QUEEN OF EGYPT
G.P. Gottlieb ....BATTERED
SMOTHERED
CHARRED
Lansford Guy ....THE GUARDIANS
Wayne E. & Sean P. Haley ....AN APOLOGY
TO LUCIFER
David Kruh ....INSEPARABLE
Shawn Mackey ...THIS WORLD OF LOVE AND STRIFE
Jeanne Matthews ....DEVIL BY THE TAIL
C.K. McDonough ....STOKING HOPE
Fidelis O. Mkparu ....SOULFUL RETURN
Phillip Otts ....A STORM BEFORE THE WAR
THE SOUL OF A STRANGER
THE PRICE OF BETRAYAL

335